SHOOTING STAR

DEEPANSHI TIWARI

Copyright © Deepanshi Tiwari
All Rights Reserved.

This book has been self-published with all reasonable efforts taken to make the material error-free by the author. No part of this book shall be used, reproduced in any manner whatsoever without written permission from the author, except in the case of brief quotations embodied in critical articles and reviews.

The Author of this book is solely responsible and liable for its content including but not limited to the views, representations, descriptions, statements, information, opinions and references ["Content"]. The Content of this book shall not constitute or be construed or deemed to reflect the opinion or expression of the Publisher or Editor. Neither the Publisher nor Editor endorse or approve the Content of this book or guarantee the reliability, accuracy or completeness of the Content published herein and do not make any representations or warranties of any kind, express or implied, including but not limited to the implied warranties of merchantability, fitness for a particular purpose. The Publisher and Editor shall not be liable whatsoever for any errors, omissions, whether such errors or omissions result from negligence, accident, or any other cause or claims for loss or damages of any kind, including without limitation, indirect or consequential loss or damage arising out of use, inability to use, or about the reliability, accuracy or sufficiency of the information contained in this book.

Made with ♥ on the Notion Press Platform
www.notionpress.com

Contents

Acknowledgements — v

1. Chapter 1 — 1
2. Chapter 2 — 7
3. Chapter 3 — 18
4. Chapter 4 — 28
5. Chapter 5 — 40
6. Chapter 6 — 48
7. Chapter 7 — 54
8. Chapter 8 — 62
9. Chapter 9 — 77
10. Chapter 10 — 89
11. Chapter 11 — 101
12. Chapter 12 — 117
13. Chapter 13 — 129
14. Chapter 14 — 140
15. Chapter 15 — 147
16. Chapter 16 — 155
17. Chapter 17 — 163
18. Chapter 18 — 171
19. Chapter 19 — 179
20. Chapter 20 — 190
21. Chapter 21 — 197
22. Chapter 22 — 204
23. Chapter 23 — 211

Contents

24. Chapter 24		218
25. Chapter 25		225
26. Chapter 26		232
27. Chapter 27		241
28. Chapter 28		251
29. Chapter 29		257
30. Chapter 30		264
31. Chapter 31		274
32. Chapter 32		285
33. Chapter 33		292
34. Chapter 34		299
Epilouge		311

Acknowledgements

To start with if I don't thanks GOD for the work I have done then its not me, so thanking the lord for sowing this seed of creativity in me that today this book is finished and coming into existence, if not his constant blessings I would never had done this in my life ever.

Then comes the pillars of my life my parents without them I'm nothing, I'm truly thankful for each and everything you have done and still doing for me, as a child I can never thank you enough but I'm constantly trying to make you both proud and I will one day. one special thanks to my mother who never fails to support me in anything I do in my life, thank you for always being there mamma.

I can never finish without thanking my backbone who bear all my tantrums and listen to my ideas for countless number of times, Thank you so much Ankita if today I'm able to write then you are one of the biggest reason behind this, thanks for pushing me into this I'm always greatful to you.

Last but not the least a warm thank you to each and every one who supported me in this wonderful journey of writting this book Hope I did some justice with the art called WRITING.

"Sometimes in our life some one special appears like a shooting star to fulfill our wishes in such a way in which even the real ones are not capable enough"

Sometimes sitting quietly with ourselves, remembering our priceless memorable time spent with the one who touched our soul to its depth where no one could ever reach. It is the most blissful feeling anyone could ever experience. Thinking about her, I took out a big photo album from my cupboard this album is the witness of the most beautiful time of our life, at the moment I opened its first page automatically a smile crept on my face holding the album in my hand I sat down on the swing placed in my balcony with a mug of tea in the other hand. Seeing the first picture of her in which she was wearing a white knee-length kurta with blue denim, I remembered how much she used to love this outfit, even though I did too. The typical artistic look in this picture dragged me back to the time when I first met her. She was wearing the same outfit.

****

A boy was sitting in the Tire 1 AC compartment of a train looking out of the glass window, keenly observing the trees that were moving behind. He was drowned in his thoughts. He was looking calm, but his eyes were showing that some sort of storm was running inside him. It was looking like he was trying to find out if the trees are the ones leaving behind or if he was leaving behind somewhere. Getting irritated by his thoughts, he put on the headphones and started listening to songs.

The train was moving at full speed. There were very few people in his compartment, so he was feeling relaxed. Somewhere around 2 hours later, the train stopped at a random station and people started going in and out of the compartment, but the boy was still in his seat. He just took a cup of tea from a little tea vendor roaming on the train and started looking out of the window again, waiting for the train to start. He was thinking deeply about something when suddenly a girl entered the compartment with her 2 bags with great difficulty. She was struggling to keep her bags under the seat but due to some reason; she was not able to do that. Finally, getting pissed off, she glared at the boy.

"Argh...... How shameless a person you are.... Here I'm trying so hard to settle my bag. Don't you think you should move a little and help me" she said annoyingly. Hearing her, he came out of his thoughts and got up from his seat to help her.

"I'm sorry, I was thinking something" while saying this, he adjusted her bags under the seat. "Thank you so much for your help...... and sorry," she said meekly "Sorry for....?" "I didn't want to say anything bad to you and I don't mean it..... Because of frustration, I said that..... So sorry again" she replied, adjusting back to her seat right in front of his seat. "Oh, no need to be sorry, it's fine," he said

Slowly the train started moving again on its track, and again the boy was drowned in his thoughts. The first hour went by in complete silence, but the silence was irritating the girl, so she abruptly started speaking.

"Well, where are you going...?" She asked to start the conversation. He shifted his attention from the trees to that girl. "Jaipur..." he again kept quiet and started looking out

"Oh, I'm also going to Jaipur......"

"What is with this weird boy...... not speaking a word..... Now how will I pass this long journey?" she thought, pouting cutely. She waited for sometime patiently, but losing her patience, she chose to start the conversation all over again.

"Are you going to Jaipur for work or home?" she asked, breaking the silence again.

"Just like that..." he replied.

"Just like that......? What kind of answer is this..... No one goes anywhere just like that" she asked, shock and confusion was visible on her face.

"When you feel filled up or start feeling suffocated by your surroundings...... and especially when there is no one to hear you or to understand you..... One should leave for somewhere just like that," he said, looking straight at her.

"Umm..... Very deep actually..... In life, one should spend a little time with oneself too..... What if life doesn't give that opportunity again.... What and when life will show we can't predict.. So yeah, it's better to sometimes leave just like that"

"Your thoughts are very deep," he said, genuinely getting impressed by her thoughts.

"No, no, it just came with the flow..... I said what I felt...... well, if you don't mind, can I ask you one thing"

"Yah sure...." he replied, a little hesitant about what she'll ask.

"I've been watching you since I came. You are lost somewhere, is there anything bothering you...... I'll try to help you out if I can," she asked like a caring friend.

"Why do you think that I'm upset....? And even If I am, then how will you help me"

"I can see it on your face that you are not ok and about helping, it gives me happiness by helping others.... If I am capable enough to help anyone in any way, then what is better than that" she said, smiling contagiously. By now the boy was a little impressed with her thoughts that someone strange to you is so eager to help you with your problems, those problems which are nothing in the eyes of your close ones.

"I am not upset...... it's like I'm in a dilemma..... Just not able to understand where I should go," he told her honestly.

"Very simple..... Just go where your heart is taking you"

"Sometimes ignoring the requests of our heart, we have to make decisions considering our mind..... Well, let it be" there was a glint of sadness in his voice.

"hey..... See, we have been talking for a long time, but we didn't even introduce ourselves...... hi.... I'm SHRISHTI...." she said, forwarding her hand.

"Hi...... I'm KABIR..." he replied, taking her hand and shaking lightly)

"Kabir," there was a slight smile on her face while pronouncing his name.

"Why are you smiling...... is there anything funny in my name?" he asked with a cute frown on his face.

"No, no..... I found your name unique, or should I say different.... That's why" she said, smiling.

"Ahh........well, usually there are many people on trips.... But you are alone on your trip" he asked wondering.

"Yes.... As I told you before..... One should sometimes go on some random trips just like that.... Where no one is with you, but you are with yourself." While saying this, there was a bright smile on her face.

"It seems like you are a very happening person, isn't it?"

"Maybe me or maybe it's the time who made me like this, see it's dark already. I think we should sleep now," she said while looking out of the window.

Saying this, she lay down on her seat, covering her face with a blanket. But sleep was far away from Kabir's eyes. The whole night he was sleepless...... fighting with his own heart and mind. Night passed like this, and soon he was seeing the sun peeking out from behind the trees slowly. Shrishti was still sleeping..... but her sleep got disturbed by the voice of the tea vendor getting irritated. She kept the blanket on one side and sat in her seat, crossing her legs cutely.

"madam chai (tea)....." the vendor asked, showing a cup of tea.

"one please"

Taking her cup from him, she turned and found Kabir already sipping his tea but she wondered as he ordered one more cup. After giving him one more cup of tea, the vendor left from there.

"good morning"

"Good morning," he replied, while taking a sip from his cup.

"don't drink this much tea, this will affect your health." she suggested.

"Nothing will happen to me...." he chuckled a little. "this is the only reason for my life you know" there was amusement in his voice.

"it seems like you are a chai lover (tea lover)" she chuckled

"deadly chai (tea) lover," he said with enthusiasm.

Both burst into laughter. The whole day passed while talking on some random yet deep topic. Both were somewhere enjoying talking to each other. Around 5:45 in the evening, their train reached Jaipur station. After taking their luggage out from the train, both said goodbye before moving on their path.

"Ok then goodbye Kabir...... it was nice meeting you Or I can say nice talking to you," she said.

"true... ok then goodbye.... See you soon" saying this there was a smile dancing on his lips.

"We don't even know if we will meet again or not and here you are saying see you soon." she laughed at his line.

"this world is small, madam... the ones who are meant to meet some or the other way" he gave a meaningful look.

"yaa right. Ok bye, my cab is here...." she said, looking back at her cab.

She left waving her hand... Kabir was also waving his hand back with a heartwarming smile..... he felt a weird change in him..... just a day before he was not even uttering a single word, but now he was smiling.

"Something is different about this girl..... I don't know why but I wanna meet her again if possible......... God." he looked up at the sky, which was now turning dark in shade of blue.

2

Kabir was in his hotel room sitting ideally and continuously staring at the wall blankly. On the other hand Shrishti also reached her hotel room. She quickly adjusted her luggage in the wardrobe and opened the big windows of the room. The night beauty of Jaipur was attracting her to go and get merged in that, but she was tired because of the journey, so she simply chose to stay in the room only for the time being and take a rest.

Time passed and around 10 PM she felt something like hunger, so she thought about going to the restaurant of the hotel except ordering food in the room. She got up lazily and after setting her messy hair; she opened the door of her room. The moment she opened it, she was shocked to see the person coming out from the opposite room. The reaction of that person was also the same.

"You...!" both of them exclaimed at the same time.

"see told you na.... the world is so small," he said amusingly

"seriously...... biggest coincidence of my life," she said dramatically. "well where are you going...?"

"to throw something in my stomach... before it starts growling" he chuckled at his statement.

"Ooo..... so would you like to join me.... I'm also going on the same mission" she said like a spy.

Kabir thought something for a minute, then agreed to go. Soon, both were sitting in the restaurant. After ordering their food, they started talking.

"So what is your plan, from where you'll start?" she asked excitedly.

"What...?" He gave her a confused look.

"sightseeing..... that's the thing for what we are here na, I'm already dying to explore this city" there was excitement on her face like a small kid.

"sightseeing!!..... well I don't have any plans to be precise" he stated like a universal truth while pouring himself a glass of water.

"What...! then why are you here in the first place?" she asked, shockingly, gaining some attention from people in the surroundings.

"Just like that..... told you," he said plainly.

"Are you crazy...... you are here at this wonderful place just like that...... what will you do..." she asked, getting more curious.

"nothing..... just sit back in my room," he said while looking at his plate.

"you are kidding, right.... If you had to sit back in your room wondering why you spent this much money on this useless trip of yours... you must have your room at your house na..... why didn't you utilize that.....what are you even doing here after spending this much"

"PEACE......." he said, looking to another side

"Don't take me wrong, but you'll not find PEACE in your room.... you are here at this such a beautiful place... explore it... I'm sure you'll get your peace and you'll enjoy it too......" she suggested genuinely.

"How are you so sure......?" he asked, looking at her.

"Because I'm also here to find that thing... called PEACE.... Which I think I'll get for sure" she said, determination filled in her eyes. He didn't say anything further. After finishing their food, they quietly left for their rooms, and after wishing them a good night, they closed the doors.

Kabir silently lay down on the bed and was in deep thought. He was trying to figure out whether what Shrishti said was right or what he was doing was right. The whole night Kabir was in deep thought and finally, he decided that sitting alone in the hotel room clueless is not a good idea. He should also go and explore the city....... Called pink city.

The next morning, around 7, Shrishti heard someone knocking on the door. She lazily got up and went to open it and found Kabir standing there, almost ready to go somewhere.

"hey... good morning," he said with a smile on his face.

"good morning.......what's up," she said, while still trying to open her eyes.

"Ceiling," he said, chuckling.

"What...?" he asked, confusingly.

"leave it..!!.... I wanted to ask you something"

"yes say"

"as you said last night, I can find peace with myself... I just need to explore myself and I felt that..... so I'm here to ask you would you like to go sightseeing with me.......as we both are alone" he asked

Shrishti was silent for a while. Maybe she was trying to decide if she should go with a stranger or not....

"it is completely fine if you don't wanna come with me..... I understand......no problem" he turned to go.

"Ok done..... we are going together" she replied happily. He turned again happily. "Are you sure?"

"yes...... two are always better than one... well, otherwise you don't look like a kidnapper.... So yaa... let's go together. It'll be fun" he laughed at her joke. "Just give me 30 minutes to get ready then we'll leave, OK?"

"Sure...."

After having breakfast, both of them left for sightseeing...... Firstly, they went to the most famous place, Nahargarh palace.... Both were in awe seeing the beauty of the fort..... Shrishti wandered like a kid, each corner of it in detail and side by side she was telling Kabir in detail about the fort like how it was made and to whom it belonged and everything..... he was wondering how she knew this much about this place but he didn't ask. Soon they went to Hawa Mahal. Kabir was just roaming clueless, but Shrishti was enjoying every single bit of it. Seeing her clicking pictures through her camera, he sat on a side and seeing her only how happy she was, her face was showing another level of calmness.

"How can someone be this happy..... or is it me who is not understanding or maybe doesn't want to understand anything..... why even after trying hard I'm able to find peace.... Why am I stuck in the battle of heart and mind...... just whyyy....." he thought bitterly to himself.

He came out of his thoughts, feeling a tap on his shoulder. It was Shrishti.

"hey.....!! Kabir, what happened? Where are you lost" she asked.

"no.... no.... nothing...... just was thinking something..... you tell are you done with your photo session" he tried to change the topic.

"yeah, come let me click yours too..." she asked excitedly.

"oh no no.... no need..... actually I don't like clicking pictures of mine especially" "why? Everyone likes it..... c'mon.... go stand there... fast." he made a face but seeing her cuteness, he agreed, "very good"

She clicked many pics of Kabir, and on her insistence, he also clicked her. Soon it was night and both of them decided to go back to the hotel. While walking towards their room, both were discussing the places they were going to visit the next day.... Kabir was only listening, Shrishti was telling him everything as he was unaware of the places. Soon after wishing good night to each other, both went into their respective rooms..... today Kabir was feeling a little relaxed after roaming clueless with a person like Shrishti who was living her every moment in the present without any tension of the future and any regret of the past.

Sometimes we don't get the peace that we seek from our close ones but unexpectedly receive the utmost peace and calmness from a stranger...... Kabir was sitting on his bed crossing his legs.... He was thinking about the whole day he spent with her and with himself indeed..... automatically he sighed calmly with a little smile of satisfaction on his face.... He was about to lie down and sleep, but his phone started beeping abruptly.

"MOM" was flashing on the screen. He ignored it and lay down facing the window. his eyes were closed but he was not asleep yet again his phone rang. This time "DAD" was flashing, getting irritated he got up and sat again crossing his legs, and waited for the call to get disconnected. As soon as the call disconnected he switched OFF his phone and again lay down hugging a pillow.

"I know why you are calling me again and again but I'm not gonna talk to you both till I'm here at least" he mumbled laying on the bed, Soon he fell into a deep slumber.

shrishti was wide awake, there was not a single sign that she was planning to sleep. She was sitting near her window and was wondering about the beauty of the city. Getting excited she took out her diary and started writing her experience of the past 2 days. She was writing with complete focus but suddenly she stopped remembering Kabir as she was writing about her meeting with him she dropped the pen and fell into deep thinking.

"I don't know what but there is something with Kabir....... he is here all alone even I am here alone too but he is sad.... What's the matter..... I don't know why but his eyes show the pain he is suffering internally but after all who I am to ask...... we are just together on this trip for merely 2 or 3 days..... but I'll try to make him happy..... yeah....!!" thinking all this something shines in her eyes. She got up from the chair and drowned herself in the bed and soon she was in deep sleep.

The next 2 days passed in a very exciting way both enjoyed a lot, in actual means Shrishti forcefully made him enjoy all the moments keeping everything aside finally last day of their trip came and now Shrishti was banging door of Kabir's room from the past 20 minutes as they were getting late, Finally Kabir opened the door setting his hairs.

Shrishti was staring at him fuming in anger yet she was looking cute like anything making him chuckle and seeing her fuming yet cute face.

"What happened, a tsunami is coming or an earthquake or sky is ready to fall?" he asked sarcastically, smiling at her.

"Are you even serious..... like seriously I'm banging on this door for 20 minutes.......can you please enlighten me kindly what were you doing for this long" her voice was stating the fact that how mad she was at that time.

"umm…. I was setting my hair," he said, adjusting his curls. Shrishti stumbled at her feet listening to him "hey hey…. Are you ok"

"Are you out of your mind…. You took 20 minutes for your hair…… even girls don't take this long man" he scratched the back of his neck looking here and there "ok ok now if your hair and makeup are done then shall we leave…… we are already late" she said sarcastically.

"just a minute… let me lock the room…"

Both of them visited a few leftover places till 2 in the afternoon and then only at Shrishti's insistence did Kabir also agree for roaming in the local market of the city as now they were free. For almost 2 hours Shrishti was continuously shopping some little things for herself, some for her sister, and some for her parents, Kabir was shocked that how can she do this much shopping without getting tired. he was busy in thoughts and came out of his thinking world listening to the scream of Shrishti and feeling a jerk on his hand.

"Hey what happened……?" he asked, confused.

"not what happened…… it's what I found" she said dreamily

"whatever…. What on earth have you found…… please enlighten me too"

Shrishti pointed her finger towards a tea stall where Mirchi pakoras (chili fritters) were also displayed nicely.

"What are you showing, girl."

"aagh…. Are you seriously dumb or is this just to show me" she said getting mad.

"what……?? Dumb and that also me?" he asked dramatically, widening his eyes.

"Whatever…… now we'll stand here and continue fighting or will go and enjoy those heavenly fritters with mesmerizing ginger tea" she was already jumping in excitement.

"How are you so sure about ginger tea?" he asked comically.

"I have superpowers..... I can know everything.... Now come" she said dragging him along with her

He helplessly went behind her holding her bags, as he was a gentleman who can't let a girl carry her shopping bags. Both sat on stools given by the stall vendor and kept on stools in between to place their plates and cups, putting one piece of fritter in her mouth Shrishti felt like heaven, seeing that she was so careless and innocent at the same time Kabir chuckled.

"Why are you laughing...... you to eat.... I bet you'll just love it" she forwarded a pakora toward him.

"no no I can't bet because I have nothing to lose," he said dramatically

"Now let's finish this quickly and leave..... only one place is left on my list"

"what.....!! don't tell me there is one more place to go, I'm already tired. I just wanna die in my bed till next morning"

"Kabirhhhh......!!" she yelled in anger

"What happened?" he asked getting a little worried

"See I know we are here together just for today and after reaching Mumbai we have our different ways...... and this is also true that I'm no one to you......... but....(she sighed heavily) but still I'm giving you a suggestion as a human being or you can say as a well-wisher....... Please don't use the word die, death, etc ever...... and make sure you can teach others the same.........now let's go..... we are getting late, if you trust me then follow me you'll surely love that place"

Kabir didn't say anything and he started following her, after 15 minutes of walking they reached an isolated place which was looking like a hilltop. Kabir was amusingly looking here and there, finally, they stopped walking as they reached the edge of the hill. Both of them were completely silent for approximately 10 minutes. And finally taking a deep breath Shrishti started speaking.

"So tell me, mister, how do you like this place...." she asked, smiling widely at him.

"I'm speechless yr...... I have never seen this beauty of nature ever....... Thank you so much....for bringing me here" he said looking at her but she was busy checking her watch.

"Come let's sit here. The sun is about to set in just 5 minutes..... that view will be very beautiful"

Both of them sat there looking at the beauty of nature without uttering a single word. Shrishti was ready with her camera; she didn't want to lose the opportunity of recording the sunset. Soon the sun eloped behind the clouds and from the other side of the sky a beautiful moon peeped out. Following the moon, within a few minutes, the whole sky was filled with stars. None of them wanted to go back leaving the view, So both of them sat there quietly. There was a serene smile on both of their faces and both were drowned in their thinking world. Suddenly Shrishti screamed due to excitement which pulled Kabir back from his world.

"what just happened.... Did you see any ghost" he asked, terrified at her reaction?

"you stupid..... just look there" she makes him look at the sky where a star was falling from the cosmos and becoming a SHOOTING STAR.

"What to do then?" he asked cluelessly.

"you dumbo..... shooting stars are very rare you know..... whatever wish you'll ask.... It'll be fulfilled" she joined her hands and closed her eyes and silently said her wish and then she opened her eyes and found Kabir looking at her in the place of making his wish.

"why are you looking at me..... why didn't you make any wish...... see it's just disappeared now" she was looking disappointed like a little kid who lost his chance to eat ice cream.

"Wish," he said with a sad chuckle

"What happened?"

"We ask for any wish when we have faith or you can say trust that it will be granted...... but when I'm already very confident in my fate then why should I make a wish" all the while he was looking at the sky with something like pain in his eyes.

"Kabir see......I know that it's your personal space and I should not ask you anything but now I can't control myself...... please tell me what your problem is...... what is there which is making you this sad..... this disappointed..... this dissatisfaction from your life......"

There was complete silence for a few minutes as if he was debating in his heart and mind if he should open up or not but finally, he spoke.

"you know shrishti...... when a person feels strongest and happiest when there is someone who can understand his feelings, his likes and dislikes..... but in my case, there is no one........ I'm the one who is suffering with my thoughts, likes, dislikes, needs, everything all alone....... There is no one to understand me....... And now I just know clearly that no one in this world understands the other one. ``His voice began to break because of emotional turmoil in his heart, so he stopped talking.

"It's not like what you are saying Kabir..... in our life there is always a person who can understand our feelings, our inner turmoil, our happiness just by looking at our face..... it's just sometimes that person just appears automatically and maybe sometimes you have to find that person....... I'm damn sure you'll too get that one for you.... That too very soon" she tried to motivate him with her warm smile at the end.

"How are you so positive, Shrishti," he asked, turning his head towards her.

She was looking directly at the sky and absorbing what nature was pouring out. "sometimes situations convert the person into one..... which is completely different from its personality...."

"can I ask you a question"

"hmmm ask," she said shifting her gaze from the sky to him

"that time when we were sitting at that tea stall.... Why you shouted like that...... mere using a death word won't cause me to di...." before he could complete she kept her palm on his mouth and nodded negatively.... She immediately pulled her hand back and looked at the sky with moist eyes.

"this word, it is very easy to use this word na..... but its reality is way more bitter and devastating..... The most bitter truth but the truth of life is this only....that it can come anytime without any notice.... And if it came then there is no other option..... that's why don't use these words..... leave it..... let's go It's already very late, we didn't even realize that time is 9 already"

"what? we have been sitting here for the past 3 hours" he asked shockingly.

"Yes sir, now let's go..... we have a train to catch tomorrow," she said, stretching her arms while getting up from their sitting position.

3

Soon they were back in their respective hotel rooms, and as both of them were tired they fell asleep immediately. The next morning both of them checked out from the hotel and reached the railway station exactly 15 minutes before the scheduled time train. Shrishti was waiting excitedly for the train but Kabir's face was showing something else. Soon their train arrived and coincidently their seats were in the same compartment but not together, a boy was sitting on the opposite seat, Kabir. Kabir requested that the boy exchange his seat with Shrishti's seat. That boy also agreed easily so after doing all the adjustments both sat in their respective seats.

As soon as Kabir sat on his seat he was again in the mode in which he was when he was coming to Jaipur, he was again continuously staring out of the window.

"Kabir...!! Have you sworn on something...... like the moment you'll step on the train your heartbroken mode will get automatically on" she asked in all seriousness

"No not at all...... and also for your kind information madam I'm not heartbroken," he said, cringing.

"Well yes, a heartbroken person didn't get one girl.... But the kind of face you make it looks like you didn't get 10-12 girls at once" she said jokingly.

"oh my god girl..... a person is not always sad because of not getting a girl no girls..... There are many other reasons too... to get sad" he said with a sad smile on his face.

"see..... even if there are a thousand reasons to be sad..... but this smile of ours.... This should never disappear.... We can solve 100 problems with just a simple smile on our face"

"How.....?"

"see..... suppose you have lots of problems.... You are stuck somewhere you don't wanna be.... But you are helpless to do anything then just let everything be and smile" she said bringing a smile to her face.

"why....?"

"because even if you'll not smile, the problem is not going anywhere..... but if you'll face those problems with a smile then it'll be easy to deal with them". There was a genuine look in her eyes saying this.

"Hmm, well. You are right" he nodded in acceptance.

"I always say what is right sir," she said, raising her fake collars and smiling all wide.

He shook his head in disbelief and smiled looking out of the window. Time passed very soon for both of them to talk together and discuss some philosophical topics that they didn't even realize how they reached Mumbai so soon. The train stopped at one of the platforms of Mumbai railway station. Both of them took out their luggage and came out of the station to book cabs for themselves.

"It was a great time with you Kabir.... I enjoyed your company"

"you enjoyed my company hahaha..... What a joke, I should say that I enjoyed your company, seriously you are the most positive person I have ever met and surely this trip is going to be unforgettable for me."

"definitely....... For me too" she smiled.

"you know what when I went there na.... I was very confused in my thoughts and very sad too..... But thanks to you who taught me the meaning of smile...... thank you so much" there was a heartwarming smile on his face "ok then my cab is here bye" he turned to go waving his hand at her.

"one minute." he turned and gave a questioning look "always keep smiling like this, you don't know but your smile is very beautiful"

he nodded blinking his both eyes together "ok bye see you soon"

"Again, how are you so sure..." she asked with disbelief in her voice.

"you never know" he smiled and left towards his cab

She was smiling idiotically without even blinking her eyes and then she realized that her cab is here too...... She took her bags and moved towards her cab.

Soon Kabir reached his home. Well, he didn't want to go inside but he half-heartedly pressed the doorbell. His mother opened the door and gave him a shocked expression, without saying anything he started moving towards his room but his footsteps halted listening to the voice of his father.

"Finally you remember that there is a house of yours too..... how many times have I called you, why don't you pick up that damn phone of yours..... are you even listening to what I am saying," he said sternly, anger evident in his voice.

Alas, Kabir turned with a plain face.

"I didn't want to, so I didn't pick up the call..... and I'm not a kid anymore that I have to give me every update necessarily," he said plainly with a dead serious face.

"but at least you are accountable for telling about your whereabouts" his dad hissed

"I was in Jaipur..... now happy.... Now you got to know"

"Kabir!! Is this the way to talk to your dad..... on the first place you are wrong and not even accepting it" his mom said

"let it be.... There is no use saying anything to him..... he's just out of his mind..... I'm not just able to understand what on earth is going on in his mind..." his dad said with disappointment filled in his voice.

"That's the problem....... no one understands me and does not even try to.... Everyone is just ready with their opinion about me.... No problem... I'm cool" he said with no emotions trying hard to not show his weaker side.

"That's all..... no more discussion on this topic..... and yes.... The way you eloped leaving all the work behind it has already caused a lot of pending work.... Finish it as soon as possible" his dad stated.

"dad.... I have told you earlier too and again saying this.... I don't want to handle your company..... I want to fulfill my dreams..... why are you not understanding"

"I know your useless dreams very well..... which don't have any future and don't have any benefit..... this is my last decision, you are joining the office again from tomorrow that's it" he was not in the mood to listen anymore.

"I will not go and that's final for sure"

"you make him understand before I take any strict decision. I don't know when this boy will become mature," he said to mom and left.

Kabir also left for his room without uttering a single word.

Here Shrishti reached her home, her father was already waiting for her at the main gate of their house. Shrishti stepped down from the cab and hugged him tightly.

"paaa......"

"shrriiii, how's my tigress," he said caressing her head

"Now tigress will be like one only na." she giggled, smiling wide at her dad.

"Come let's go in..... Your mom and sister are waiting for you for a long"

"hmmm...... let's go"

Both entered the house and her mom and di welcomed her like a queen coming from another kingdom, four of them talked for many hours. Shrishti told each and everything about the trip and distributed their gifts too, as she was tired because of the journey she had her food a little early and went into her room, after taking a shower she directly jumped onto her bed with her camera.

Here Kabir was sitting expressionless in his room, he didn't even realize that time was past 10 PM already. He came out of a trance listening to the opening of the door of his room, it was his mom with a plate of his favorite cheese sandwich in her hand. He stared for a moment then looked away.

"Kabir... Leave this anger na.... see it's already very late and I know you must be starving" she said sitting beside him "come Let me feed you with my own hands"

"no need...... I'll eat on my own.... You say, for what you are here...... I know dad had sent you here..... Right?" he said looking to another side

"It's not like that son...... at least look at me first" she made him look at her.

"See, I understand that you are not interested in handling the company and you want to fulfill your dreams..... but at least once think about your dad.... Once, look at him too...... he has many hopes from you..... now you'll do like this then it will be fair enough..... you are only a single child of ours, now if you'll back out like this then what will happen to us...... tell me..."

He closed his eyes in frustration........

"You have to do it, Kabir........ You indeed have responsibilities as a son and you can't back out..." his mind said.

"But what about my life, my dreams, my goals....." His heart said.

"Sometimes we have to leave our most precious thing just for the sake of family...... and this is the time..... You have to sacrifice Kabir" his mind said.

Kabir opened his eyes and took a deep breath he said......

"ok I'll do this......I'll go to the office tomorrow yet again..... Please inform him too..... Now it is fine?" he asked his mom who was looking at him with hope-filled eyes.

"you are happy..... Are you Kabir?" she asked, caressing his head.

"Now it is ok the way it is," he said, blankly.

"ok now eat.... Wait let me make you eat"

She put a morsel in his mouth. He didn't say anything and finished his food by taking it from his mom's hand...... after feeding him mom left for her room. Kabir was sitting blankly with a sad face and was staring out of the window then he remembered her words....... Shrishti's words......

"Suppose you have lots of problems.... You are stuck somewhere you don't wanna be.... But you are helpless to do anything then just let everything be and smile......Because even if you'll not smile, the problem is not going anywhere, But if you'll face those problems with a smile then it'll be easy to deal with them ...."

"you were right Shrishti, now there is no other option in front of me..... Except one...... smiling......" He smiled sadly "but now it's enough of being sad..... Now I'm not gonna permit anyone to make me sadder" He got up energetically and started packing all his things in bags. Shrishti was chuckling seeing the pictures she clicked on the trip.

"what is it shrii darling..... Looking very happy..... Show me also whatever you are seeing" Monika, Shrishti's sister said entering her room.

"When I said no......huh.... come" She patted the space near her indicating her to take a seat beside her on the bed.

"It seems like this trip was very awesome," She said sitting beside her.

"Really....... See how beautiful these pictures are" She said, showing her the camera. Monika was swiping the pictures but was stuck at one pick..... It was Kabir's picture.

"Who is this boy..... Why are you having his photo" she said squinting her eyes

"oh, madam over thinker..... There is nothing like you are thinking ok..... He is just a friend.... The poor boy met me on the train.... He was very sad so I thought why not boost him up then we enjoyed the trip together as we both were alone"

"Is it...." she asked, still squinting her eyes.

"Of course," she said in a duh tone.

"well don't you think you help strangers more than required madam shrishti"

"I like actually, I enjoy helping others...... it gives me peace," she said dreamily looking upward.

"Ok now.... Time to sleep it's already very late.... You must be feeling tired" Shrishti hugged her and then slipped under her blanket, Monika left after switching off the lights.

Next morning

Kabir woke up on time and went to have breakfast with mom and dad. He was eating silently and suddenly his dad started speaking.

"I'm glad that you are going to the office...... again...... I'm hoping you'll not elope again" he taunted.

"Now please leave this na...... He is going at least" his mom tried to save him from further taunting sessions.

"yes, I'm going.... See there." he indicated towards the servants who were bringing his bags.

"Now what is all this.... Where are you going.... Tell me fast" his mom instantly turned into freaking mode as she can't see her only child going away again.

"What is this Kabir..... Say something" his dad asked sternly.

"Don't worry please...... I'll go to the office too.... I'm just shifting to the house near the office, that's it" he casually answered while having his food.

"And who made this decision?" his dad asked, getting more impatient.

"I...... you want me to handle your company..... No problem, I'll do it..... But I want peace and to live alone..... as a grownup I can too.... There is nothing to worry about"

"ok do what you want" his dad finally gave up as his only concern for the time was his company which however Kabir was going to handle.

"how the hell do what you want..... You are going nowhere," she said, fuming as her child was going away from her.

"Mamma, please no emotional blackmail, I understood your point so please try to understand my point too," he said standing up from his seat and adjusting his blazer "ok then, I'm leaving..... Bye," he said, hugging his mom and leaving not before giving the order to the workers to shift his luggage to another house where he is going to live alone.

Shrishti got up from her beauty sleep and ran toward her mom for a morning hug as her mom is her energy booster.

"from where the sun rose today." her mom said dramatically looking out of the window to check the direction of the sun "how are you up this early madam"

"just like that..... I thought why not give you a surprise.... Let's make tea.... Where are dad and Di (sister)"

"Elsewhere, they definitely will be sitting in the garden with their serious discussion on world economics as today is a holiday you know" there was a sarcastic smile on her face.

Soon after making tea both Shrishti and her mom came out to the garden where Monika and dad were sitting together arguing on some general topic.

"presenting hot tea shrishti special..... Now no more discussion on your world economics" She said teasing her sister and dad

"Sure sure" both of them raised their hands in surrender.

"umm.... Papa, I want to talk about something" she hesitantly started the conversation.

"yes, say"

"see.... I know what I'm doing is going well, but recently I sent my portfolio to Mehra fashion ltd..... And that got approved.... So can I join from next Monday" she said with hope-filled in her eyes as somewhere she had an idea that it'll not be easy to make her parents agree to this?

"What is the need to change the job in the first place shrii..... I'm saying, "Leave your job and stay at home." her mom stated in a little authoritative manner.

"Mamaaaaa...... please don't tell me that, every single person dreams to work in that huge company, and on top of that, I got the direct post of head designer..... Please, mamma.... Papa Please.... Say yes.... We don't know what is there in store for me, please let me do what I want..... I request....." her puppy eyes were already complimenting her statement and she was sure, now they will finally say yes.

"ok fine.... Only for you.... Now Happy" her dad said before her mom can give her more lectures.

"Very happy." She said hugging him and showing her tongue to her mother playfully "you are the best papa"

Here Kabir reached his office after many days. He was standing at the main gate of the building, somewhere something was breaking in his heart but taking a deep breath he stepped into the office, all started wishing him good morning, while replying to everyone he moved towards his cabin...... where his PA was already present.

"Good morning Sir," she said smilingly and professionally

"morning Khushi...... what's up...... all good." he asked, taking a seat on his chair.

"yes sir..... How about you"

"Well I wanna escape from this planet but aliens are not ready to grant me a plot on mars...." he said chuckling at his line "leave it, I'm sure a lot of work must be pending. So go and begin to prepare a list and give it to me as soon as possible....ok....."

"Sure sir, I'll do that..... One more thing I wanted to inform you"

"go ahead...."

"Our previous designer had left the company in your absence so one new designer was appointed. She'll join from Monday...... she is the best sir..... All were shocked seeing such talent at a very young age, I'll give you her file please check it once"

"ok sure, give it to me"

"Sure sir" said she left his cabin, to begin with, her work leaving him with the pile of files to which he was least interested in working.

4

Shrishti was busy convincing her mother to let her join the new job. She was following her mom like a 5-year-old kid in the whole house holding the drape of her saree from behind.

"mamma at least listen to me. For god sake let me speak one time. she said while running behind her

"why? Should I listen to you.... Have you ever listened to me... no..... So I'll not listen too" she was adamant about not listening to shrishti

"hey..... di..... why are you laughing..... say something na..." she pleaded to her sister who was laughing at her condition.

"Now what do I do when I know very well no one of you is going to listen to me..... Please carry on"

"haww.... Very bad.... I'll also not help you when you come to me.... Try me" she threatened Monika while walking behind mom

"mamma please give me chance at least" she requested entering the kitchen

"what....? Say it fast," she said, crossing her hands near her chest with a straight face.

"See, I know you are worried for me but please agree to it.... It is my dream and on top of it they appointed me on their own, not many people get a chance to work in such a big company." She said taking out her cutest puppy face "please, sweet mamma, cute mamma says yes........"

"done with your emotional drama.... What do I do with this girl" she said dramatically, throwing her hands in the air.

"yeah....... Means you are fine with this..... Right?" shrishti squealed hugging her mom from the back

"hmm..."

She went towards her room dancing like a maniac, leaving her mom and sister with moist eyes.

At the office,

Kabir's Pa handed him over the portfolio of the new designer to check it once so he was busy checking it, immediately he was very impressed with the designs..... After checking the whole file he was about to check the name of the person but suddenly his phone started ringing so he closed the file and kept it aside and picked up the phone call.

On call:

Kabir: hello.....

Person: where are your feet man... let me take your blessing..... Who knows if I'll meet a bigger idiot than you ever or not (sarcasm was dripping from his voice)

Kabir: ya, you to call me an idiot...... others also give me this honor why will you stay behind..... After all, who I am to you..... (He said almost saddening voice)

Person: see I knew it, you and your emotional drama..... are you drunk already in the early morning....

Kabir: not at all man, these office boys never give me tea on time.... I repeat never... (He was complaining like a nursery kid who didn't get his favorite chocolate.)

Person: don't even try to change the topic ok..... Tell me.... Where you eloped suddenly..... No text no phone calls..... What is this behavior..... Don't you love your life......(he said with a hint of anger in his voice)

Kabir: Aaditya Bro, will you please now stop getting angry...... if you wanted to talk only, then why did you call me..... At least let me also speak a word or two..... (He said comically)

Aaditya: why should I not get angry.... Who disappears like this without informing even once.... Do you have any idea how worried I was for you idiot......

Kabir: aww....... See only you are the one for me, who thinks about me like this..... ok now don't be mad I'm sorry I went to find Peace

Aaditya: oh so did you find it.....

Kabir: what.....?

Aaditya: peace idiot......

Kabir: yeah..... kind of.... Ok, now I'll call you later. I have a lot of work to finish.... Wait, why don't we do one thing.... Come to my home near the office we'll enjoy our bro time and as a piece of news, I shifted there only..... so yeah come tonight.

Aaditya: Ok done..... I'll come.... Bye

Kabir: Bye....

Call cut

After talking with Aaditya Kabir left for a meeting..... In a conference hall.

Here after getting permission from both mom and dad Shrishti was feeling very happy so she decided to make a painting. She put her canvas on the stand and took out her painting colors and paint brushes. She started painting and after 3 hours she was done with her painting. she was smiling seeing the painting she had made 5 minutes before, unknowingly she made the scenery of 2 people sitting on a hilltop witnessing a shooting star, she came out of her trance listening aww from Monika.

"awww...... shrii..... What you just made girl..... This is so beautiful" she chided like a teenage girl.

"I don't know what, I just painted, what came to my mind," Shrishti said, still adoring the beauty she created. "how can this be possible.... This is the same scene where I and.... And Kabir was sitting on the hilltop......" she thought, wondering if the fact just clicked in her head.

"Maybe that day that view settled in my heart in a way that I didn't even realize what I was drawing," she wondered.

"oh my Picasso...... where are you lost...." Monika chided

"no....no.... nothing..... I just remembered something" shrishti tried to act normal but still her mind was busy wondering.

"ok, now It's already very late..... Go and sleep" Shrishti makes a disgusting face hearing the word called sleep "see, no need to make this face ok..... Without any tantrums go and sleep otherwise I have nuclear weapons too..... You know" Monika said smirking

"Ok, my lord....... Going.....I know both of you very well.... You and your Nuclear weapon...huh" Shrishti taunted with a scoff.

Making sure that Shrishti slept, Monika left the room after switching off the lights.....

Here Kabir reached home late and found that Aaditya was already asleep. Maybe he was waiting for Kabir for a long time.

"Oh, my dear god..... What I have done to you..... I only have one single friend that too is like this" He said looking upward dramatically "now he is sleeping like a baby and I don't have the heart to wake him up..... Aaditya bro I'm leaving you now but will not in the morning." After murmuring to himself Kabir left to change.

He did his dinner and slept because to whom he had planned to talk the whole night was already in the lap of deep sleep.

Next Morning, Aaditya woke up before Kabir. He went to prepare breakfast for both of them. As Kabir loves grilled sandwiches made by aaditya. Soon Kabir also woke up and after getting fresh before he could leave the room Aaditya came in the room with a tray in his hand.

"Hey Aditi you are awake already, Where are you, man?" Kabir chided.

"see..... If you called me that one more time..... then my dear friend I'll eat all these sandwiches alone..... and yes you're this most loved tea that too I'll have myself." He said in all seriousness.

"hey..... Hey..... No...no no no...... don't please don't do this injustice with me..... I'm sorry sollyyyy" He started his drama earning an eye roll from Aaditya

"ok ok.... Now enough of your drama..... Come sit.... Otherwise, this will get all cold" Aaditya called him to eat breakfast.

"yeahh..... That's my Aditii" he bites his tongue "sorry sorry, Aaditya" he said holding both his ears cutely.

Both of them enjoyed breakfast together and made plans to pass their Sunday happily.

Here Shrishti was very excited about her new office and was planning everything for her first day in the office. Seeing her so happy her family was also very happy. The whole day passed like this, at night Shrishti decided to sleep early so there should be not a single chance of getting late.

Monday morning

"mamaaaaa......... where is my white shirt..... I'm not able to find that" She was shouting like a little kid "oh, that...... I threw it in the washing machine..... wore something" Mom said from the kitchen while preparing her breakfast

"damn it.... that was my lucky champ.....I wanted to wear that only on my first day at the office.... Now what do I do"

Finally, Shrishti selected a decent shirt with a pair of jeans, Left her hair loose, and wrapped a matching scarf around her neck. She took her famous artistic look and came out of her room to have food and after listening to thousands of do's and don'ts from mom she left for the office which was 30 minutes away.

Here in the office, Kabir came on his regular time and started his work according to his to-do list. While he was working Khushi entered with a basket in her hand.

"may I come in sir"

"yes..... Come in." he said working on his laptop

"Excuse me, sir..... Someone sent this for you from a pet company" she said showing the basket she was holding.

"oh!! So finally it is here....... Keep it on the table...." He said looking at her with excitement dancing in his eyes.

"But sir..... What is it"

"Just give me a minute." He kept his laptop aside and took the basket from her hand

He opened the basket with a heartwarming smile. And a little LHASA pup jumped out and directly landed on Kabir and started licking his whole face. He was enjoying her cute antics.

"hey...... easy...... easy..... Baby... stop" surprisingly she stopped on his single command

"aww..... sir.... She is so cute....." Khushi said happily.

"hmm...... So let's give her a name than" he thought for a minute then exclaimed, "this is my CHIKU" he said kissing her and Chiku moved her little tail to show her happiness.

"ok sir I'll take your leave"

Kabir thought to play a little with chiku and then continue his work.

On the other hand, Shrishti reached the office and asked the receptionist about her appointment. She guided Shrishti to meet Khushi. Shrishti went near the little chamber of Khushi to ask her about the further proceedings.

"Excuse me..... Miss"

"Yes," she replied in a professional tone.

"good morning..... I'm here for the post of design head..... Here is my appointment letter" she forwarded her letter to Khushi.

"oh, so you are Shrishti.... Glad to meet you madam....... sir is waiting for you..... For the leftover little formalities, you have to meet him"

"Yes, why not..... Where is his cabin.......?"

"let me show you"

Khushi led Shrishti towards Kabir's cabin and after leaving her at the door she went back to her chamber...... Shrishti took a deep breath and opened the door.

"May I come in sir...?"

She found a curly-haired man standing there facing the other side. His face was not visible but somewhere he was looking like someone familiar to her. The man (Kabir) turned and before she could register the identity of the person, Chiku jumped from his hands and ran towards Shrishti. She screamed her lungs out and started running into the big cabin, Like a little kid saving her life while chiku was running behind her. To save the girl from chiku without noticing her, Kabir started chasing chiku, three of them were playing "ring around the roses" in the cabin, and finally, both of them noticed each other.

"Shrishti you here" surprise was clearly evident in his voice complimenting his wide eyes.

"Hey, this should be my question," she said while running cutely here and there in the cabin to somehow save herself.

"what do you mean....?"

"First stop this, please...... I'm tired..... Please.... Please" She said pointing to chiku who was in no mood to back out.

Finally, Kabir caught chiku and held her tightly, well she was wriggling to get free from his grip but he didn't leave her, here Shrishti due to utter shock got almost unconscious. After tying chiku with his desk,. Kabir made Shrishti sit on the couch so she could calm herself down after a few minutes he gave her water to drink, meanwhile, chiku was innocently looking at Shrishti with her puppy dog eyes which were enough to freak shrishti out anytime.

"Now feeling good," he asked while taking a seat beside her.

"hmmm..... Finally"

"Now tell me what you are doing here," he asked, being all curious.

"I'm appointed here as the design head. Today is my first day, so I'm here to meet the head of this company Mr. Kabir Mehra. See what a coincidence you are also Kabir he is too Kabir, ok leave it please ask sir to come. I'm eager to meet him. she was getting excited as if her dream was going to come true finally.

"oh...... so you are the one who is appointed as a designing head...... hmm I see"

"yes...... now call him na..... And you didn't tell me what are you doing here...... wait do you also work here......?.... It'll be fun na working together here under the name of such a big company, now will you please call me my lord" she ended dramatically.

"I am only Kabir Mehra Miss. Investigator" he thought, smiling mischievously. He got up decently and with a heartwarming smile, he forwarded his hand.

"Hello…….. Shrishti….. Welcome to our company…… myself….. KABIR…… KABIR MEHRA…" Her mouth opened in a perfect O shape but she immediately controlled her shocking expressions.

"You are kidding me right…? I know the names are just a coincidence…… now c'mon please call Mr. Mehra" she whined like a kid helplessly at the end.

He gave her "are you even serious" look "why would I lie to you Shrishti……? I am Kabir Mehra…… trust me"

"my god…….. I can't believe this……."

"See….. I told you already….. "YOU NEVER KNOW," he said with a proud smile showing he was right.

"I don't know how this happened but…. Leave it….. Nice to meet you again…….. Sir……" she suddenly changed her tone from friendly to professional and extended her right hand for a shake.

"same here"

"I hope you have already been through my portfolio….. So from when and where I can start my work sir"

"yes, I have seen it already…… you are a very talented person Shrishti…..but wait a minute…. What is this sir……?"

"You are my boss here so I have to call you sir no……" she said in a duh tone.

"No, it's Kabir for you remember this"

"why anything special…..?" She said mischievously

"yes…… because you are my friend first and then an employee here"

"oh so I'm your friend…?" she tapped her chin with her index finger as if she was trying to figure the fact out.

"why? Are you not my friend...... or we are enemies......I THOUGHT you taught me many things you had surely done all those things for me as a friend........ Or you did it as an enemy" He squinted his eyes at the end for the extra effect.

"ha-ha...... enemy and you..... No... No, I can't afford any kind of hostility against you specially..... So yes we are better as friends" She said dramatically

"very good"

In between all their discussions chiku was feeling left out so she barked in her little cute voice due to which Shrishti jumped on her place and then she remembered she is in a highly insecure place, so she was back to her defensive mode ready to run anywhere.

"oh my god..... see my chiku is feeling left out, she's trying hard to gain our attention....... wait, kiddo I'm opening you"

"noooooooo...... no no no" She screamed, literally screamed frightened before he could open Chiku's tie.

"What happened....?"

"Please don't open her ties otherwise I'm dead next moment"

"chill Shrishti...... chiku is very friendly in nature..... she doesn't bite at all" he tried to assure her but it was working opposite to her.

"Is it....? If she is that friendly, why was she running behind me....? I'm sure I'll be dead meat next moment"

"because she was trying to play with you...... wait let me introduce both of you" He got up from the couch and after picking chiku in his hands he again sat beside Shrishti "see.... How cute is she..... Hold it"

"no no..... Very.... cute.... But keep it to yourself please" She said, still being afraid. "she'll not do anything..... Just hold it once" he assured

Before Shrishti could protest he placed chiku in Shristi's lap and surprisingly she (chiku) adjusted herself comfortably in her lap and slept within seconds.

"Aaaaaa........ How can she sleep instantly...... Kabir, please pick it up...... otherwise I'll start crying" She was already on the verge of freaking out.

"why are you getting so afraid..... See how cutely she is sleeping in your lap...... caress her back once.....you'll feel good" he moved his palm on chicku's back trying to teach shrishti.

"what if she bites me......"

"she'll not..... Trust me....."

Finally, slowly Shrishti caressed Chiku's back, and feeling her touch she moved a little and opened her cute little eyes and started licking Shrishti's hand...... firstly Shrishti got frightened but then she enjoyed playing with chiku.

"see.... I told you na she is so cute and friendly"

"Sorry for reacting like that..... Actually, I'm dog phobic"

"But see, now you are playing with it" he replied smilingly, seeing chiku sleeping cutely.

"thank you...... for this new experience.....Ok.... we talked a lot; Now tell me my work..... So I could start working" and here she was back filled with enthusiasm to start her work.

"ok...... so as you know you are designing head from now onwards so you have to handle all the big projects by yourself and other projects will be handled by your department"

"got it...."

"Come with me, let me show you your cabin"

Kabir led Shrishti towards her cabin which was on the opposite side of his cabin. Shrishti happily followed him. Shrishti entered her new cabin and was in awe seeing its beauty. She came out of her dreamy world listening to Kabir.

"So from now onwards this is your cabin Madam Shrishti....... Feel free for anything" He declared smilingly

"thanks..... And yes, one more thing..... I'm glad you took my advice seriously and started smiling"

"How are you so sure that I'm smiling because of your advice.......?" he asked amusingly.

"I know......" she shrugged.

Without saying anything he left for his cabin and Shrishti started studying the files kept on her desk so that she could understand the needs and demands of the projects.

5

Everything was going well. Shrishti was super enjoying her work as it's her dream job, everyone in the office was also enjoying working with her as she was very friendly with everyone. The situation of Kabir was constant. He used to work the whole day with a warm smile on his face but deep down in his heart, he knew that he was not happy at all, almost 15 days passed like this. Now Shrishti was used to her work in the office.

One fine day she was working till late so after finishing her work she locked her cabin and was walking towards the exit but she glanced towards Kabir's cabin and found him still sitting there alone, With his face resting down on the desk. First she thought to go near him but she decided to not invade his privacy. Next few days she noticed the same thing... He was sitting till late in the office even without any work.

"I don't know but I'm sure something is bothering him...... I think I should talk to him and probably I can help him.... Otherwise, he is also my friend so as a friend I can ask him his problem......" The same thought was revolving in her head the whole day. She finished her work and went towards his cabin and knocked on the door.

"Come in," He said while rubbing his palms on his face, Meanwhile Shrishti came and sat in front of him "oh

Shrishti...." He said again with his heartwarming smile.

"How are you Kabir.....?" she asked with a serious face that was already telling him that she suspected something.

"I'm good..... Why are you asking," he said, not looking in her eyes.

"then why are you smiling fake"

"what....?? Ha-ha..... Why would I smile fake"

"Because you are not fine but you are pretending that you are very happy....."

"no Shrishti nothing is like that...... you are overthinking..... Don't stress your mind because of me.... Well, I indeed give tension only to everyone..... But still saying don't take tension for me...... I'm fine"

Again he tried his best to not look directly in her eyes.

"ok then very good.... If you are fine..... You should be.... But I'm saying again whether you accept it or not you are not fine Kabir." She said standing up "now don't sit like this here..... Go home.... Your family must be waiting..... You'll get sick if you keep on sitting here till late..." She left saying this before giving him any chance to speak.

"Nobody is waiting for me..... if I go home or not doesn't matter..... How come she knows that I'm not fine..... How did she understand me.....? How she understands everything going on in my mind" He closed his eyes and took a deep breath. Finally, he also decided to go back home as it was getting late now.

Here Shrishti reached home and after having food she directly went into her room and sat on the swing placed on her balcony and started staring at the moon that was shining among the clouds Sadly, almost 30 minutes passed, She abruptly spoke up to herself.

"why am I sitting here like this.....? What just happened to me.... He is the one who is sad..... Not me"

"Because you can't see anyone sad shrii," her heart said

"Hmmm..... I can't see anyone sad around me..... and in fact, he is my friend..... What do I do to make him happy.... How do I know why he is troubled?"

Kabir was also sitting on his balcony with chiku in his lap and a mug of Tea in his right hand. He was thinking something very deeply when he broke his silence himself.

"Enough is enough....... now I can't take it anymore..... I need someone to talk to.... Who can understand my feelings.... Who may not laugh at me.... Who may understand what I want..... but who is this who....? Shrishti..... yes she is very sincere, she'll definitely understand my point and maybe help me too.... But... but how do I talk to her.... Let it be.... I'll talk to her anyways....."

While thinking all this he finished his tea and after keeping chiku on her mini bed he also slept.

Here Shrishti also slept thinking about Kabir's problem.

Next morning.

Everyone started their day, as usual, everyone was doing their work in the office, Shrishti was thinking that how to ask Kabir about his problem, and on the other side Kabir was also thinking about how he'll talk to Shrishti, finally, he decided to take her out on some café so that he could talk freely with her.

The whole day passed, and finally, in the evening around 5 PM, Kabir went to Shrishti's cabin. Before entering he knocked like a gentleman.

"Come in," She said while working on a design, After a few seconds finally she looked up "oh Kabir it's you...... you don't need to knock we are friends remember...."

"It's ok Shrishti, ethically I should..... Ok, leave it.... I'm here to ask you something" he asked, fidgeting with his fingers.

"yes say"

"not as a boss but as a friend I need to talk to you..... if you don't mind can you come with..."

"ok..... After office, we'll talk whatever you want"

"Please continue your work tomorrow right now, come with me.... It's urgent"

"umm ok fine...... just give me 5 minutes..... Let me wrap up my work at least"

"ok I'm waiting in the parking lot to come soon"

"O.k.," she said smilingly. Soon Shrishti finished her work and left towards the parking lot where Kabir was already waiting for her.

In the car

"Yes, say what you wanted to say......" she asked, suddenly curious.

"hmmm...... yes I had to talk about something," he said calmly

"yes.... And I'm asking that something only.... What is it.... Tell me..."

"umm..... Yes.... Telling..... Take a breath first...." He said a little hesitated

"what do I say..... How do I start..." he thought, scratching his head.

"I know Kabir, what you want to talk about..... I know you are disturbed and need someone to talk to, And I know too that you are feeling difficult to speak about. I think I should start" she thought, studying his unsaid words.

"Kabir.... We never talk about our families... you know in my family we are 4 members..... Mom, dad, di (sister) and me.... And among all of us, I'm the most mischievous one....." She said chuckled "you also tell me about your family, how many members are you all"

"We also have a small family..... Mom, Dad, and me..." he said plainly

"Oh..... Don't you have any besties....."

"yes.... Aaditya...... We have been buddies since childhood..... he is the one and only friend of mine" while telling about Aaditya there was another kind of excitement in his eyes which she had never seen before.

"Then who am I a potato?" she said, narrowing her eyebrows.

"hey no.... it's not like that.... Let me finish first.... I was saying that after Aaditya, you are my friend who listens and understands my things maybe from the heart....." he finished with a genuine look in his eyes.

"What is this maybe from the heart.....? Don't you trust me" she said controlling her laughter

"Now you too will make fun of me..... Very bad....." he pouted

"Friends are only there to make fun sir.... Don't you have knowledge about this...." she said moving her eyebrows up and down

"you know what? You are impossible....." he shook his head dramatically.

"I know......" she said, smiling widely and raising her fake collars.

"You are irritating me intentionally.... Don't you....?" he asked raising an eyebrow

"Ummm......" she started thinking seriously after 1 minute she said "a big YES" with this she burst into laughter.

Seeing her laughing like a maniac he also started laughing. "Shrishti you are, seriously impossible girl"

Finally, when she calmed down she looked out and found that the car was moving on the seaside road, she exclaimed

"Kabir......"

"hmm say"

"See the beach is near and the sun is about to set.... Come na let's go there, it'll be soothing"

"but we were going to the caf....." he finally agreed, seeing her pleading puppy eyes "ok done......"

Within 5 minutes both were standing on the beach. There was a different kind of happiness on Shrishti's face. She was happy like a kid who got his favorite chocolate. Seeing her happiness Kabir was automatically smiling, he didn't even realize it when she dragged him with her towards the area where the waves were brushing their feet.

"See how beautiful and soothing this sunset is" she excitedly squealed like a kid waving her both hands in the air.

"Hmmm......" he said, deeply inhaling the fragrance of wet soil near them. "You say, would you have felt this same serenity and soothing feeling in any 5-star cafe which we are feeling sitting here on these rocks with waves brushing our feet"

"Never Ever" he replied gazing at the vast sea in front of his eyes.

"Ok so finally, spill what is bothering you and what you wanted to talk to me about."

he closed his eyes and said feeling every word

"Thehro Zara samait lun is khushboo ko main, kya pata phir kabhi naseeb ho na ho"

"Wow, Kabir I really didn't have any idea that you are a poet too...... quite impressive to be honest...... may I add a line or two if you say" he nodded encouraging her

"Bade naseeb se milte hain lamhe sukoon ke, fir kya pata kal hum ho na ho"

"Actually I'm not any poet or something, it's just sometimes it just comes out of flow, maybe when something touches my heart it comes out automatically then, well you too are not bad you know," he said scratching his head.

"No, you said just like that sitting casually which is very good, if you try you can do well, and about me..... Haha it's just like a time pass sometimes." she said looking at the sun that drowned in the sea

"If I say about doing, then I can do a lot in many fields, but nobody allows me...... well, leave it right now my mood is very good and I don't want to spoil it because of some stupid thoughts"

"Well, you are CEO of this big renowned company, even India's youngest CEO, so just out of curiosity can I ask something"

"Yes, of course"

"Was this your DREAM, to be what you are today in your life"

"DREAM...!!" he chuckled sadly

"hmmm......"

"We'll talk about this some other time, you'll be late for home, let's get back hmm..." he tried his level best to avoid the question, pretending as normal as he could.

"Okk......"

Soon Kabir dropped Shrishti at her home and then he left for his home.

After reaching home Kabir played with chiku and was feeling a little relieved after talking with Shrishti. By the way, he was not able to talk about the main topic but he was feeling good. Happily, he had his dinner, and finally, he slept peacefully after many sleepless nights.

After reaching home Shrishti was also happy but she was not sure of the reason...... After dinner again she took her dairy and sat on the balcony as per her habit...... and wrote about her whole day...... after writing the last line there were tear droplets in her eyes but she silently wiped them off and slept.

6

After breakfast Shrishti hurriedly left for the office, she was already late for the office but the Mumbai traffic was also there to greet her.

Here in the office, a big storm arrived when Shrishti reached office. Everyone was running here and there, after keeping her stuff in her cabin she approached Kabir's cabin...... he was also very busy with his work. Soon the meeting was over and Kabir grabbed the deal on which he had least confidence and now everyone in the office was very excited for the new deal..... All were working very enthusiastically here Kabir was sitting in his cabin and was drowned in lots of work suddenly his phone rang..... Dad was flashing on screen.

On call:
Kabir: yes dad... good evening.... (he started)
K/dad: how was the meeting.....
Kabir: good.... We bagged the deal......
K/dad: seriously...... very good Kabir... proud of you....
Kabir: thanks..... (He was about to cut but dad interrupted meanwhile Shrishti was also standing at the door of his cabin)
K/dad: son, it's been many days at least once, come home..... If not for me, at least come for your mom.

Kabir: I'm not coming dad...... and yes I'll talk to mamma too.... Bye.

Call cut

Shrishti fake coughed to gain his attention. "hey Shrishti come....why are you standing there" he tried hard to change his mood instantly.

"I came to show you some designs.... If you have a little time" she said, waving her tab in her hand.

"yes, show me...." he took the tab from Shrishti and started taking the overview of the designs

"All the designs are good, finalize them."

"Think like It's already done." she smiled.

"Ok then, I'll talk to the modal for the photo shoot and the dates," he said while looking at something in the cupboard of his desk.

"ok..... Now I'll take your leave"

She stood up and walked towards the door but she turned and said something which left Kabir speechless.

"Kabir........ See resentment is ok.... But please never hurt your mother, because a mother cannot see her child sad..... You should go to your mom" Saying this she left.

Hearing these words he was in deep thought. But keeping his thoughts aside he again continued his work. The whole day passed by casually working and after finishing her work on time Shrishti left for her home. Because she was hungry like anything, she hurriedly reached home and found everyone was having tea with her favorite snacks. Seeing this she started her mellow drama.

"Oh, my dear god.... See what's going on on the earth...... Here a person is starving and heartless family members are eating alone and enjoying....." She said dramatically.

"Please join in madam...... We were waiting for you only, and please keep this over acting with you for future purposes." Monika sarcastically called her toward them.

"huh…. First, at least see here there is a plate for you too" her mom called her shaking her head in disbelief.

"Why are you both just behind my daughter…. Come shrii sit with me." his dad fake scolded them and patted the space near him on the sofa calling shrishti to sit with him.

"Very good, the moment she comes you just jump at her side" her mom complained like usual but both father-daughter duos ignored her royally and started munching their snacks.

"Very bad dad……" Monika whined.

"No dad, very good." she said stuffing her favorite snack in her mouth and all of them burst into laughter

"Ok now, jokes apart….. Shrii how your office is going, they are treating you well…. Right…?" dad asked with concern for his little princess.

"Yes dad, everything is going great, and everyone in the office is very humble and soft spoken…. My boss Kabir he's my friend too. I didn't have any idea that I'm going to work in his company." She told everything all excitedly and happily.

"That's great"

On the other hand in the office Kabir also finished his work on time and went into the parking area to take his car. After sitting in the car he remembered what Shrishti said earlier, Unknowingly he turned his car towards his parent's house. After 30 minutes of driving, he was standing in front of his parent's house…… hesitatingly he pressed the doorbell Luckily his mom opened the door. Seeing her one and only child standing in front of her after many days tears automatically dwelled in her eyes, seeing her like this Kabir immediately hugged her tightly, but in response, he earned soft slaps from mom on his head.

"you are very bad..... very bad..... I'm not gonna talk to you, you came very soon to meet your mom, why didn't you delay it a little more....... I would hai died remembering you....." Before she could complete he placed his palm on her lips to prevent her from saying anything further.

"Enough scolding pretty mom.... Keep it safe for the future why waste all the scolding in a single day" he said slightly smiling

"oh yes..... I forgot it's dinner time, you must be hungry come I'll feed you" she said dragging him into the house holding his one hand like he was again her small baby.

"someone was not ready to talk to me..." he asked, wondering while looking here and there controlling his smile.

"oh, c'mon I know all your drama" she scolded again and kept on dragging him with her. He smiled and entered the dining room with his mom where his dad was already sitting waiting for dinner to arrive.

"Great kabir that you are back, come sit we'll eat together," his father said with a smile when she saw him entering the dining area.

"I'm here for tonight only..... I'll leave tomorrow morning," he said plainly.

"ok, we'll talk about that tomorrow only, live in the present, don't think much about the future..... And you wait for a little, I'll be back, don't eat this food..." his mom said indicating the food kept on the table

"But why....? I'm hungry mamma... where are you going"

"Just wait for 10 minutes I'm coming"

He nodded and mom walked towards the kitchen. After a few minutes, she came back with Kabir's favorite cheese sandwich in her hand, seeing that Kabir became very happy. "You went to make this," he asked, becoming a little emotional.

"So.... My son is back after so many days. I had to make his favorite food. Who knows if you eat well there or not, don't know whether Shanta is taking good care of you or not.

He hugged her while still sitting on his seat..... Unknowingly a teardrop fell from his eye but he didn't let anyone know.

"thank you, mamma"

She caressed his head and he happily had his food.... After that, he went to his room to sleep. Next day Kabir left early in the morning for his house to get ready for the office while driving he got a call from Aaditya.

On call

Kabir: yo bro, say....

Aaditya: where are you, man......?

Kabir: going back home.

Aaditya: going back home early morning..... Where were you the whole night sir?

Kabir: went to meet mamma......

Aaditya: whatttt......??

Kabir: why are you reacting like I did something illegal, man

Aaditya: didn't you say you'll not go.....

Kabir: umm...... someone said not to hurt mamma so I went to meet her.... And If I say truly I felt good too seeing that smile on mamma's face

Aaditya: oh..... well who is this someone (he interrogated)

Kabir: someone special......(he said teasing him)

Aaditya: Tell me fast.... You know very well you can't hide anything from me

Kabir: she is my friend......

Aaditya: she means, she is a girl.... You made a friend that too, a girl, and didn't think to tell me even for once...... you traitor (he said getting angry a bit)

Kabir: hey why are you getting mad..... She is a girl only I didn't make alien, my friend

Aaditya: I'm feeling complex now..... other than me you have one more friend.

Kabir: ok now enough of your drama, now hang up I reached home, I need to get ready quickly and leave for the office we'll meet later then I'll tell you everything in detail..... Now happy?

Aaditya: ok, for now...... bye

Call cut.

Kabir shook his head at the childish antics of his bestie...... he hurriedly got ready and left for the office.

7

Shrishti left for the office listening to a lecture from her mom about her eating schedule but ignoring her she ran out of the house. Soon she was checking all the designs finally before sending them for making actual dresses as they have very less time to prepare for the deal. How, half a day passed she didn't even realize. She was about to go to have her lunch but Kabir stopped her on her way towards her cabin.

"hey..... Where are you since morning no see

"I was just busy checking the final designs of the dresses," she replied tiredly.

"oh..... so now you are done with the work"

"yes.... Almost...... but firstly I'm hungry so I'm going to throw something in my stomach before I die out of hunger" she said, rubbing her hand on her stomach.

"what are you saying madam," he said holding his laughter

"Sorry I can't help, once I start feeling hungry then my mind stops working then I speak rubbish which even I can't understand." she shrugged.

"oh, I see..... Come let's have lunch together" he proposed.

"But how Kabir..... I'm an employee here, it is not right..... You are CEO.... Not possible" she simply stated the fact and was about to walk out but his words stopped her.

"But you are my friend too.... And I don't care about anything we are having food together and it's final let's go"

She was already hungry and not at all in the mood to argue so she agreed and both went to the cafeteria. Both were having food silently but the reasons were different for both of them. Kabir was quiet because he was trying to thank her but Shrishti was focusing on her food because she was really very hungry. A few minutes later Kabir abruptly spoke up.

"Thanks, Shrishti" she was busy savoring the taste of her food.... Listening to him she stopped and looked at him shooting a questioning glare

"thanks...... But, for what" she asked, raising her eyebrows.

"Just like that, I had to say...." he shrugged his shoulders.

"But for what at least tell why...... otherwise I'm not going to accept your thank you" she stubbornly replied.

"Because of you I met my mom after almost a month. If you hadn't told me what you said to me yesterday I don't think so when would I have gone to her" he sincerely said looking down at his food.

"you.... Why do you take my advice so seriously Kabir" she genuinely asked as she was amazed by the fact that someone really takes her advice so seriously and applies it in his life too.

"that I don't know but one thing I'm sure of is that..... your words give me positivity and motivation to fight with my problems," he said looking into her eyes as if he was trying to show that he means what he is saying.

"What, is it..... I never even thought that in life an idiot like me can motivate someone" she said laughing at her own.

"no Shrishti..... Please don't say like this... what you are you don't even know...... seriously.... Take my advice do value yourself" he said

"The same goes for you, Mr. Mehra..... You also do value yourself" she said genuinely like a friend who cares.

"how do I value myself.....? When my own people don't do..... If they had cherished me too..... Maybe I would have somewhere else"

"You know what Kabir, I don't know what your main problem is but what I understand is that what you are, Where you are, what you are doing, you are not happy..... Say.... I'm telling the truth...... right?"

"I'll tell you everything.... Maybe another time" he said smiling slightly "as of now dresses are ready, go and check if it is everything or if it requires any changes or something till then let me finish my work.... Ok" She nodded and he left for his cabin. Seeing his retiring figure Shrishti went into deep thought.

"I don't know why but this pain on your face, this pain in your eyes gives pain to my heart." she thought to herself and sighed deeply

"Because you are his friend Shrishti....."(Her mind said)

"No you are just concerned for him that's why you are feeling bad seeing him in pain" (her heart said)

"concern......!! From when, I started being concerned for anyone...?"

Keeping her thoughts away she got up and went to check the ready dresses. After working the whole day both Kabir and Shrishti went back to their homes. Kabir was ok but Shrishti was drowned in very deep thoughts or I can say she was drowned in Kabir's thoughts. She didn't even realize how and when she slept very soon, not like her daily routine.

Next day in the office all things were set and Shrishti and her team were waiting together for the model to arrive for the photo shoot, But she was late.

"God when this modal will come, we have been waiting since morning and it's already afternoon." she sighed frustratingly

"Madam, let me confirm with Kabir sir actually he is the one who has conversed with her about this" her assistant suggested.

"ok do it fast it's already late"

She went to have a word with Kabir meanwhile the modal arrived. Shrishti was already pissed because of waiting so long."oh finally you are here Miss. kritika......good morn... well good afternoon please get done with your makeup fast as the shoot is already very late," Shrishti said casually

"First of all it's kritika madam and secondly I'm not here to follow your orders miss. Whatever" she said in a complete attitude-filled voice.

"I'm sorry kritika madam.... But sorry to say this again as we are getting late please get ready fast for the photo shoot"

Here in Kabir's cabin Kabir was busy with his work when Shrishti's assistant entered his cabin. "excuse me, sir"

"yes"

"sir, miss. Kritika is not here yet. We have been waiting since morning and it's 1 o'clock already....... Shrishti mom is getting very angry" she stated everything in detail.

"what Shrishti is angry..... means fight is going to happen for sure because of the ego issue of kritika and shrishti will not back off easily, Let's go.... I'm coming with you..... Come fast...." he said while walking out of his cabin hurriedly

Both were walking towards the shooting hall, Meanwhile here kritika was throwing tantrums at the makeup artist and other helpers who were helping her with her dressing and other things, seeing her useless tantrums Shrishti's temper was almost on its edge.

"God knows what this girl thinks of herself, if the shoot was not getting late then I had told her how to respect others," shrishti thought glaring at kritika who was busy throwing tantrums. She was sitting silently in her seat when she heard kritika shouting again.

"how stupid these dresses are, who the hell designed these dresses, how can you call me to wear these useless pieces of cloth, I would have never used these clothes even for moping, did Kabir appoint designers or cartoonists"

That's it by now Shrishti was controlling her anger but now kritika was getting on her nerves she was crossing her limits, she approached her with full anger.

"Now enough is enough, miss. Kritika.......firstly You can't judge anyone's work just like that without knowing anything...... secondly you are here for a photo shoot not for buying these dresses alright..... These dresses are made according to the preferences of the customer so please do your work"

"How dare you talk to me like this...... speaking like these dresses are made by you only, now say, what happened speechless or something.... Who the hell you are, tell me first, what you do here....." kritika was insulting shrishti but she was quiet just because she didn't want to create a scene there.

"She is designing heads and yes all these dresses are designed by her...... any problem," Kabir said in a loud tone standing at the door of the shooting room, the disappointment was evident on his face because of kritika but still he was controlling his temper.

Kritika got shocked listening to this on the top of it from Kabir. She knew that she was overreacting but still she was not accepting her fault.

"Yes, I have a problem..... Your so-called designing head doesn't have the manners to speak.... She is insulting me... and blaming me for coming late...". Kritika said, still not accepting her fault and continued insulting shrishti.

"First of all her name is Shrishti..... got it and secondly can you please tell me what was your call time." she became quiet "ok let me tell you.... Your call time was 10 in the morning and now it's almost 2 don't you think she is right"

"ok, I accept that I'm late..... But she was talking to me disrespectfully"

"oh is it..... But I heard everything, so don't even try to act innocent in front of me...... you are the one who was disrespecting her.... Now apologize to her first and then start the photoshoot"

"Kabir.... You too are saying that I am wrong, that too because of this girl..." She said shooting a disgusting glare at Shrishti

"who is wrong is wrong...... and who is right is right..... Now apologize, I don't have the whole day here for your stupid drama" he said checking the time on his wristwatch.

"Kabir.... There is no need, please.... Let it be...." shrishti pleaded to him through her eyes, nodding at him negatively.

"no.... now cam on kritika do it fast"

"I'm not gonna apologize...... I'm not gonna do this shoot either..... I'm leaving" she arrogantly picked up her bag and was about to leave but hearing Kabir she stopped right away.

"you can't Miss. Kritika..... you are already paid for it so you can't back out..... Now c'mon apologize and complete your work" she stated "ok fine...... I'm sorry for my behavior..... Shrishti" she huffed and finally said as if she was doing some favor.

"Shrishti mam......" Kabir corrected.

"I'm sorry Shrishti mam," she said again gritting her teeth

"it's ok kritika" shrishti politely said so that she dont get more annoyed. She left stomping her feet, to get ready

"Was that necessary kabir....?" shrishti asked as she doesn't like to make people apologize in front of her forcefully to be precise.

"definitely..... Now you come with me..... the work will be finished on time now she'll not do anything stupid" Both walked out of the shooting hall. "you said too much unnecessarily kabir..... She got mad, you should not have reacted like that" she said while walking towards their cabin.

"It needed shrishti, she is the daughter of dad's friend, I unwillingly approach her every time because of dad, and the stunt she pulled today is her regular drama..... Today it was getting over my head so I did that"

"Oh so Mr. Mehra too gets angry," She said comically

"why don't you get angry?"

"I do.... Didn't you see just a few minutes before? But now it went away" She said smilingly shrugging her shoulders.

"Oh, so that was your anger whom I met on the way towards the shooting hall." She looked at him and shook her head in disbelief.

"you are mad Kabir....."

"it is said you get influenced by your company," He said in all seriousness as a matter of fact.

"yes true," She said smilingly but when reality hit her she looked at him frowning "am I mad, do I look like a mad person to you"

"I didn't say anything, you are the one admitting it," he said, controlling himself from bursting into laughter.

"you.... I'll tell you later you just wait and watch." she said, crossing her arms in a challenging way.

"why later, is there any problem in enlightening me right now" And here he earned a deadly glare from Shrishti "you know what..... Ok leave it I'll tell you later......"

Both laughed at each other and left for their cabins shaking their head on their stupid pointless conversation.

Days were passing well, The bond between Kabir and Shrishti was growing more and more day by day. Their friendship which started from just friends now turned into best friends, The hesitation between them was waved off, they use to make fun of each other in the office also all the staff started loving their bond.

8

One fine day Shrishti was working in her cabin and she listened to some chaotic sound from the main hall where all workers work. She halted her work and came out from her cabin and found that Kabir was standing in between and all the other employees were surrounding him.

"Hey guys, what's going on here?" she asked curiously.

"Oh great, you came on your own, I was about to send Khushi to call you" Kabir chided like an excited child.

"why? What happened, why have you collected the whole staff here..... Have you won some lottery or something" she joked "ok jokes apart... tell me what happened"

"ok so everyone please pay attention....... As you all know the fashion industry organizes a big competition where fashion companies from all over the world participate, so the thing is our company too applied for participation in that competition and hues what.... We are selected" kabir announced with enthusiasm

"what!! this is great news Kabir....." she said excitedly.

"yes....... I'm really excited for this...... and today I'm very happy and because of that, I'm...." Shrishti cut him in between.

"So guys, as kabir said he is very happy today so he'll give a treat to everyone present here, right Kabir," she said smiling widely to tease Kabir.

"what treat......?"

"yes.... A cup of tea from your side to everyone"

"Are you even serious Shrishti.... Really tea"

"Oh only tea is not ok, no problem one sandwich too, now happy," she said more comically this time.

"ok now enough, listen guys there is no use of treats or something like that..... Today I'm giving half a day to you all..... so enjoy" Hearing this everyone's face lit up. "thank you so much sir" everyone cheered.

"but..... As we are going to participate in world level competition so tomorrow everyone has to work hard...... ok"

"Okay sir," all said smilingly

"Ok then back to work," he said and returned to his cabin.

"congratulations Kabir sir......" she said sir deliberately to rile him up

"We'll say congratulations after winning the competition to each other too" he smiled simply, his face was telling how happy and hopeful he is from this competition.

"Hmm" "Khushi arrange a meeting about this competition discussion tomorrow.....ok"

"ok sir"

As he declared a half-day holiday so after some time everyone started leaving the office, after finishing his work Kabir was also leaving for home but he noticed Shrishti standing at the main gate of the office all alone, he stopped and stepped down from his car.

"hey shrishti, why are you standing here alone.... Don't you have to go home?" he asked, stopping his car in front of her.

"of course.... Actually, you announced a half-day suddenly so I'm just waiting for the cab.... But I don't know why it's not here. It has already been long" she replied while continuously looking at her phone screen to track the location of her cab.

"but why are you waiting for the cab, you drive on your own isn't it"

"Dad dropped me so.... That's why"

"oh..... No problem, come I'll drop you.... Till when you'll stand here alone, come" he offered.

"no no it's ok, I'll manage why are you troubling yourself for me"

"oh, madam...... Sit here without any argument, don't even try to do formalities with me.....huh" he said in a duh tone leaving no space for argument.

"you'll not listen to me right" He nodded negatively. "shall we, my lord"

"Of course, sir, do I have any option" she took a seat in the car and Kabir started driving towards Shrishti's home.

"So what do you think about the competition?" She casually started the conversation.

"To be honest, right now nothing is in my mind.... We'll discuss it tomorrow in the meeting. From tomorrow we have only 10 days to prepare for it" he replied, focusing on the road.

"what.... Only 10 days.... Then why do you declare a half day off today..... We already have on our plate, Kabir" she asked, freaking out. "so that employees come back getting fresh after a little break and work more efficiently" he said genuinely.

"You are a very good boss you know, who thinks this much for his workers" "have learned from you only," he said looking into her eyes, She smiled slightly.

"so finally here is your home madam"

"come inside, I'll introduce you to my family"

"no shrishti, sorry actually if I didn't reach on time then Aaditya will eat me raw, and you know it's not age to die, right," he said showing his fake frightened face "some other time I'll come for sure"

"ok, no problem.... Bye, drive safe" She stepped down the car and after waving her hand towards him she entered her house.

The next day everyone was very excited in the office for the upcoming competition, as per the already decided meeting all the main personnel of all the departments gathered in the meeting hall.

"a very good morning everyone" he started enthusiastically

"Good morning" everyone present there replied.

"So first of all let me clear all the details about the competition and then we'll discuss how to proceed further, So yes.... First of all, we have only 10 days for everything..... Secondly, we need to decide on an interesting theme..... third and best is the team which will work on this will go paris for the competition" Hearing this all became happy who were present in the meeting "that is really awesome, we'll work super hard to win this competition sir" someone from the employees exclaimed, Kabir, nodded giving a professional smile.

"I have one theme in my mind for this" shrishti exclaimed while thinking about the theme in her mind.

"great..... Make a proper detailed note on that and start working on that as soon as possible..... And try to complete the designs within 2 days hardly...... because It'll take time in the stitching of dresses" Kabir said

"Hmmm, I'll let you know about this by afternoon" she assured.

"Sure" Soon the meeting ended and everyone went to work on their assigned work.

As soon as Shrishti entered her cabin she started working on the theme she thought for the competition, after almost 3 hours she was done with the overview of her theme to present in front of Kabir. Soon she collected her stuff and approached Kabir's cabin.

"impressive...... you are done even before the time given to you" he praised.

"I prefer my work to be completed on time and with full perfection," she said dramatically raising her perfectly shaped eyebrows.

"oh I see"

"ok now focus here...... see, this is the overview of our theme..... Which is......? Proper Indian culture...... how's it....."

"Very nice..... And especially it's unique...... because of world level competition most of the companies choose something stupid most of the times"

"So it means shall we lock this right?"

"for sure"

"ok done.... Let me go because time is already very less and I have to work a lot on the designs" she hurriedly got up to run back into her cabin.

"ok....."

She went back to her cabin and gathered the best designers of her team so that they could work on the designs perfectly, she supervised all of them and started working on the showstopper dress on her own. Whole day passed working continuously, around 7 in the evening. Finally she wound up her work for the day and packed everything to take home with her but remembering something she again sat on her chair with a sad face. She was thinking something clueless.

After sometime everyone started leaving the office, soon Kabir was also walking towards the exit but he noticed that Shrishti is still sitting in her cabin whereas most of the staff is already left, to make sure everything is ok he went in her cabin and found her sitting with a sad face. He knocked on the door to gain her attention. She abruptly looked at him.

"Hey, Shrishti everything is ok...... what happened.... Why are you sitting alone and with this sad face?" he asked with concern filled in his voice as he never saw shrishti this silent and lost in her own thoughts.

"actually" She wanted to speak but again she stopped thinking about something.

"Shrishti.... Girl, tell me what happened why are you sitting being this sad, now you are scaring me" he said sitting in front of her

"I can't go with all of you......for the competition," she said, closing her eyes as she desperately wanted to go but there was a reason she couldn't go.

"what.... why....? How we'll handle everything without you, you're our head designer without you it'll be total chaos there"

"I know..... But.... I know them very well they'll not send them there....." She said looking at him sadly, he immediately knew that she was talking about her parents.

"why what's the reason that I'm asking"

"Because I know.... They'll not allow me to go so far from here, maybe I can convince dad somehow but mamma she'll not agree at all" She said cutely pouting, Kabir took a deep breath and sighed

"you tell me one thing..... Without giving a thought to any other thing.... Do you want to go.....?"

"of course why not...... what type of question is this...... who doesn't dream once to go Paris..... I too have a dream" her eyes were looking like twinkling stars while saying this.

"That's it...... you are coming with us.... And it's final." he said, getting up with determination filled in his eyes and voice at the same time.

"But how?"

"I'll talk to your parents" before she could speak he again begins "trust me I'll convince them," He said with a serene smile on his face expecting the same smile on Shrishti's face too but she didn't smile.

"Now smile madam shrishti..... I'll convince them in fact get up we'll go now only"

"what.... Now?" She suddenly got frightened as she was already convinced in her head and heart that her parents would not allow her to go to Paris.

"Of course..... Get up..... I have learnt from you only that we should not delay to make someone happy and you are not mere someone..... Right..... Now come on" he said, almost dragging her to come with him out of the cabin. Finally, she smiled slightly and both of them left for her home. Whole time Shrishti was quiet in the car because she was 99.99% confirmed that her parents are not gonna allow her to go to Paris.

Finally after sometime they reached before stepping down the car Shrishti looked towards Kabir with hope filled in her eyes..... Kabir smiled calmly at her "don't worry, Hmmm" She nodded slightly, and then both of them approached the main door. Shrishti hesitatingly pressed the doorbell and within a minute monika opened the door, Assuming Shrishti only shouted comically at her without looking at her.

"shrii why are you this late girl...." She was about to start her rant but she stopped looking at Kabir

"Di, at least let us come in...... ok let me introduce you both......di this is Kabir.... Kabir Mehra my boss and my friend too and Kabir this is Monika Sharma my di"

Both of them smiled slightly at each other and then three of them moved towards the living hall. Where Shrishti's dad and mom both were sitting, Kabir went near them and touched their feet as they are older than him.

"Dad this is......" her dad cut her sentence in between saying "Kabir, Right?"

"yes..... But how do you know uncle? " Kabir asked amusingly.

"she talks a lot about you.... It was quite easy to identify you" He said pointing towards Shrishti, Kabir looked at Shrishti squinted eyes as if he was asking.......IS IT...... but ignoring him she looked here and there.

"Come son, have a seat" her dad offered a seat beside him. "so guys, how's work going"

"uncle actually I have to talk to you about this only."

"talk to me about your work..... but I don't have any idea of your work Kabir" taking a deep breath he looked at Shrishti "uncle actually our company is participating in a world-level competition"

"Great that's too good to hear"

"but the thing is that our team needs to go to PARIS for the competition..... Shrishti too as she is our designing head, so I came here to talk about that only." Kabir said clearly without beating around the bushes.

"PARIS" Before her father could speak Shrishti's mom begins

"sorry, but Paris so far, we can't send shrishti this far that too alone" she stated just in her single sentence authoritatively

"Aunty Shrishti will not be alone..... She is our head designer we need her with us for every tiny bit of detailing"

"Still, we have never sent her alone this far, how she'll manage there alone" There was a concern in her voice and some kind of fear too.

"aunty shrishti is really mature and understanding..... She is surely capable of managing 10 more people along with her" He tried to convince Shrishti's mom but she was not at all ready to get convinced by his words, Finally he spoke something which convinced her father instantly.

"you are concerned for shrishti, this is the main point right, if I promise and make you believe that I'll myself will take care of her, then too will you not agree for this," he said with complete determination in his voice

Before her mom could say something her dad spoke,

"ok enough of the discussion on this topic..... Kabir, I'm trusting you...... shrishti will go with you all" By now Shrishti was completely sure that her parents will not allow her so she was sad to try once she whined like a baby

"dad please say yes, I'm not any small kiddo...... please.... Please...... pleassssss......" She said hugging his arm and closing her eyes tightly

For completely one minute there was pin drop silence, feeling the silence she opened her eyes cutely one by one and found everyone staring at her "what happened?" No reply "at least speak up, anyone......." She said getting impatient. Looking at her pissed face everyone burst into laughter, Seeing everyone laughing at her she made a face and was on the verge of crying.

"idiot girl...... we already said yes, now what do you want more...." her dad asked making fun of her

"Seriouslyyyyyy..." She screamed in excitement "seriouslyyyyy." He too said in the same manner to make her believe. "really...... you are the best dad..."

"only dad..." her mom said looking on the other side faking hurt expressions.

"no no, you too..." She said hugging both her mom and dad seeing her happy with her family Kabir felt very happy but somewhere he was craving for the same love from his dad too a drop of tear brimmed in his eyes but he immediately wiped it off.

"Ok, then Shrishti madam finally...... now get ready to fly," He said comically "ok uncle aunty now I should leave.... My work is done here..... Also, it's getting late too"

"not possible...... it's already dinner time, eat and then go....." Shrishti said more like ordering him and everyone chuckled.

"no no, it's fine I'll eat at home you all carry on"

"No son, we are not leaving you this easily, now get up..... Everyone to the dining table" her mom too insisted. Finally giving up Kabir too agreed to the dinner, After having dinner he greeted Shrishti's parents And left Shrishti too joined him at the main gate.

"thank you so much, Kabir"

"what for..." he asked as if he had done nothing. "Now don't be innocent ok..... it was really difficult to make my parents agree, how hard you tried to convince them, thank you so much again."

"It's ok, see there are two reasons for what I did, I'm a little selfish. I wanted you to be there with us throughout the competition and...." suddenly he stopped thinking about something.

"And....." she asked, looking straight at him.

"And... you only said na it's your dream to go there, so when you'll get a better chance than this, so that's why....."

"you know what..." she smiled at him but didn't complete what she was saying.

"What...?" he asked innocently

"Well leave it, maybe some other time," she said looking towards the sky trying to absorb the peace that the starless sky was radiating. He didn't say anything and left with a serene smile on his face, here Shrishti too was smiling dreamily.

"I don't know why but it's feeling very nice here....." she kept her hand on her heart "it feels like something really good is going to happen in Paris...." she sighed and looked upward at the sky again "Let's see god what are you planning for me" Shrishti went back inside and excitingly sat on her working table happily she started working on the designs which she was making for the competition as she had only one day left with her to complete the designs

The next day in the office finally the designs she made were approved and sent for the making process. Now the team working on the competition was focusing on the models and the rehearsals were also going on. Finally, the last day of their preparation came, and the whole team was busy checking the arrangements. Kabir was giving instructions to the models.

"So guys.... Finally, the time is here..... we are flying to Paris tomorrow morning.... We have done all the required work from our side now it's your guys' responsibility to proceed further, so hope for the best.... Ok, then we'll meet at the airport tomorrow.

All greeted him and left happily for their home. "Now I just pray that everything goes well," shrishti said, getting a little worried which was quite obvious for her as it was her first international event.

"don't worry..... Everything will be fine, and why did your face drop like this hmm, where is your smile..... Be happy girl, you are going to visit your dream destination" Kabir tried to motivate her as he didn't like her sad face even a tiny bit. She smiled happily and seeing her happy he too smiled.

"No doubt I'm very happy and all this is because of you, Thank you so so much," she said, her eyes turning glassy, Kabir made a serious face at which She gave him a questioning look.

"What happened...?" he didn't reply "say something, will you"

"Now you'll say thank you, that too to me..... From when this thank you and sorry started between friends"

"Ok, my lord noted..... I will never say thank you now, happy?, but please don't ever make this face..... You..." she placed her palm on her mouth to prevent herself from bursting into laughter.

"Me what?" he asked squinting his eyes

"You, you look like an angry bird that is too red one" she giggled, and controlling herself hard she burst into laughter.

"Is It?" he asked, raising his eyebrows.

"Yes" she replied winking at him

"Don't you think you are getting more naughty day by day?" he asked, keeping his hand on his waist dramatically.

"Naughty and me? Not at all" there was mischief clearly visible in her eyes which were twinkling like small stars.

"So, you are saying you are not naughty.... Hmm," he asked, stepping towards her.

"Not at all" before he could understand anything she ran ruffling his well-set hair. "Shrishtiii..... You.... wait I'll not leave you, you spoiled my most precious hair" he said chasing her.

"First catch me then we will see" she challenged while running on the whole floor like a small kid saving her life, there were only two of them left and all the other employees were already left. She was running and noticed that Kabir was not behind her so she reduced her speed but she was continuously looking backside whether he was following her or not but abruptly she bumped into someone and he was none other than Kabir. He held both her hands blocking her way, he asked wiggling his eyebrows up and down comically.

"Tch tch tch..... Now where will you go....." he flashed his perfect white teeth to annoy her more. "Hehe.... I was joking yrr, you took it seriously"

"Ohh, I guess just a minute before I was an angry bird, right?" the way he was blocking her way he was not at all in the mood to let her go so easily. But Shrishti cleverly tried to mislead him so she started looking behind him with a frightened face seeing her scared he also got a little concerned.

"Hey, shrishti what happened?" he immediately changed his tone from mischievous to concerned.

"Umm...... that.... That..... Behind yo...you" she tried to pretend as scared as she could and stuttered more for the better effect.

He turned to look behind him leaving her hands and taking advantage of the moment she began running again. "Oye dumbo...... no one is there" she giggled while starting her marathon again, Seeing her giggling he got the point and again started chasing this time at a faster pace, and this time poor Shrishti was trapped.

"Now, what will you do madam shrishti," he asked, wiggling his eyebrows up and down.

she looked cutely here and there to find a way for her to escape but there was no way so she surrendered finally with her best puppy eyes possible. "sorryyyy........ This will not happen again, I'll never spoil your hair again.... Now let this poor child go"

"Oh, really....."

"Yes, yes promise" she pinched her throat like a little kid god promise.

Seeing her cute antics Kabir burst into laughter, seeing him laughing at her she made a cute face, and looking at her cute face soon he was laughing like a maniac. "Now if you'll not stop laughing then I'm not gonna talk to you.... Huh," she said with a grumpy face he immediately stopped laughing.

"Hey please never ever do anything like this shrishti, you don't have any idea but you and your talks are very important to me" he was giving her a meaningful look from his eyes at which she smiled genuinely as she understood what he meant by his words.

"Ok, now we should leave, we have wasted enough time, tomorrow morning we have a flight to catch and still there is some packing left for me to do," she said with seriousness.

"What?" he exclaimed horrified, keeping his both hands on his either ear dramatically. "What now, why are you reacting like this, as if I just stated some rocket science"

"you are still not done with your packing....... You girls......" he exclaimed again loudly.

"what we girls!!" she asked, raising her eyebrows with a tight smile on her lips. "N-nothing..... Nothing, why did you become serious so fast girl"

"Oh, so I get serious, that too very fast..... I see" she said, crossing her hands at her chest. "Oh no my lord, you just come with me, let's go, why are you sticking to one topic only..... Come come" he dragged her out of the office with him trying to save himself from her outburst.

"Thank god, this little don left that topic... otherwise I was gone today," he thought, Finally fighting on silly topics they left for their respective homes.

9

Shrishti was really very excited about the trip to Paris and obviously for the competition too. She was getting ready happily when her mom entered her room with gloomy self "Shrii, you are not ready yet" she said plainly clearly showing that she was sad because of her departure.

"Only 5 minutes mamma, I'm almost done but wait why are you looking sad hmm," she asked, shifting her attention from the mirror to her mother. "Nothing, just like that" "It's not just like that, c'mon fast tell me what's the matter" shrishti asked adamantly.

"Oh god, it's nothing my baby, it's just you going na so the mood is little low today, but also I know that you are hella excited so forget everything and enjoy there ok and yes win that competition too" she took out her love caressing her cheeks lovingly. "You know what? You are the best" shrishti said pulling her mom in a tight hug being emotionally riled up.

Soon bidding goodbye to her family she left for the airport with her dad. Kabir also after getting ready quickly went to meet his mom before leaving for the airport. "Kabir, you here early morning"

"Mamma, there is a competition in Paris and our company is also participating as you already know, so I was just leaving for the airport so, I just thought to meet you once before leaving" he said taking her both hands in his.

"You did really good that you came, wait I'll come" Saying she went to bring curd for him as it is a good omen to have curd before leaving for anything good. "Oh lord, now I have to eat this" he made a disgusting face but his mom was adamant to make him eat that as she was a great believer in good or bad omens, especially for her child.

"Yes, you have to eat, now without any drama eat this" she made him eat curd with her own hand to which he could not deny "well, when you became this sensible to think to meet your mom before going" she asked keeping her hand on her waist dramatically.

"Umm..... can't say if I became sensible or someone knocked this sense in my head" he chuckled, listening to Kabir and her mom talking, his dad also came downstairs.

"So, you guys are leaving today for Paris right?" his dad asked with his usual cold demeanor.

"Yes," Kabir replied with difficulty as if he had any problem while speaking."Best of luck... for the competition.... To you and your team"

"Thanks" he said plainly "Ok, mamma I'm leavingotherwise I'll get late."He hugged his mom and left without even sparing a look at his dad.

Soon everyone from the team gathered at the airport, Kabir also reached and following him within a few minutes Shrishti also reached with her dad.

"Good Morning Uncle." he said, touching his feet to take blessings.

"Stay blessed son, you guys leave now, the boarding announcement is already done" her father said casually but there was some sort of tension in his eyes which was not unnoticed by kabir at all. "You guys go ahead I'm coming" he indicated to his whole team, "Bye papa, see you soon"

Shrishti hugged her dad as she was ready to go in with her luggage.

"Bye, my little tigress.... Take care..... Go and win the competition" he said caressing her head

After everyone left, Kabir turned to talk to Shrishti's dad. "uncle I know you are worried about Shrishti..... And I completely understand as a father you should be.... But I'm assuring you I'll take care of her don't worry..... She'll come back as she's going" he said, taking his hand in his hand to assure him.

"I trust you kabir, You are very sincere and sensible that's the only reason I agreed for this.... Ok now you too go hmm..... Good luck" he caressed his head and left.

Soon everyone was sitting on their seats. Kabir and Shrishti's seats were together. She was sitting on the window side seat and was enjoying the view very much. "it seems someone is already very happy"

"Indeed I'm happy" she squealed but suddenly composed herself looking at her surroundings.

As it was a long journey everyone got busy with their phones, ipads etc. after sometime Shrishti noticed that Kabir was sitting completely quiet and was in deep thought, looking at him she slapped her forehead.

"Kabir......" she said, jerking him with little extra force. "What is it," he said coming out of his trance. "Have you really sworn or something" he gave her a confused look then decided to ask "about what?"

"That, whenever you'll travel your deep thinking mode will be on automatically by your system" He chuckled listening to her. "Now what is there to laugh," she asked, getting annoyed.

"Your talks are really very entertaining sometimes," he said again trying to hold his laughter back "Ok on a serious note, I was just thinking something casually, otherwise also you were busy in enjoying the view so what are you expecting me to talk to myself like a mental case"

"Ok, leave it..... Tell me what you want to talk"

"Tell me one thing if you try to forget something and nothing is working, what to do," he asked cutely, raising his eyebrows. "to whom you are trying to forget Mr. Mehra," she said in a teasing manner.

"Oh Einstein, it's nothing like what you are thinking..... As a human being, we have a lot more things to remember and to forget" he was serious while saying but shrishti was not ready to stop teasing him.

"Really"

"Oh sadly yes, not say"

"See, the more we try to forget something the more it keeps on revolving in our heart and mind, So.... Just don't try to forget that thing or person just let it be.... go with the flow..... with the passage of time you'll realize that the thing you were trying to forget is now not bothering you" Shrishti was speaking continuously without noticing that even he is listening her or not, few minutes later when she didn't get any response she looked at him and shook her head in disbelief.

Kabir was already fast asleep, he was sleeping with a little open mouth. she laughed silently looking at him as he was looking cute while sleeping. Feeling that he might feel cold she took out a blanket given by the airlines and covered him feeling the warmth of the blanket he adjusted himself without opening his eyes and fell into a deep slumber. Shrishti also covered herself with the other blanket and she also fell into the lap of a slumber. After a long flight, Kabir and Shrishti with their whole team landed at the international airport of Paris in the evening, all of them were grinning ear to ear and their excitement was clearly visible on their faces. Soon the whole team reached the hotel.

"so guys finally we are here..... as we all are tired so you all go and take a rest in your respective rooms, after today we have two days for prep tomorrow and the day after tomorrow am I clear"

"ok sir"

"cool..... we'll meet tomorrow morning..... there is a room allotted for all the participating teams so we'll continue our discussion and everything there....... Now you all can go to your rooms after taking key cards from the reception....." Everyone nodded in agreement and went to take their key cards. Meanwhile, Shrishti was wandering like a lost puppy keenly observing each and every detail of the atmosphere, Kabir patted on her shoulder and then she came out of her lala.... World....

"Earth to madam, where are you..... Don't you wanna go to your room" he asked, finding her still lost in her dreamland.

"Damnnn...... I can't believe I'm finally here, I really don't know if I should be happy or sad" she pouted cutely wondering.

"Obviously happy girl, why sad" he butted in a duh tone.

"See, I know that I'm here at my dream place but what's the use of having a hell lot of work when I'll explore this beautiful city" she cleared the thing which was revolving in her mind to kabir.

"Oye dumbo, we had a show after 2 days and after that we have 4 days in total before we fly back to India, what will you do then?" she smiled wide on the realization. "In fact I'll join you too, remember our experience of site seeing together is great" he asked wiggling his eyebrows.

"Oh, yes yes..... I forgot it completely.... Sometimes I really feel I'm mad" she slapped her forehead earning a chuckle from kabir.

"I was saying the same, I guess...."

"What did you say...?" she asked, squinting her eyes at him.

"That, we should go to collect our keys genius, everyone is off to their rooms and here we are blabbering nonsense.... Come come" he cleverly changed the topic and dragged her towards the reception

He silently thanked god that she didn't flare up on his joke as he knew very well how difficult it is to handle her if she's riled up. Coincidently this time both of their rooms were adjacent. Both of them went into their rooms and kept their luggage. Shrishti was already very excited because of that sleep was miles away from her so she thought to go and roam on the streets, firstly she thought to go alone but it was night and she was unknown from the country so she decided why not to ask Kabir about this, after changing and freshening up she went and pressed door bell of Kabir's room.

After a good 5 minutes he opened the door, yawning and with his half open eyes.

"Now what do you want?" he asked, letting out a cute yawn again.

"You"

"Whattt?" his sleep was long gone hearing this.

"You come with me, please"

"God, at this time where do you wanna go?" he asked, a bit annoyed bending a little back to watch the time on the wall clock.

"To roam on the streets, please let's get going" she pleaded.

"Ehh..... go and sleep na, and let me sleep too.... I'm tired, bye" he was about to close the door but she interrupted.

"No, I'm not sleepy, please come na, we'll come back soon" she literally pleaded like a kid.

"Shrishti, we have work tomorrow if you remember" he tried to bargain.

"It's only 9 man, we'll be back in an hour max, please come na" she grabbed his hand and started jerking like a baby who pleaded it's parents for his wish.

"stubborn girl...." she smiled widely and he shook his head at the childishness of her "Ok, give me a minute.... I'm coming...."

"thank you soo soo soooo much....." she squealed.

"Ok, ok now no need of buttering.... huh"

Soon both of them were walking on the streets of Paris, they were silent for more than 10 minutes and were silently observing their surroundings. Taking a deep breath, Shrishti started.

"Kabir"

"Hmmm"

"don't you think roaming on these streets in some other country where no one knows us, is giving very calm vibes? Don't you think our mind is feeling a little calm..... peaceful......." she asked, looking at him like she meant each and every word she said. He remained silent for some time, sighing calmly.

***"Kabhi kabhi sukoon hum dhundte hai dar badar.......
Ehsas bhi nahi hota hai dil ko ki milega vo sukoon kis kadar......"***

"You are right...... very right sometimes we find our peace at the place where no one is available to give us sympathy but our own self is capable enough to make us feel peaceful"

"Bhale ye duniya sath ho na ho...... Khud ke sukoon ke liye hum khud hi kafi hain......"

she said looking at him with a slight smile, which he returned with a heartwarming one.

"Come let's have ice cream..." he said pointing towards the ice cream parlor "okiii..." she squealed like a kid.

"you know what....?" she raised her eyebrows in response "you are a kiddoo..... Be always the same as you are" She smiled widely nodding again like a kid to make him chuckle. Soon they were walking back towards their hotel licking their Ice creams, after reaching back they went into their respective rooms wishing good night to each other.

Next morning, Everyone from the team was gathered in the room allotted to them for preparations.

"Guys, we have 2 days for final preparations...... so if anyone has any kind of doubt please clear it right away...." Kabir asked like a boss which he was.

"Do you know anything about the schedule of the competition?" shrishti questioned.

"not yet.... But they'll tell us soon about that...... anything else"

"no..... then let's start the final rehearsals of walk on the ramp and about the sequence and all" shrishti suggested and everyone agreed. Without wasting a minute the whole team was engrossed in their work, all were busy in their respective work.

Two days passed in a snap and finally the day of competition arrived, all were busy with their work. Shrishti was checking all the dresses of the models, while Kabir was checking about the schedule and the other things which required his attention.

"Ok, guys for the final time check your outfits. I don't want any chaos at the last moment, am I clear? "Shrishti informed the team of models, Meanwhile everyone was checking their outfits. A team came from Spain and was observing all the outfits of team India. Their company was a leading fashion company, firstly they were confident with their outfits but seeing outfits of team India they were feeling complex and somewhere they were getting the vibes that they were gonna lose the show.

The Head of Spanish ordered his assistant to call the main showstoppers of team India. "sir, is this ethically right to talk with the participants of another team" his assistant asked in a trembling voice.

"Just do what I say...... understand, don't just use your brain" , the coldness in his voice scared the poor assistant which left him with nothing but to agree with the head.

"ok sir..... As-as you say" She went to call the showstoppers of team India.... Firstly both of them hesitated but then went with her.

"Hello.... Please take a seat" the head of the Spanish team said with nothing but a straight face.

"Hello..... Sir " both of them greeted him politely and immediately he was straight to the point without beating around the bush.

"can you both do a favor for us" the seriousness in his voice made both of them a little hesitant but still holding themselves they started the conversation.

"What do you want from us?" the boy asked.

"backout from your team....." the tone he used was not pleading one but the ordering one which left both of them in utter shock.

"how can you even say this.... Why will we back out from our team" the girl said, freaking out.

"don't freak out, I will give you many things in your favor..... if you both will do this..... you will get permanent placement as a model in our company and 10000 dollars respectively........ now decide wisely....." he said with finality in his voice. Both of them looked at each other to decide what to do, they thought the deal is worth accepting

"ok but what is the proof we'll get what you are saying"

"your money will be transferred within 10 minutes in your accounts and as models you guys are appointed I'm giving you my words"

"done"

"Now without talking with any member of your team..... just escape from here" both of them nodded in agreement and left after giving their bank details for the transaction to happen. After some time all the teams were preparing for the competition, all the models were getting ready soon, all the guests and owners of the companies and judges, everyone was settled in the audience sitting area.

Total 15 teams were present there and team India's turn was lined up at no. 10...... finally the show started and meanwhile here Shrishti was trying to find the showstoppers of their team, But they were nowhere to be seen.

Eventually the panic she wanted to hide started showing on her face she was actually freaking out as without showstoppers how will they step on stage. "khushi.... Go and find them asap..... Meanwhile I'm also doing the same " she nodded and left to do the work assigned but shrishti. Almost 30 minutes passed but they were nowhere..... Khushi returned helplessly.

"Oh lord, now what do I do? Within 2 hours it's our turn on the stage" she was getting hopeless but finally she decided to enlighten kabir about the situation. "Now, I can't handle this anymore I need to tel kabir, khushi you stay here with the team I'm going to talk to kabir"

She hurriedly left towards the sitting area from the backstage, she was trying to figure out that where he was but she was not able to find him,. finally she called him, but at first he didn't answered the call she was helplessly trying to call him again and again, when she was about to return back hopeless she saw that he was walking towards her only, Looking at him her eyes started getting moist, as now she was looking some hope in him.

"hey Shrishti..... what happened.... Why did you call me this many times.... And why are you looking disturbed..." he asked in a concerned filled voice as her eyes were glistening with tears and he already knew something had happened.

"Kabir, our..... Oh my god..... Our " she choked on her own voice which made him more concerned about her he tried to calm her first.

"Easy easy..... First breath and then tell me, what's the matter?"

"Our showstoppers are nowhere to be seen, I've been looking for them Since long....." she said, almost on the verge of crying.

"What? What are you saying shrishti? "His expression saying that he was shocked was an understatement at that time.

"The truth..... They are nowhere to be seen..... Now what will we do?" she asked with moist eyes. "Ok first you calm down, let's go to the team first then we'll think" Both of them entered the room where their whole team was sitting with sad faces.

"Guys don't be sad don't lose hope like this, we are trying to figure out what can be done right now" he tried to cheer up his team which was now sitting with the surety that they are going to lose the show.

"We don't have time Kabir, only two hours left for our turn. What to do? I'm not able to understand anything right now, "Shrishti said again on the verge of freaking out.

"Have you guys tried their number?" Kabir asked.

"yes sir.... But their cells are switched off" one of the team members said.

"God.... now what do we do" he sighed.

"Now we can do only one thing, we have to find two new people who can take their place" shrishti suggested.

"But the thing is where we will find these two new people..... We don't have time.... If we were in India we could have managed but what to do here? "Kabir objected.

"If you don't mind.... Should I say something sir? "Khushi asked.

"yes of course..."

"sir..... why don't you and Shrishti mam take their place" she presented her idea.

:what are you saying khushi..... how can this even be possible...." shrishti exclaimed unbelievingly.

"Exactly" kabir too agreed with shrishti

"but sir we don't have time and we don't even have their substitutes..... If we have to participate then this is the only single option left with us" khushi tried to explain her point more clearly.

"Well, sadly she's right, Kabir," shrishti said, looking at him with defeated expressions.

"Ok then if there is no other option than what can we do, let's do this only" kabir finalized the idea making everyone sigh in relief.

"Great then you both go and get ready in the outfits' 'Khushi chirped after a long time as the environment was really depressing for some time. both of them nodded and left to get ready.

10

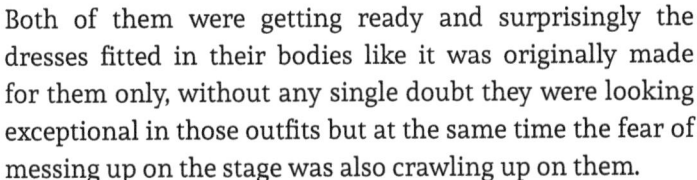

Both of them were getting ready and surprisingly the dresses fitted in their bodies like it was originally made for them only, without any single doubt they were looking exceptional in those outfits but at the same time the fear of messing up on the stage was also crawling up on them.

Here the head of the Spanish company was relaxed that their biggest competitors are now almost out of the race but soon he got the news that now two new people are taking the place of the showstoppers.

"what the hell...... now what to do.... I was relaxed that now everything is in control and here comes another problem"

"sir now there is only one way left," his assistant said

"what......??"

"We have to ruin their dress somehow....."

"and how is it even possible....". he asked seriously like it was the most useless idea ever.

"that you leave on me...... I'll do something at that point when they'll be short of time.... Almost before their arrival on the ramp"

"ok do whatever you want"

On the other hand, after getting ready Kabir was waiting for Shrishti to come out of the green room, finally, after 15 minutes his wait came to halt as Shrishti appeared from behind the door.

She was wearing a very elegant white colored lehenga, Paired with pearl jewelry and her hairs were tied in a very elegant bun and white flowers were wrapped around the bun beautifully, basically she was depicting the proper Indian culture from her look. Suddenly the world stopped around Kabir. He unknowingly fell in the mesmerizing world of her beauty. He tried to look away but it was looking like some spell was made on him, she was not looking less than any goddess that came straight from heaven. He came back into senses feeling a jerk on his wrist and then he found that she was dragging him somewhere.

"Damn you Kabir, why are you walking at the speed of snail, come fast we have to do little rehearsal before going on the ramp" her annoyance was visible in her voice at which he chuckled silently.

"Ohh....." was what he said stopping where she abruptly stopped dragging him

"What ohh.... Now c'mon" she said, keeping one hand on her waist cutely making look like a small white angry bird, making him chuckle again at which she shook her head in disbelief. Soon both of them started walking in the way they were going to walk on the ramp and finally only 30 minutes were left for their turn they were busy in their practice when assistant of the head of Spanish team came with a bottle of liquid black eyeliner in her hand and spilled it on Shrishti's dress intentionally and pretended like it was accidental. Seeing her dress ruined in front of her eyes, Shrishti started fuming within seconds and the other reason was that they didn't have time left for anything.

"I'm really very sorry mam........ This was an accident" she tried to fake apologizing by hiding her smirk.

"what rubbish it was an accident.... First of all why the hell are you roaming here with a bottle of liner in your hand and secondly can't you see two people walking....." Shrishti tried, keyword tried to say keeping her calm but the calm was nowhere in her voice.

"I'm really very sorry mam" she continued her drama like a pro.

"Oh god, now what do I do" she said holding her head in her hands "Kabir now what?" tears started brimming in her eyes "it seems like god is also in mood to play with us today" her voice was choking as she was trying hard to not cry but finally a traitor tear fell from her eye, A tear was again about to fell from her eye but her prevented it placing his finger on her face and nodded negatively.

"don't freak out Shrishti.... Let me see if I can do something" he tried to assure her but she was nowhere looking like being assured.

"hun mera dimag kharab ho reha hai...... main char chand la deniya es kudi de..... challi ji na hove tan..... tu khad ja put tennu tan main dassangi hun...." she said, pointing her index finger towards that girl fuming in anger.[Now I'm really mad.... I'm literally feeling like giving a tight slap to this girl..... Nonsense..... You wait girl let me tell you.... What you will get for what you did to my poor dress]

"Hey shrishti, girl relax..... She doesn't even know Hindi and you are lecturing her in Punjabi, it's useless..... Leave it..... You come with me" he started dragging her with him before she could start yelling again at the poor girl who was not really poor but a cunning employee of her boss.

"Now you are also blaming me, what we will do.... I'm blank, literally blank..... This was my favorite outfit and she ruined this......" she stopped in between the track where he was taking her and started freaking out seeing her already on the verge of crying he sighed and made her look at him

"First please come with me, I'm saying na that I'll do something"

Finally Kabir and Shrishti reached their green room,.he made her sit on the makeup chair and started looking here and there to find something but when he didn't get what he wanted he asked her.

"I need brush"

"Now what will you do with them?" she confusingly asked.

"Girl! We are not here to play KBC..... we'll play some other time you just find brushes for me" the trace of annoyance in his voice made her do what he said as she didn't want to make him more upset than he already was.

She searched and found some makeup brushes, he immediately grabbed those brushes from her hand and started stroking the brush on the area where the liquid liner was spilled. Shrishti was looking at him very keenly and was observing the moves he was doing with the brushes. Soon the patches of the liquid liner turned into beautiful designs, Seeing that Shrishti was shocked and relieved at the same time, But again she was sad.

"Now what? "I don't understand why your face fell like this again."

"You fixed my dress, that's great..... But we were supposed to do twinning and right now see our dresses....." she sadly told him looking at their outfits.

"Hmm.... you are right," he said observing his outfit in the mirror "ok no worries you just give me 5 minutes and see" He find a bottle of liquid liner and poured it a little on a plate and used that as a paint he created similar designs matching with Shrishti's outfit on the end of the sleeve of his sherwani and on the pocket near his collar.

"see..... now is it ok......"

"huff..... Finally... it's beautiful"

"Ok now no more getting sad..... smile and let's go we only have 10 minutes left......" she nodded and silently stood up from the chair.

"Let's go," she said with a small smile playing on her lips.

"May I say something...?" she nodded "you are looking very beautiful" the look in his eyes was telling her that he mean it, Listening to those words for a moment she felt something flutter in her heart, she just smiled in response and then both of them left towards the backstage where their whole team was present and was only waiting for them.

Last round of some team was running on the ramp and here Kabir and Shrishti was standing all set with the team to go on the floor, Finally it was the turn of team india both Kabir and Shrishti wished their team good luck and happily everyone started going on floor very confidently as time was passing Shrishti was getting nervous bit by bit, She hold Kabir's hand tightly in nervousness he was looking at her amusingly.

"Shrishti...." he tried to gain her attention but it was looking like she was lost somewhere still she hummed in response.

"Are you ok...." There was concern in his voice not for his employee but for his friend, the friend who was always there with him since the time came in his life.

"Hmm...."

"Then why is your face saying otherwise like you saw some ghost or something" he chuckled at his own lame joke just to make her feel somewhat good.

"I'm scared man" she looked at him with her puppy eyes and he realized that she was actually scared somewhere.

The same fear was in him too but he composed himself before saying something.

"Why so...."

"First we don't have a tiny bit of experience of this ramp walk thing and secondly our outfits...." she voiced her fear looking at him.

"Khudi ko kar buland itna ki khuda khud bande se ye pooche, bata teri raza kya hai....."

She directly looked in his eyes "don't look at me like this.... These are not my lines but very appropriate for this moment.... Be confident and see the world will be yours..... And also we have done our best rest god will see... throw this tension out of the window and smile" he finished his mini speech just to get a humming response from her.

"What hmm? Now smile..... If you'll go with this poker sad face on the stage people might get scared you know" he joked

"Do I look scary...... huh" the hint of anger was visible in her voice so he immediately came into his defensive mode.

"Please my lord please don't get angry now" he dramatically folded his hands in front of her "now please have some mercy on me and smile.... And please don't worry whatever will happen, happen for good.... Ok now be ready we have to go in a minute or so" he motivated her and grabbed her hand to mark their entry on the ramp.

She took a deep breath and after giving a glance to her hand which he was holding securely she moved towards the ramp, the moment they stepped on the ramp together royally the whole hall filled with clapings and hootings, Both walked on the ramp gracefully and posed beautifully at last, all the judges were also in awe seeing the beauty both of them were carrying together.

After finishing their round they went backstage again, after them there were 5 teams left so they had plenty of time to take rest as both were restless from the past few hours. Whole team was sitting in the room allotted to them and Kabir and Shrishti were sitting in the green room given to them with a serious face. Almost 30 minutes passed but none of them spoke even a single word.

"Oh god for how long I have to sit with this serious face..... I need to do something..... But what" he thought to himself making stupid faces.

Getting bored he took out his phone and started scrolling instagram Suddenly a video played abruptly or it can be said he played it on full volume intentionally to grab her attention who was sitting like she came after fighting some war or something like that.

"duniya main aye hain to jeena hi padega...... jeevan hai agar zeher to peena hi padega"(funny version)

"What on earth are you doing Kabir?" she asked, getting annoyed with the irritating song he played.

"What am I doing.... Passing time dude, no one here is talking to me so I have to do something right? Well why is someone not talking to me" he pretended like he was saying the last part to himself.

"Here I'm scared like hell and someone is busy being comical I see" she shook her head and glared at him.

"Now again scared but what for?" he finally asked, composing her grinning self.

"That's what will be the result" she pouted cutely saying that.

"Tell me one thing" he kept his phone back in his pocket and shifted his complete attention to her "now whatever will be the result can we change that"

"No"

"Then tell me is there any use of taking this stupid tension and hurting your brain"

"No." she said looking down

"You know what we can do many productive things here other than being tensed for nothing"

"Like," she asked innocently.

"Like....umm.... Yeah Photoshoot, now when we'll get a chance to get ready like this, don't you think we should make some memories" he asked, moving his eyebrows up and down comically.

"hmmm......well, It hurts saying this but you are right."

"Then get ready for the photoshoot mam" he smiled wide and took out his phone and pretended like a photographer.

"But as far as I remember you don't like clicking pics na.... then how this change in behavior came," she asked remembering the incident of him refusing for the pictures in Jaipur.

"Oh that, actually someone told me, if we face any situation with a smile then everything goes good" he looked here and there to avoid any kind of eye contact for the moment.

"Is it..... Well, which great personality tells you about this" she asked, wiggling her eyebrows.

"Someone told me.... Why do you care" he played along as both of them clearly remember it was shrishti only who said those things to him.

Talking this way both of them got busy clicking pics of each other and finally, time passed and the time of the final result came, all the head designers and CEOs of companies present in the competition were gathered in the hall for the result announcement.

Three judges were there to announce the results, they took over the stage and began announcing.

"Firstly, we would like to thank all the companies participating in the competition...... all were very good and preparing the result was really a hard task for the three of us...... so Mr.James will announce the result," the first judge said in the mike.

"So without wasting time let's announce the name of the team who bagged the 3rd prize....... So it is team no. 3 teams came from Bangkok" the second judge announced and the hall echoed with the sound of clapping for the team. Listening to this Shrishti breathed heavily and Kabir was also a little tense now for the result.

"So yes the team who got the 2nd place is team no.13 team came from England" the other one announced.

By now Shrishti and Kabir both were hopeful that maybe they'll get 2nd position as they were not expecting 1st at all because there was a fault in their dresses but they became sad listening that some other team bagged the second position.

"so now it's time to announce the name of the team who won this competition" both Kabir and Shrishti were tensed completely by now, they closed their eyes and joined their hands "This team attracted us towards their designs that three of us were unable to resist from tagging them as winners.... So we'll not keep you all in suspense much the team who won this competition is TEAM INDIA......."

The moment these words fell in the ears of Kabir and Shrishti their eyes opened wide because they were not able to accept the fact that they really did it, Both of them were in utter shock to respond to anything. They were shocked to the extent that they were not even able to hear the announcement made to call them up on stage because the judges announced again to call them and finally hearing that they came out from their shocking state.

"Shrishti"

"Hmm" she hummed, controlling her tears that were dreading to fall from her eyes out of happiness.

"We did it." he said holding her hand "let's go......" He took her on stage with him and the whole hall erupted with hootings and clappings for them. Judges handed them over the trophy and the prize check.

"congratulations..... MR. Kabir Mehra...." one of the judges congratulated.

"thank you so much...." After thanking everyone, both Kabir and Shrishti were about to leave the stage but the judges stopped them. "Just a minute please...... we would really like to mention one main thing. The main reason for choosing team india as winner.... These small beautiful designs made with black on complete white dress is just amazing" one of the judges said.

"Your designs are really amazing and as an extra award and honor for your hard work we want to give you guys a contract for designing the outfits of our company for the next year," the other one said.

"oh god.... That's huge.... Thank you thank you so very much sir" he said as it was never done before by the organizers.

"your team really deserves this"

Finally soon the event went over, Kabir and Shrishti with their team were happily returning to their hotel....... While walking towards their room both were making plans for sightseeing as the first purpose of coming to Paris was achieved.

"I can't even imagine that finally, we did it...... thank you so soo soooo much god" shrishti squealed

"Yes, finally it's true that we are the winners...... well if all is well that ends well." Kabir replied wiping the sleep away from his eyes as the day was really hectic for him and his team too.

"So now," she asked with her twinkling eyes.

"Now what?" he pretended like he forgot about their plan of sightseeing.

"What what? We have to go sightseeing, did you forget?" she almost yelled in frustration as she couldn't take a chance with her sightseeing at all.

"No your honor, I didn't forget, you get really excited about this sightseeing thing, I have noticed this recently"

"And why should not I get excited, already time is less" she rubbed her eyes violently meanwhile.

"Means," he asked, giving her his whole attention.

"Oh einstein, we have only 4 days and lots of places to visit"

"Oh, now leave that I'm just gonna sleep tight and then will think about everything in the morning." he was yawning a little showing how tired he was and he noticed she again was rubbing her eyes not quite normally.

"Ya ya you go take rest, also I don't want any excuse tomorrow, got that" she asked rasing her an eyebrow then was about to open the door of her room.

"One minute look at me..." he made her look at him directly in his eyes "shrishti girl, why your eyes are turning red..." he asked in a very concerned way while observing her eyes "you are ok right"

"Hey hey, don't take tension, I'm completely fine.... It's just because of doing work the whole day then the huge stress for the show is nothing much.... It'll be fine once I'll get some good sleep" she said smiling wide to assure him that she is fine but at least he knew that she was a very good actor when it came to hide her pain.

"Are you sure, otherwise we can consult with the doctor too" he suggested looking at the crimson hue in her eyes.

"Oh no no..... I'm fine.... Now just go to your room and take a good sleep" she said, pushing him into his room as he was adamant to take her to the doctor.

"ok good night.... But please if there is any problem just do tell me" he said sincerely as he knew even if she was a grownup, her parents had sent her after trusting him and she should reach back home all good like before. She nodded and pushed him into his room again..... after that she lazily went into her room and she slept the moment she hit the bed.

The next morning Kabir got up on time, without wasting a minute he went to get ready as he knew the consequences of getting late especially when it comes to going out with Shrishti. After checking everything the last time he went to call her, he was pressing her doorbell for the past 20 minutes and in response he got nothing. Soon he started worrying if she was fine or not.

"Oh god, she was not looking well yesterday.... I don't even know whether she is fine or not" he talked to himself and Getting worried he started pressing bell more frequently at last Shrishti opened the door, he was about to shout on her but looking at her condition he abruptly stopped, She was looking very dull and weak before he could ask anything she stumbled a little to prevent her from falling he hold her before she fell on the floor, in no time she fainted in his arms.

11

"Shrishtiiii"

For him everything stopped for a moment, he was not able to decide what he should do. Immediately he carried her and after placing her gently on the bed he covered her with a blanket and rushed to call a doctor. The staff of the hotel arranged a doctor within minutes meanwhile Kabir was restless could be an understatement. While the doctor was checking Shrishti he was pacing in the room agitatedly, finally, the doctor was over with his examination.

"Doctor how's she..... she is fine right?" he asked impatiently

"don't worry she is fine," he said with a small nod.

"Then why did she faint," Kabir asked, freaking out as it was his first experience dealing with an unconscious person.

"calm down gentle man...... she fainted because she is very weak and I'have checked her eyes its totally red maybe she hadn't took rest or a major headache could be a reason..... but don't worry now I gave her an injection she'll wake up within 30 minutes" the told him calmly.

"are you sure doctor...... and is there are any precautions to be taken"

"yes yes.... Don't worry..... just try to make her rest when she wake up and give her healthy homemade food to eat" "actually doctor we are on a business trip and staying in this hotel only homemade food is not possible"

"it's ok then you can switch it with boiled vegetables and some low sodium soup" the doctor suggested.

"ok.... I'll make sure what you said is fulfilled"

"ok then now I'll take your leave" "thank you doctor"

After sending the doctor out Kabir came back into the room and silently sat on the couch placed just a little distance from her bed. He was waiting for the past 20 minutes for her to wake up. These 20 minutes were the hardest 20 minutes for him ever, he was not able to look at her bit by bit he was drowning in guilt that because of him she worked continuously without taking any rest and ended up getting sick. While he was drowned in his thoughts Shrishti stirred a little and he immediately became attentive. A few minutes later she opened her eyes. Maybe she was trying to register what just happened, she was about to get up but Kabir interrupted.

"no no no..... There is no need to get up..... Just take a rest" she looked at him innocently trying to figure out why he was behaving like that. After making sure that she is ok he sat back on the couch again with a grumpy face. Firstly she was observing him silently then finally she asked.

"Kabir...." he didn't look at her "hey am I audible.... Sir..... why are sitting here making your face like a donut"

"My face is my choice," he said, showing his grumpiness.

"Ok leave that, let's go, didn't we have to go sightseeing.... See I'm fine too now, now get up and I'll too get ready quickly" she was about to step down from the bed when he warned her

"dare you to step down..... do you really think that after what happened I'm going to take you on sightseeing"

"But I'm alright na.... See I'm fine"

"we are going nowhere and that's final...... understand now take rest..... I'm ordering food for us" he strictly said and turned to order through the intercom. She didn't say anything and quietly sat in the blanket only with a pout on her face. Soon their food arrived, Kabir passed her a bowl filled with boiled vegetable soup seeing that Shrishti made the most disgusted face ever.

"Wasn't there anything more disgusting available to order" she scrunched her nose shaking her head.

"I ordered what the doctor told me..... now no drama, eat it quietly" looking at his straight face she somehow took one sip and made a more disgusted face than before.

"Eww..... This is yuk... I'm not eating this" she said with finality making him lose his calmness.

"If you'll not eat it on your own then I'm bound to make you eat this forcefully," he said with a plain face and tried to threaten her but she was adamant. "You are saying as if it is some delicious dessert which I am denying to eat...... before forcing me why are you not trying a bit.... Huh" she said crossing her arms adamantly

"I have also ordered the same for myself too..... now no more drama....eat it..... after that, you have to take medicines too" Finally giving up she started having the soup, Kabir was also having the same because he didn't want to make her feel alone eating tasteless food, soon they were finished with their eating and now looking at medicines placed in front of her she shoots a questioning glare at him.

"what....?? Have this and don't give me that look" She knew that there was no room for arguing with him, so took the medicines and was about to talk to him but he opened his phone and pretended like he was busy now she was getting mad at his behavior.

"Kabirhhh"

"what...?"

"why you are not talking to me"

"nothing like that...."

"Are you angry with me" he didn't reply "at least say something..... Please" she requested with a sad pout as feeling ignored was the last thing ever wanted in her life.

"Yes.... yes I am angry.... Now happy"

"But why.... What did I do wrong" she asked looking at her hands that she kept in her lap.

"Seriously..... You are asking what you did wrong..... Shrishti are you out of your mind.... You were suffering from the pain the whole night. I told you in advance too that whenever you feel that you are not well or feeling sick you'll tell me straight but no, someone has to be self-dependent and all...... if something would have happened to you then..... What I would have answered to your parents han after trusting me they sent you here and then this is happening here"

"Oh.... so you are getting tense for me..... I see" she joked.

"I'm not in a mood Shrishti"

"Ok sorry na..... This will not be repeated ever..... Why are you getting so tense..... See I'm all ok.... See" she said, flashing a bright smile at him so that he could feel a little better.

"I'm getting tense because you don't have any idea how I felt when you fainted right in front of me..... You dumbo.... My mind was not working. I was freaking out like an idiot. On the top of it I shouted at the poor doctor....." he said embarrassingly.

"But why....."

"Some people in our life come and unknowingly become a very important part of our life.... To whom we can't see in pain and for me you are also like that important person...." the genuineness in his eyes and voice simultaneously was showing how he meant each and every word she said.

"Sorry yaar," he didn't say anything. "Now please smile…. If you'll sit like this grumpy face then….." Before she could complete he glared at her "Ok I said sorry right…. This will not happen again…."

"Promise"

"Promise"

"ok….. now sleep and take a rest"

"Nooooo……. I don't want to sleep," she said, shaking her head like a kid.

"How not like that you will not sleep…..you want to stay like this only, no right…. So sleep" he said, lecturing her like a mother and she whined exactly like a child to not let her sleep forcefully.

"Please naaa….."

"You are sleeping or do I call aunty," he asked, flashing his phone in front of her eyes to threaten her she gave him an are-you-even-serious look.

"Why on earth everyone threatens me with the name of my mom, first di and now you too" she sighed frustratingly in disbelief.

"Because you are stubborn…" she made a sad face "Now what"

"How I wanted to roam here carelessly and explore this city but here I'm sitting being sick" she was already on the verge of crying.

"Ok ok don't make that face now, take a rest for 2 days then we'll go sightseeing on the last day…… I promise"

"Well, why are you sitting here uselessly on the place of going and enjoying your trip, why are you wasting your time….. Don't spoil it because of me"

"Is there an idiot written on my face…." she shook her head negatively "Then why are you asking this stupid question.... How even this came to your mind that I'll leave you here alone" she looked at him innocently "Now sleep.... Don't keep me busy in these talks I know your tactics you know" Finally she lay down on her bed and covered her face with a blanket but didn't sleep because she was not feeling sleepy.

Kabir thought she slept so he sat on the couch lazily and started scrolling his phone. He was busy scrolling his phone. Suddenly his phone started ringing. It was from his dad. He didn't want to talk but half-heartedly he picked the call.

On call:

Kabir: yes dad.....

K/dad: congratulations Kabir.... Congratulations to you and your team..... really proud of you son.

Kabir: thanks, dad..... Thanks but as a CEO of your company but not as your son......(he said plainly)

K/dad: what happened son why are you talking like this..... Are you not happy with this success?

Kabir: Happy, now there is no meaning of happiness for me at least..... Yes as the CEO of your company I'm more than happy..... But your son is not happy.... And now you don't need to think about him also..... He's fine the way he is now.

K/dad: don't say like this Kabir I am really proud of you Son......

Kabir: no dad..... you are not proud of your son you are proud of THE KABIR MEHRA CEO of your company not of simple Kabir....... If I tell you the truth your son doesn't do anything to make you proud because he's not allowed to..... Better we don't discuss all this..... You should rest at this time there will be night..... And please take care of mamma... bye.

Kabir sadly threw his phone to one side and covered his face with the pillow and cried silently...... Shrishti also became sad as she listened to the whole conversation.... She was in deep thought that what is the exact problem from which Kabir is suffering, she decided that she'll find out finally what is bothering him before going back to India.

2 days passed and now Shrishti was fine but Kabir was still treating her like a little baby.

"Oh please Kabir.... Now enough na I'm fine now..... You are literally treating me like a kid" she was sounding frustrated but it didn't affect him a bit "I'm not gonna eat this Yuck food now... and that's final" she adamantly.

"I see..... But sorry my dear.... You don't have any option.... I can't take any kind of risk so you have to eat this only"

"You know what you are giving me completely my mom's vibes.... It feels like mom had sent you with me after giving full fledged training to annoy me.... Am I right"

"Now don't tell me that yrr..... I'm also here eating the same thing right with you..... So now cut your drama and eat" Finally she gave up and had her food making ugly faces, seeing that Kabir wanted to laugh very hard but he controlled himself because he didn't want a swollen forehead in return. After finishing she sat sadly with a really sad face seeing her sad Kabir got worried.

"hey Shrishti what happened"

"Dammann...... We are in Paris.... Can you imagine from the past whole week, but still we haven't seen Eiffel tower... and also now we don't even have time" she pouted disappointingly.

"Hey it's not like that... we still have 1 and the half day we can at least visit the most famous places," he said smilingly to make her smile

"Really..." she squealed like a kid.

"Of course, now get up fast and get ready, and then we'll leave"

"You are not joking right?" she confirmed one last time as she was thinking if he was pulling some prank on her or something.

"of course not.... Now go and get ready fast I'm also going to get ready... ok..." saying this he went into his room,

Soon after getting ready both were now in the taxi and moving towards the Eiffel tower within 30 minutes, they reached there, Shrishti was hell excited and so was Kabir

"Kabir.... Come let's go to the top... I want to see the view" she excitedly started pulling his arm.

"Hey no.... Are you mad"

"What happened"

"This is too high...... If you got scared then"

"Huh.... you don't know me till now Kabir... I don't get scared of anything, are you scared or something" she asked, raising her one eyebrow to tease him.

"I'm scared that's the reason I'm denying genius," he thought, making an annoying face.

"No no.... Why would I be scared.... I was saying because you must be scared so... It's fine na.... We'll see from here only"

"I told you na I'm not scared of anything.... Now let's go, we don't have a lot of time to wasted" she dragged him with her into the elevator to reach the top of the tower. It was a working day and off-season for tourists so few people were there. As the lift was moving upward Kabir's nervousness was also increasing, he was rubbing his hands continuously as sweat was forming in his palms.

"What happened, Kabir.... Are you ok"

"ya ya.... I'm fine...." he replied with a little confusing smile.

Finally, they were on top of the Eiffel tower, Shrishti stepped out of the lift before Kabir and started getting mesmerized by the view in front of her, in all this she forgot someone is missing.

"Oh god.... Where is this kabir left now" She was finding him here and there and luckily, she saw him standing beside the lift's door with a plain face. "Oye why are you standing here like Devdas"

"Yrr, firstly I'm not Devdas," he said, closing his eyes to prevent himself from seeing anything there.

"Ok ok, you are not" she chuckled "but at least come forward, are you planning to stay here to adore this lift of something" ignoring her sarcastic comment he simply replied. "No, you go I'm fine here"

"You are scared right?" he didn't reply, "say" she was teasing him but he didn't actually care for that at least for that moment, but eventually giving up accepted.

"Yes, yes I'm scared.... I'm scared of heights"

"Nothing will happen, Kabir, see I'm with you right?"

"No you go I'm fine"

"I'm saying na, that nothing will happen.... Don't you trust me"

"I DO..... but" She cut him in between "no if no but..... Now come" She held his wrist and dragged him under the open sky, because of nervousness he closed his eyes again. He was standing still without opening his eyes. Shrishti noticed that he was really scared so she held his left hand with her both hands, to calm him down.

"Kabir don't be scared yrr...... its nothing ca mon be a brave man...... open your eyes" she said calmly but trying to cheer him up.

"no I'm not gonna do that..... Whatever you wanna see, see it fast and then let's get out of here quickly" he literally pleaded still with his eyes closed.

"Please na.... At least open your eyes once, I can bet you'll love it.... Really" she again tried, but seeing him not even budging she sighed. "Please trust me....... and don't worry I'm here only with you" collecting all his courage Kabir slowly opened his eyes and the beauty in front of him was enough to make him awestruck, he was looking at the view without even blinking his eyes.

"So Mr. Mehra, how do you like it?" she chirped happily seeing his positive reaction. "It's beyond beautiful..... seriously..... I have never thought that I could do this ever.... Thank you so much buddy"

"kabhi kabhi zindagi hume vo tazurbe de jati hai jiski kabhi kalpana bhi na ki ho....."

"literally..... this happened because of you Shrishti...... thank you so much"

"really..... because of me?" she asked, raising her one eyebrow in a questioning manner.

"of course...."

"We'll discuss this matter sometime later, now c'mon let's click pictures... I'll show them to mom dad and di" she excitedly handed him her phone and started posing for the pictures.

"Sure madam sure, come let's do your photoshoot" He started clicking her pictures, almost after 30 minutes Kabir was tired clicking pics continuously but Shrishti was not done with her poses. "Oye, how many more," he asked, tired of clicking pictures continuously.

"Just 2-3...."

"Are you sure"

"Yes yes"

After clicking pictures Kabir handed her over the phone to check the pics, while she was busy checking pictures he taunted her intentionally. "Why don't you do one thing, hire a personal photographer.... The way you like clicking your pictures it'll be better"

"Oh yes, you are saying right.... Do one thing you only become my personal photographer, you also click pictures ok ok so it'll be good" she giggled seeing him shocked yet comic expressions. "Haww..... Do I click only ok-ok pictures"

"Yes.... and don't worry I'll give you a salary too" Saying this she ran from there as she knew she had put fuel to the fire. "I'll tell you now, you wait..... Let me show you how to click pictures" he said while chasing her, after chasing each other like tom and jerry both of them got tired. "ok ok I surrender," she said raising both hands in the air.

"good for you......"

"Ok, come now let me click your pictures too" hearing this he made an annoying face "You already know that...." she cut him in between "yes yes I know that you don't like yourself clicked... but please do it this time... for me.... If not many at least 2-3" she was pleading through eyes because she wanted him to live his life cheerfully and that was the reason why she was pushing him, Seeing that he was not able to refuse so he posed and Shrishti took some good pictures of him and then dragged him for taking selfies.

Finally, both of them climbed down the Eiffel tower..... Kabir was feeling hungry like hell but there were zero signs of hunger visible on Shrishti she was busy adoring their surroundings.

"Shrishtiii......." he whined getting irritated as the hunger was getting the best out of him "what?"

"Are you a robot...?" "no.... I'm an alien..." she said with a wide smile

"Oh, so you are Jadu, that's why getting charged with sunlight right" the grumpiness was clearly visible on his face as his stomach was growling uncontrollably.

"What exactly you are trying to say, sir?" "Damn.... You don't feel hungry or something" he asked making helpless face. "Yes I'm damn hungry"

"Thank god, let's go we'll eat first otherwise I'm not going anywhere"

"Ok ok, let's go" remembering something she stopped abruptly in her tracks. "Now what happened to you girl" " make a promise" she forwarded her right hand towards him "promise...what promise" "first promise then I'll say"

"How can I promise something just like that.... If you asked something weird then"

"Oh, so you trust me this much only that you can't even promise without knowing"

"No, it's not like that..... Ok, promise.... Now even if you'll ask my life that too I'll give you"

"Really....." she asked, raising her eyebrows.

"If you want to try then just ask...... Kabir never backs out from his promises" Kabir said looking straight into her eyes.

"hehehehe..... I'm not gonna ask that.... Don't worry Mr. Mehra..... Just listen to this now as you have promised me so" she mischievously smiled rubbing her palms together. "Soooo" he knew that smile very well, he was sure about something fishy cooking in her brain.

"Soo, I'm not gonna eat that yucky food today..... Got it.... And that's final...." she announced. "Hey this is wro...." she cut "nothing is wrong, come" she held his wrist and dragged him with her on the other side of the road, Both of them were cluelessly walking on the street to find a good restaurant.

"Shrishti.... Why are we walking like this.... We can eat in any restaurant no..... see there are many"

"No"

"Can I ask why?" he was getting irritated because his stomach was growling badly. "because I'm trying to find an Indian restaurant"

"But what for..... We can eat anywhere right"

"Because I'm tired of eating these sandwiches, burgers, and pizzas.... And not to forget that boiled yuck food from the past 3 days.... Now I for sure want my favorite typical Indian food"

"actually yrr..... you are right...."

"I'm always right Mr." she raised her fake collars praising herself.

"Is It?" "Oh yes"

"Ok then, find some Indian restaurant quickly.... If I didn't get food asap I'm sure I'll go mad"

"As if you are not" In return She earned a deadly glare from him acting innocently she pretended like she was finding the restaurant, and finally they found an Indian food restaurant.... It was an open-roof restaurant. As both of them were super hungry so they immediately selected a table for themselves and started looking at the menu card for ordering their food.

"Excuse me, meanwhile mam is deciding what to order please bring 2 cups of ginger tea" meanwhile she was ordering he ordered tea as he was dying to have authentic Indian tea.

"You wanna have tea?" "Obviously, it's been an eternity since I had my darling tea," he said in a duh tone. She shook her head in disbelief and continued looking at the menu card. At last, Kabir's tea arrived and he began enjoying it.

"oho, ho hoooooooooo........ It's fab... just fab..... Feels like heaven" he said, enjoying his tea. She looked at him trying not to laugh but helplessly she asked the question bugging her head. "Is it that good that you started daydreaming"

"It's just I'm feeling peaceful after having this wonderful kadak chai.... Last time had in India...... Oh no.... I'm suddenly feeling emotional god..." he said wiping his fake tears earning a head shake from her.

"Do you love your chai very much"

"Much more than very much" again he took a sip from his cup enjoying the aroma of tea.

"People nowadays don't even love their girlfriends this much you know, as you do to your chai" she laughed at her own statement.

"Oh yes, that's true," he said, playing along.

"Don't you worry, I'll make you and your chai get married ok...." he didn't pay any attention to her words and continued drinking his tea.

"Come Mrs. Chai Mehra...... Let me see how much tasty are you"

Taking one sip Shrishti's reaction was as same as Kabir's

"So, didn't I say that it's heaven?" he asked, wiggling his eyebrows in a comic way. "Seriously man, this is really heaven"

Both burst into laughter and after some time their food too arrived they enjoyed their Indian authentic food and at the end again after having one one cup tea they left the restaurant. The whole day they visited the popular places which were possible to visit for them and finally after the whole day they were returned back to their hotel. In the cab, Kabir was busy checking the pictures they clicked the whole day but he noticed that Shrishti was sitting with a gloomy face.

"Now what happened to you madam.....?"

"Nothing...."

"Is it?..... Nothing.... Then in what happiness are you sitting with this gloomy face"

"Tomorrow is our last day here.... Then we'll go back right.... After that maybe i'll never get this chance again to come here..." she looked out trying to avoid showing her gloomy self to him.

"Hey, why are you saying like this..... Well is it like you want to settle here with your kids and husband..." she tried to joke to lighten her mood but in return, he got her deadly glare. "what.... Kids.... Husband... youuuu......" She was about to beat him but he held her hands to stop her. "Easy easy girl.... Why are you getting angry.... In the future, you'll have your kids and husband na.... Don't you" he comically said, making fun of her. She shot a deadly glare at him, and then abruptly tears brimmed in her eyes.

"Hey..... what happened.... I'm sorry if you felt bad.... Please don't cry yrr" he suddenly was in a panic state. "I'm not crying, you idiot.... Something must has gone in my eyes" she said while rubbing her eyes, But in reality, she was emotional which she didn't want to show him.....

"oh....."

"what.... Ohh.... Help me"

"oh yes yes...." He blew in her eyes and after a minute she was ok.

"you know what.... You don't ever scare me like this" he said, showing fake fear on his face. "Do I scare you"

"Obviously, you get angry in a snap.... My poor soul gets scared.... Umm one minute, I have an idea"

"what idea......"

"Your name, Let me give you a nickname..... But what..... Yes DON..... you are don.... Wait wait everyone calls you shrii.... So from today, you are DON for me ok.... great..... how creative I am" he said, raising his collars. "Don, seriously, you are seriously mad.... Who gives this kind of nickname" she shook her head unbelievingly.

"Me" he smiled wide. "Whatever" she started looking outside the window, He chuckled looking at her grumpy yet cute face. After some time both reached their hotel and wishing good night both ran into their rooms as they were tired a lot.

Shrishti changed quickly and fell asleep immediately but here Kabir was thinking something, Very deeply sitting in the gallery of his room.

"she is not happy...... I can feel it... I know we don't have much time here but maybe I can do something for her, something memorable" Suddenly he remembered something and opened his laptop and started surfing about that. Finally he was done with making plans to surprise her on the last day of their trip and also to create a memorable moment. Thinking all about his plan he went to sleep with a serene smile on his face.

12

The next day, According to their schedule Kabir and Shrishti left for sightseeing. The whole day they enjoyed themselves a lot and finally came back to their hotel. They were about to enter the hotel but Kabir stopped Shrishti.

"Shrishti"

"Yes"

"Don't go inside"

"why..... is there anything left," she asked, yawning.

"yess very big thing"

"now what more, let it be na..... let's go in"

"No.... not at all.... We are going and that's final"

She sighed and agreed finally, he smiled widely and dragged her with him. "Do we have to walk to the place you are taking me, see it's already late"

"Yes, why are you scared..... What if your ghosties met" he chuckled at his own joke. "hihihihi..... not so funny" she rolled her eyes as she had no other option. "It's ok just come with me" After almost 20 minutes of walking, they reached an area that was surrounded by trees only.

"where we are going yrr..... at least tell me..." she whined while trying to meet his pace. "What is the fruit of patience deer shrishti?" "Sweet" she pouted, getting annoyed.

"yess.... Very good..... You are also getting intelligent finally" she gave him a serious look and he looked here and there to avoid eye contact, After a few more steps Kabir tied a blindfold on her eyes.

"hey..... now this is for what"

"for surprise kiddo"

"What surprise?"

"Can't you keep quiet for a few minutes.... You talk too much girl... is it kbc going on.... Even mr. bachan don't ask these many questions"

"Ok then, let me see your surprise first and if it came out something stupid then you are so gone Mr. Mehra" she was threatening him with the blindfold on while he was chuckling seeing her cute antics. He held her wrist to lead her the way as she was blindfolded, finally they reached a lake which was surrounded by trees on three sides.

"We reached right.... Then please open this damn thing"

"Yes, my lord.... Just a second.... Ok see you open your eyes in slow motion ok" she nodded in agreement. He went behind her and slowly opened her blindfold. The moment she opened her eyes she was awestruck. For almost 5 minutes she was looking at the view in front of her without even blinking her eyes.

"sooooo..... how do you like it"

"Do I need to mention" she turned towards him with her emotions flooding in her eyes ``this is the best surprise anyone gave me in my entire life..... I just can't express how I'm feeling right now...... thank you so much Kabir...... you made my day..... no no my entire trip..." she tried her best to control but her voice ended up getting heavy.

"Hold on girl.... Don't praise me this much, it's just I wanted to make my Don happy..... if you liked it what more do I need" the look on his face was showing the genuineness in his words she gave him a wide smile asking him to sit there for some time. "Can we sit here for some time" "yes, why not…" They sat there dipping their feet in the water, both were silent but the silence was speaking a lot. Though there was no need to talk to share the peace they were having but still shrishti chose to speak as there was a lot going on in her mind which she wanted to ask him before leaving paris.

"Kabir"

"Hmmm"

"May I ask a question"

"Of course"

"That day when my outfit got ruined because of that liquid liner, then you made those flowers on the dress right?"

"Yes"

"how your strokes were so professional…… means it was looking like you are a master in that art" the confusion yet curiosity in her eyes was twinkling and he knew that it was time when he had to tell her because she was nowhere looking in the mood to leave the topic.

"Remember you asked me many times, what actually is my problem, why I roam like Devdas as you always say…. This is what my problem is, Painting is my problem"

"Means"

"Since childhood, I have had only one dream…. To become a successful artist, I wanted to open my art gallery….. But" his sudden silence made her more curious whereas he was in turmoil about whether he should say all this or not. "But what Kabir," she asked softly, keeping her hand on his shoulder.

"But, my parents or if I say my dad rejected it completely…… According to him, my dreams, my feelings , everything is useless…… he only wants me to do what he says….. And the most painful thing is my mom too take his side always, for her he is everything and he can never be wrong"

"But being an artist is not useless....." the hurt was evident in her voice as she was a great supporter of any art form, for her art was something more precious and dear than anything on earth. "But for him, It is, because his reputation will be ruined in this so-called society if his one and only son will not handle his company"

"That's why you have conflicts with your parents" he looked at her quizzically "sorry but, that day when you were talking to your dad i was not sleeping, I heard your conversation"

"I don't have conflicts. I love them very much but......" abruptly he stopped as his gaze fixed on the sky filled with stars "It hurts..... It hurts badly, the only thing I feel is loneliness. I'm helpless. I'm not able to understand what I do, if I choose my dreams then it'll be unfair to them.... Or if I suppress my dreams then it'll be wrong with myself..... Very wrong" listening to him she was stunned but she didn't want to overpower that thing on her as she was there with the motive to make him feel good not worse. "Can I say something?"

"Obviously..... Who is there except you and aaditya in my life who can say anything to me"

"You can make everyone happy together..... yourself and your parents too" "How"

"You can continue your passion side by side and also handle your business, you and your parents both will be happy"

"do you really think I didn't try this" "then what's the problem" hearing her innocent question he chuckled sadly "only one thing...... they don't understand me..... I told you na for them what I do from my choice is always useless........ And now I'm done..... I'm tired of explaining myself everytime..... Now I can't do this anymore" the tone of his voice was clearly showing that he was feeling defeated, again the silence but the comfort fell in between them, By now Shrishti was feeling tired she unknowingly rested her head against his shoulder..... as he was drowned in his talk he didn't even realize it and continued pouring his heart out.

"You know, they never made me feel special, they never made me feel loved... for my dad his business is everything and for my mom my dad is everything...... My friends used to say that I'm a single child so all my wishes and demands used to be fulfilled... it's true though..... But to date, they never ever asked what I want..... Where is my happiness.... They were so busy with work that they never even celebrated my birthday with me...... Birthday huh well.... It's gonna come yet again.... And I'll be alone ye again" a sad yet sarcastic chuckle escaped his mouth, he was laughing at his own destiny that even after having everything he has nothing which can make him feel content and happy "But now it didn't even affect me...... sometimes I feel for then I'm just their hire, who'll handle his company.... But what they don't know is in all this they lost their son way long back..... Who's not gonna come back....."

"Dil agar begane tod jaye to shayad sambhal bhi jaya karte hain... lekin apno ke diye zakhm kahan bhula karte hain....."

A teardrop fell from his eyes and he wiped it immediately trying not to show her but, then he realized that Shrishti's head was resting on his shoulder, and didn't know when she was sleeping. There was a serene calmness on her face, seeing that a small smile formed on his face too, his heart was somewhere pleading to stop the moment right there for eternity, he didn't have any idea why but he didn't have the heart to wake her up, So he too closed his eyes to feel the cold breeze. He was unknown about the reason but somewhere his heart was feeling calm, relaxed, and peaceful. Maybe because he took out everything which was in his heart or maybe because he was sitting with the one for whom his heart was somewhere falling unknowingly.

After almost 30 minutes Kabir felt that they should leave. He didn't want to but he patted her shoulder to wake her up. For a few seconds she was not in the mood to wake up but then she cutely opened her eyes and was confused for a few seconds. "Oh no, I slept here only..... God, how foolish I am" seeing the cute antics he chuckled and calmed her down "it's ok miss. Don.... the peace is too much to handle her, that's why you must feel sleepy"

"hmm.... Maybe" she said dreamily, looking at the sky suddenly her eyes became wide "Kabir Kabir....."

"what?"

"see.... Shooting star..... Make a wish fast" she said while joining her hands to make her own wish, After a few seconds, she opened her eyes and found that Kabir was staring at her only. "Again... you didn't make a wish this time too right? I told you this wish always gets fulfilled then?"

"I too told you...... when I have complete confidence in my fate then what's the need to disturb god, also asking for wishes which I know that never gonna be fulfilled"

"Kar ke dekho yakeen kabhi khuda pe bhi zara sa..... jo qismat usne likhi hai use badalne ka hunar bhi usi ke pass hai......"

she finished but he smiled sadly yet calmness was spread on his face.

"Let's go, we'll get late.... Tomorrow we have a flight to catch.... Hmm," he tried changing the topic, She nodded and got up, Both of them were walking silently..... Kabir thought she didn't hear his whole talk but it was his delusion that she didn't hear, he was busy in his thoughts and here Shrishti too was drowned in her thoughts.

"Kabir, you have many complaints from your life na.... You think like no one understands you.... I do... and today I promise, on this birthday you'll get everything for what you have even left asking from god" she thought, drowned in their thoughts Finally both of them were back at their hotel after wishing good night to each other they went to their rooms.

The next day around 11 in the morning the whole team of Kabir and Shrishti was gathered at the airport, soon they boarded the flight and their flight took off within a few minutes. On the flight, Kabir was normal but Shrishti was lost all the time.

"Shrishti" he tried gaining her attention but she replied still being in the trance. "yes"

"where are you...?"

"at mars...." saying this she rolled her eyes and gained a "are you even serious" look from him. "I'm here only na" she answered annoyingly as she knew very well he'll not leave her alone before getting a proper answer.

"I'm asking only na, why are you sounding annoyed.... Do I annoy you?" he asked, sounding hurt. "It's nothing yrr..... I'm sorry..... I was thinking something deeply" "about whom..... Your future husband and kids?" he asked, moving his eyebrows up and down comically. "Say this one more time and I tell you" she fumed "tell me what?" He riled her up even more. "Then, I'm not done for name sake, you know better what don's do" she smirked seeing horror expressions of him.

"Oh my god..... Live threats" he said dramatically.

"Oh yes, now keep quiet" he kept finger on his lips like kids seeing her getting angry in real.

"Oh god, now what happened to this girl, we'll let it be.... She looks cute being angry" he thought to himself and covered his mouth to suppress his laughter.

Their whole flight went like this, only fighting like kids on silly topics. Finally, their flight landed at Mumbai international airport around 1 at night. All the team members happily saw each other off and then left for their houses, only Kabir and Shrishti were left there.

"Now I have to book a cab" she mumbled "kabir"

"yes"

"I need one help...."

"Order madam," he said comically.

"Please can you wait for a while here with me.... Until my cab arrives" she requested. "No..."

"ok.... No problem.... You go.... You must be sleepy" she said with a little smile covering her disappointment. "Oye dumbo..." he chuckled.

"Now what?"

"Cancel your ride..." she shoots a questioning glare at him" "do I look like a mad person to you..... Who'll let you alone that too at this time" and this time there was a seriousness in his voice.

"It's ok na...."

"You keep quiet and come with me.... There is a car outside, first I'll drop you at your home then I'll go mine" she looked at him silently "shall we.... madam"

She shook her head in disbelief and finally, both of them came out of the airport but at the moment Kabir saw who was standing with his car his face became plain and stiff, his father was there to pick him up. Half-heartedly he walked towards him with Shrishti. Shrishti was confused by his behavior but she didn't say anything.

"finally.... You are back Kabir" his dad said hugging him "I'm very proud of you beta"

"Thanks, dad..." he replied with utmost plainness in his voice.

"Namaste, uncle" shrishti also greeted him as he was elder to her and she always used to respect her elders.

"Namaste beta...... you....."

"She is designing heads.... and because of her, we won so you should be proud of her" Kabir intervened.

"well-done beta.... Great job.... I have seen your designs... it's just awesome" he praised her genuinely, she was also happy for the fact so she replied smilingly "thank you so much, uncle..."

"Let's go kabir.... Let's go home, how will you go shrishti?" Before he could ask anything more, Kabir cut him in between. "I'm going to drop her..... And then I'll go back home, thanks for coming here" he finished blankly and turned towards shrishti. His dad didn't stretch the talk further and left from there taking their car.

"lets go Shrishti..." Kabir asked and walked towards the car, She nodded and both of them after stuffing their bags in the car moved towards Shrishti's home. Whole time both of them were quiet, no one of them talked. Almost after 45 minutes of driving they reached her home, without wasting a second, Shrishti pressed the bell happily as she was excited to meet her family after more then one week. Her dad opened the door after a few minutes rubbing his eyes.

"papaa...!! How are you" without giving him any chance she hugged him and earned a great laugh from him. "Hey, my lioness is back" he mumbled hugging her back. "Oh yes" she squealed.

"Namaste uncle, see your daughter is back..... Please check if she is the same as she went or not" he joked at which her dad too joined with a chuckle. "Thank you so much son..." he said, engulfing him in a warm fatherly hug "for keeping your promise...... you have really earned my trust... thank you so much again"

"Uncle, you are calling me your son, and then saying thank you too.... Not fair" he tried to show his disappointment. "Ok ok, don't make this face.... I'll not say this again.... Now happy, now come inside you two or wanna do meeting here only"

"Oh no no uncle, I just came to drop shrishti, now I should leave you rest.... It's already past midnight"

"Ok then as you say"

"Ok uncle, good night" he hugged him "Ok don ji good night" he bit his tongue as he understood instantly what he said, he earned a deadly glare from Shrishti "ok bye bye" He hurriedly ran from there as he knew don is now in angry bird mode. Shrishti and her dad went into their rooms and fell into a deep slumber.

The next day it was a day off for the whole team who came back from paris as all were tired. Kabir made a plan to chill the whole day at home while Shrishti was totally surprised at her home.

"mamaaaaa...... What is this... this much food, are we going organize some feast"

"My baby is back after so many days, god knows what you have eaten there these days, so I made all your favorites" her mom reasoned. "Aww.... now you are making me emotional," she said, hugging her. "You know what you are best mamma"

"Yes yes only mamma is best, sister is invisible here" monika taunted her.

"Oh no no no, how can you be invisible di, you are my support system, I'm nothing without you" shrishti said engulfing her too in a bear hug.

"Ok-ok now no need to do buttering, come let's eat… we missed you a lot" "missed me or our fights di" she teased.

After enjoying breakfast with her family Shrishti went into her room and started thinking about Kabir…. The whole day passed like this only she was drowned in her thoughts the whole day all the while her mom was noticing her strange behavior, In the evening when Monika came back from her work. She told her about the same. "Monika, don't know why but I'm noticing since morning shri is behaving differently, please ask her if everything ok, and if she has any problem." "Don't worry mamma, I'll talk to her, she must be tired that's why behaving differently nothing else." She tried to convince her, and with her assurance, she looked a little satisfied too. The whole time during dinner Shrishti was busy in her thoughts and Monika noticed it too. Soon after dinner Shrishti went into her room and settled herself on the couch placed on her balcony.

Monika came and found her thinking something deeply. She sat beside Shrishti but she didn't even realize her presence so finally, she slapped her playfully on her cheek. "What dii, what happened" she whined

"What happened to you shrii"

"Nothing" she lied.

"Ok now you'll hide things from me now, huh"

"No di, why would I"

"Then speak"

"I'm just confused…. Nothing else" she tried to look cool but her inner confusion was clearly visible on her face. "May I know why?" monika calmly asked. "I'm not able to understand what I do to vanish all the problems of Kabir"

"Problems and that too to kabir, Impossible.... He's a very cheerful guy yrr, how can he be suffering from some problem" monika disbelievingly. "Sometimes what we see is not the truth.... Sometimes behind a heartwarming smile stays the heart wrenching pain" shrishti voiced her thoughts. "Ok then tell me, what's the matter," Shrishti told her everything in detail about how and why he is suffering. "Now you only tell me what to do, I really don't know why but I'm not able to see him sad, I want him to be happy and actually happy" "have you thought of something till now" monika asked. "I'm thinking do give him something precious on his birthday" "when is his birthday" "I don't know I just know it's coming soon" "so what's your plan" She told her, whole plan which she made for Kabir's birthday...... and monika was already impressed by the idea.

"very nice idea.... If your plan actually works the same way it is decided then he must be the happiest, do I ask you something" she praised her idea but then teased her at the end like her tradition of teasing her everyday. "Yes yes, ask"

"Why are you so stressed for him.... He's just your boss... ok ok a good friend too..... Or is there something else...." she raised her eyebrows comically. "What nonsense you are talking about, di.... He's my friend only, but yes I admit it he is special for me and the thing is I can't see him sad and that's why I'll do anything which will make him happy" looking at the genuineness in shrishti's voice monika asked

"you know what"

"what?"

"If someone have a friend like you na, then he or she'll don't need anyone" she passed a soft smile "ok now It's getting late you sleep, Good night" "good night" After caressing her head she left and Shrishti to slept peacefully thinking about her plan.

13

Next day Shrishti usually left for her office like her usual schedule..... everything was going well in the office, all were congratulating her for the achievement in the paris, but she was totally drowned in her thoughts about how she'll implement the plan she has made for Kabir's birthday.

"God, how can I be this idiot? I made the whole plan but damn I didn't confirm when his birthday is, you won't get any better shrii.... Now how do I confirm, If I'll ask him directly he'll immediately doubt annnndddd.... If I'll ask Khushi then there are 100% chances she'll spill in front of him then things will be as same as before....umm" she was babbling to herself all this being confused, She made a cute pout and started thinking tapping index finger of her right hand cutely on her forehead. "Idea, Kabir is quite popular. If I search on google I'm definitely gonna get to know about him.... Very good shrii... very good I am really proud of you" she patted her shoulder by herself in a manner to praise herself.

Soon she got the date of Kabir's birthday, which was the day after tomorrow. "Oh no.....means I have only one and half a day to implement the plan." she sadly pouted "now what do I do" she let out a deep sigh as she was nowhere in the mood to back out from her plan "It's ok doing anything for friends is less, I'll do this.... Now the main thing is the address from where I'll get that"

Again she was stuck in another problem, but using her clever and sharp mind she arranged the address that she required, after collecting all the info she was happy like a little kid who got everything he desired. She was over excited to start her plan and because of that she started doing happy dance leaving her design which she was making a side, she was engrossed in her happy dance and at the same time Kabir entered her cabin and she abruptly stopped looking at him with some unexplainable expressions on her face. For a minute there was complete silence, she awkwardly coughed and in response Kabir started laughing badly seeing that she became more awkward.

"Continue, continue.... I'm going"

"Hey... no.... No need to go, I was doing it just like that" she scratch her head in embarrassment "say do you have any work from me"

"Oh, actually yes"

"come sit" Both sat on their respective seats, Still Kabir was suppressing his laughter but was scared from her reaction, he very well knew she'll not leave him easily if she caught him laughing at her.

"So, yes say," she asked, arranging her files along with.

"Can I ask you one thing"

"Yes, Why not..." "why were you dancing like that.... What's the matter" he asked mischievously, showing his perfect set of white pearls.

"I was happy for you only, dumbo... but I can't tell you right now," she thought rolling her eyes "actually....umm yes, actually a very nice idea came in my mind suddenly for the next design so for that, you are getting me right"

"OH I SEE" he was clearly not satisfied from her answer but he let it just go.

"OH U SEE" she continued folding her arms "yes.... Actually it should be... OH WE SEE......funny na..." he laughed but she didn't laugh on his joke

"Ok don't laugh, I just came to ask about the update of the next project" he changed the topic towards their work for which he was there in her cabin. "everything is going good" "okk..... thatzzz rayyttttt..." he exclaimed and stood up to leave. "That's right SIR" she butted "no no its thatzzz rayytttt..." he said comically

"you are impossible...." "You too," he smiled widely and started walking towards the door. "Wait" "yes" "I need half day tomorrow" she requested as despite being his friend she was his employee too. "oh.... Ok.... No problem."

"Actually I have to do some urgent work...."

"ya ya.... No need to explain.... DON JI..... I trust you" he said, pressing the word "don" intentionally, before she could react he ran out of her cabin leaving Shrishti with a grumpy face behind him. "How bad he is, here I'm planning this much for this idiot and he is busy making fun of me.... huh"

After reaching home Kabir was sitting on his balcony with his chiku and was talking with her. "Chicku, you know what.... You are the best, you listen to me very patiently and then don't even judge me back" he chuckled sadly

"You know It's my birthday the day after tomorrow.... But no one cares" he let out a sigh shifting his gaze to the sky and started it blankly "if I say the truth.... Now I too really don't care" silence fell and he continued staring at the sky as if he was trying to pour himself out with that silence. Soon he found chiku was fast asleep in his lap. He picked her and placed in her basket and after that, he too went to sleep.

The next day Shrishti was very excited and nervous at the same time because she was confused about how she'll do what she wanted to do, till afternoon she was in the office and after finishing her work around 3 in the noon she left for her destination. Soon she was standing at the door of Kabir's home…. She nervously pressed the doorbell and after 5 minutes Kabir's mom opened the door.

"Namaste aunty" she greeted her, folding her hands together in respect.

"Namaste…… But I didn't recognize you" his mom asked confusingly as this was the first time she was meeting shrishti.

"Aunty, I work under Kabir in the office as a head designer," she introduced herself with a soft smile adorned on her face.

"Oh, come inside beta… come" She took Shrishti in with her and made her sit in the living room. Kabir's dad was also sitting there with a file in his hand. She greeted him too respectfully. "Shrishti, are you here for any work," he asked casually.

"Yes, uncle…. Actually I" his mom cut her in between "oho…. We can talk later first let me bring some snacks for you"

"So sweet of you aunty, but there is no need…. Please don't bother yourself, I just came here to talk to both of you and uncle." she requested as she didn't want to waste her time because she was well aware that it'll not be that easy to convince them.

"So, about what you want to say beta," his dad started. She took deep breaths closing her eyes and then started calmly.

"I want to talk about Kabir……" she directly came on point

"Kabir.... What happened to him... he is fine right" his mom interrupted, getting immediately worried for her son.

"He is very fine from outside, aunty.... But he is not fine from within... not at all" she said with plain expressions. "What are you saying" his dad interrupted "The TRUTH uncle, see.... I'm very young in front of you two and also I'm no one to make you understand anything or to speak anything in your family matter, But still, I'm doing this because of Kabir..... He's is a very dear friend of mine and I can't see him sad"

"Sad..... for what he's sad.... He has everything anyone wishes for in their life, house, car, money, respect....." his father argued.

"NO, he doesn't have everything..... He doesn't have real happiness, he doesn't have the love he deserves, he doesn't have peace, he doesn't have someone whom he can call mine...." she said, trying to express the important things he doesn't have in his life. "What are you saying shrishti," his mom asked in disbelief.

"I'm saying what's right.... Even if he has everything but he doesn't have the things which a person seeks in his life the most.... Have you both ever tried to understand him, have you tried to understand what he wants in his life..... In what his happiness is....."

no one replied

"You know when a person feels alone the most.... When his own people.... His parents especially don't understand him.... When he is misunderstood at each and every point.... When he is being used just as an object..." she sighed but she was determined to say everything she wanted to say so she again continued. "Have you ever spent time with him.... Have you ever asked him what he wants.... That's what's in his heart.... Have you ever asked how he feels being all alone...... have you ever asked what his state of mind..... No... right?.... You just let him alone thinking he'll handle himself on his own"

"But whatever we did we did it for him only.... What we didn't give him" his dad asked.

"The point is uncle.... That a person feels attachment with his people and their love for him, not from the materialistic things.... Have you ever made him feel like he's the most important one to you..... Like his happiness is everything for you" hearing her he became totally quiet. "That's why he got this far from you na..... He kept on falling away from you and you didn't even realize"

After 2 minutes of silence

"You are right, shrishti..... We let our son go away by ourselves, you made me realize today that real happiness is in the happiness we feel from within and not in the materialistic things of the world.... I gave my child everything but forgot to give the most important thing a father should give his child..... Now he hates me to the extent where he doesn't even like to talk to me." he said the last line defeatedly.

"It's nothing like what you are thinking uncle..... he still loves you both more than anything in this world.... He's still craving for the love and care which only you both can give him" she told them with a genuine and assuring smile seeing that relief flash in his parent's eyes. "You are saying the truth right.... And not to just make us feel happy" his mom asked with hope-filled in her voice.

"I'm telling only the truth, aunty, he's just trying to show himself tough and ignorant but deep down he's still as innocent as a child.... I have felt it that's why I'm saying all this."

"When you have already made us realize the biggest mistake of our lives then you only tell us what we do to get our son back the same as he was" his dad asked in a tone which she could not deny.

"Tomorrow it's his birthday right..... So just make him realize the love you both have in your heart for your son.... The things you have never done on his birthday do it this time..... Also, try to remove all the conflicts and misunderstandings tomorrow itself and start fresh"

"We'll surely do as it is" his dad said beaming with a true smile which was reaching his eyes which he didn't even know after how long.

"Thank you so much uncle, aunt..... For understanding my point"

"Thank you so much to you too beta..... You have made us realize that there is a very big difference between real happiness and the happiness we get from the materialistic things of this world,"

"Uncle, can I request you something?" she asked with a little hesitation. "No need to request beta, just say it"

"See..... whatever you'll do, he'll definitely ask about the sudden change in your behavior.... I'm sure, so I just have a little request that please do no tell him that I have said anything regarding this to both of you"

"How can this be possible, you have done this much for us and specially for kabir, why don't you want him to know anything about him anything" his mom asked surprisingly. "No, aunty please, I request please promise me you'll not tell him anything.... Just pretend like I never came here... simple, please"

"How we will ever pay back to you for what you have done" he was about to join his hands in front of her but she stopped him very politely with a warm smile on her face. "Uncle please don't do this, I'm like your daughter, so will you say thank you to your daughter huh" Both of them caressed her head..... Greeting both of them warmly she left for her house.

Whole day passed, around 10:30 Kabir was sitting in his room blankly and suddenly his phone started ringing, it was Aaditya he unwantedly picked up the call....

On call:

Kabir: hello.......

Aaditya: hellllooooooo..... broooo.......

Kabir: seems like someone is in a good mood, but why?

Aaditya: tomorrow it's your birthday bro, ca mon why won't be I high.... Hehe so now quickly tell me what's the plan?

Kabir: There is nothing to be this happy Aadi, it's just a normal day, at least for me and yes there is no plan, don't take a day off just to waste it on me.

Aaditya: yrr why are you saying like this..... why are you punishing yourself.....

Kabir: because birthday means nothing to me..... and you know why..... And don't pout like a stubborn kid hmm.

Aaditya: how do you know?

Kabir: Maybe someone knows you well, now go and sleep it's getting late.... Good night.

Aaditya: ok..... good night

he disheartedly hung up the call but he was feeling bad for his best friend.

"Na lagao umeeden esi jinse dil ko sirf dard mila karte hai.... Kuch kisse sapna hi reh jate hai.... Hakeekat kahan hua karte hai"

"Happy birthday in advance MR. Kabir MEHRA......lets sleep" chuckling sadly at his fate he looked at the clock once and then went to sleep.

On the other hand, shrishti was very excited at her home.... Her whole family was already fast asleep but she was getting more excited by each passing minute....... Only 5 minutes were left for the clock to strike 12..... she quickly picked up her phone and opened the call log. She was about to press on Kabir but she stopped abruptly.....

"What i was up to god, Kabir never told me his birthdate, if i'll call him right now he'll surely build doubt, and I surely don't wanna spoil his day" with a sad pout she was glancing at the clock sitting on her bed "hope I also get to wish him"

Here Kabir was sleeping peacefully but suddenly his doorbell started ringing, he got up with a jerk and started looking here and there still in his sleepy state "oh my dear god please at least let me sleep peacefully, now whom did you send at this time" Rubbing his eyes cutely he went to open the door with annoyed face, his one eye was covered with one hand, he opened the door with other, before he could ask anything two people exclaimed.

HAPPY BIRTHDAY TO YOU HAPPY BIRTHDAY TO YOU.... HAPPY BIRTHDAY HAPPY BIRTHDAY...... HAPPY BIRTHDAY TO YOU BABY!!

Listening to this his eyes opened wide in shock. Firstly he was not able to register the fact that in reality his mom and dad were standing there at his doorstep with a bunch of balloons and cake in their hand.

"You..... you two here at this time" he still asked to confirm if he's hallucinating or they were really there.

"HAPPY BIRTHDAY SON," his dad said, engulfing Kabir in a warm hug. For a moment Kabir was confused.... But he felt the warmness and love of his father towards him so he also hugged him back

"thanks dad" he was still in a half confused state.

"HAPPY BIRTHDAY kabir" his mom also hugged him and he hugged her back too. "Thank you so much mamma, but you two...." before he could complete his dad's interven "we two are here to celebrate our child's birthday and also to mend the mistakes which were unrealised for very long"

"Means I didn't get you, what are you talking about dad"

"I realized today kabir that I failed to understand you, I gave you everything but lagged behind in giving the most important thing that a father gives to his son.... I know you are angry with me and you are right very right but can you give a chance to your dad to rectify his mistakes..... Please forgive me I failed as a dad" he was about to join his hands but kabir stopped him.

"what are you doing.... Please.... No" he pulled his dad in a hug. Both of them were emotional like it was the first time they were opening up in front of each other like this, both of their eyes were moist and seeing her husband and son together his mom was also emotional.

"Hey... please dad don't cry like this.... I can't see you like this" he wiped his dad's tears. His dad caressed his head and finally his mom spoke to make the moment little light. "Oh so now you got your dad so you forget you mom right....?"

"C'mon mom, how can I forget my mom huh" he asked, pulling her cheeks. "Ok ok come let's cut this beautiful cake or we are just going to look at it"

Finally three of them sat together on the sofa..... Kabir in center.... He happily blew the candle and cut the cake. The emotions rising in him were unexplainable..... tears started brimming in his eyes but he controlled them strongly and made his dad eat the first bite of the cake and then his mom. They happily celebrated for some time and then three of them went to sleep as it was already 2 at night.

In the morning

Shrishti as usual was getting ready to leave for her office in the meantime monika entered the room. "So, Miss. Sharma, how did your plan go?"

"Plan is already executed and luckily his parents got my point..... But I'm just waiting for Kabir's reaction.... I'm damn sure he'll surely tell me.... About everything," Shrishti replied while combing her hair.

"ok.... Let's see how it goes..... well ready for the office" "yes.... Just leaving in few minutes"

14

Kabir was sleeping peacefully till late because he went to bed late.... Finally around 10 AM his highness woke up rubbing his eyes.... While stretching and yawning lazily he asked for his tea. "Shanta aunt..... Chai please" he exclaimed while brushing his teeth.

In no time his mom came with a tray in his room, when he came out from the bathroom, he realized that both of his parents were also there only. "Oh I forgot you are here also, sorry for waking up late" he said, scratching the back of his neck embarrassingly.

"No issues, here you tea.... And yes... happy birthday again" his mom said, forwarding the cup in his direction.

"thank you mamma"

"Ok now get ready quickly hmm, we both are waiting for you outside and yes no office today and it's an order"

"Are we going somewhere?" "Hmm," his mom replied. "where?"

"Surprise.... Now go get ready fast otherwise we'll get late.... Go go"

She left and here Kabir was surprised, happy and emotional at the same time..... he was not able to believe that his parents are doing all this for his birthday and spending time with him. Soon after getting ready three of them reached an old lord shiva temple.

"Why are we here dad?"

"Because in your childhood we used to come here every year on your birthday as you used to love coming here to play with the squirrels" kabir smiled hearing something about his childhood from his dad.

"Ok now again are we going to stand here and talk or go inside and do prayer" "ya ya your highness let's go inside" kabir joked while hugging his mom from behind. After doing prayer they came back home around 3 in the afternoon...... As all were tired after having lunch which was specially made as per the choice of Kabir by his mom they went to take rest for some time.

Here in the office everything was going well. Everything was normal like every other day but someone was totally lost, that someone was none other than Shrishti. "God please let everything be fine..... I just want Kabir to be happy please no chaos this time, even if I didn't get a chance to wish him but I pray let him get what he want, he has suffered enough of loneliness"

Whole day passed but because of being lost Shrishti was not able to complete her work so she was staying back for some extra hours in the office..... till 9 PM.

On the other side after getting a good sleep Kabir was moving towards the kitchen to find something edible but on the way something grabbed his attention, he started walking towards the living room. A big carton was placed there wrapped in gift wrap.

"Now what's this.... There is not a note even" Then he found that a little sticker was there on which "open it Kabir" was written.

"KABIR- only single piece kabir is me here so I should open it hehe"

Getting excited he started opening the box.... The moment he saw the things placed in the box his eyes automatically welled up and a lone tear fell from his eyes. In the box all the paintings and sketches made by him from his childhood till his college life and all his medals and trophies won by him were placed........ While he was handling himself he felt someone's hand on his shoulder..... it was his dad....

"thank you so much papa" he broke down hugging his dad like a little kid.

"I know I snatched your happiness from you son and I'm trying to return a bit of it back to you, hope you liked it" "I didn't like it, I LOVED it dad" he said, weeping again like a baby.

Meanwhile his mom too came there while kabir started pouring his heart out in front of his dad "Today you gave me what i wanted since forever.... I don't have words to express my happiness right now, thank you, thank you so much for returning me my whole childhood dad thank you so much"

"Don't you think you are getting emotional too early, there's something more" his mom said. "Now what's left mom?"

"That your dad will tell you" he looked at his who was busy shuffling some files.

"You wanted to become an artist right.... You wanted to open your own art gallery right..... So now it'll become your reality.... Here take this, these are papers of the property where your art gallery will be opened, do work hard and make me proud, and yes now I don't want to be proud on the CEO kabir mehra, I just want to feel proud for my son Kabir"

Kabir was completely speechless.... He was silent but his emotions were coming out from his eyes. He was in a state where he was thinking that all this is his dream because his heart had left expecting anything from anyone a long time back.

"What you just gave me dad, I can't even thank you for this.... I'm seriously not able to understand if it is my dream or reality, finally things are happening like I wanted...." before he could drag his emotional rant more his dad asked something which stopped him immediately

"Come back home kabir, that house is just a building without you make it home again" he looked at his dad for sometime and after contemplating for a few seconds in his mind he spoke.

"Ok.... but before that I also want to say something.... You did your part and now it's my turn, I'll surely work for my art gallery but also I'll handle our company.... I know as your only child I have lots of responsibility on my shoulders and I'm very happy to fulfill them.... Thank you so much again for everything" saying this he engulfed his mom and dad into an emotional hug, after a few seconds three of them started packing things to take kabir back home.

Kabir was happily packing his things but suddenly something struck in his mind. "Whatever happened today was best, nothing can be better for me. That too on my birthday finally I got my mom dad back..... But this huge change can not be sudden all this can not happen overnight, I'm damn sure behind all this there is a reason but what, I think I should ask mamma"

He left things as they were and went towards his parents room...... but stopped at the doorstep only listening to something totally unexpected.

"I'm so happy today finally I got my son back and all the misunderstandings are also clear, I owe a huge to god" his mom said.

"Indeed I am happy too, but we owe not only to the god but also to the person who make us realize our mistake" his dad said

"True you are right"

"I can never forget the favor of shrishti.... If not her then I still would have been sitting oblivious to everything and maybe kabir would have start hating me more, she did so much for him for us but still she requested to not tell about all this to kabir, I have never seen a selfless person like her, I owe her huge which I can't pay back by any mean in this life"

Listening to all this Kabir was shocked like anything, he was not able to believe that this 180 degree turn In his life came only because of Shrishti.... He silently ran back to his room without making any noise and directly went to the joint balcony.

"I need to meet her.... Right now.... Yes.... but.... But how.... Time" he looked at his phone screen "it's 7... I should ask khushi" He dialed Khushi's no. with passing each ring he was becoming restless and finally she picked up the call

On call:

Kabir: hello.... Khushi.....

Khushi: Hello sir..... very very happy birthday..... how are you......

Kabir: thank you thank you.... Ok everything later just tell me where are you?

Khushi: sir I'm on my way... back to home....

Kabir: Do you know anything about Shrishti....

Khushi: Shrishti mam...... yes sir..... actually sir today she is staying back in the office for some extra hours to finish her work... so right now...(Kabir cut)

Kabir: got it got it.... Thank you....(he hurriedly cut the call)

"Let's go Kabir" he said to himself while He quickly adjusted his look and ran towards the door picking his car keys..... meanwhile his mom shouted from behind. "Where to sir?"

"I just remembered something important.... I'll be back soon bye"

Here in the office Shrishti was totally busy with her work. She was getting frustrated because she was not able to concentrate on her work. In frustration she tied her hair in a messy bun and again started her work.

Hurriedly Kabir reached the office finding the whole office was empty. Lights of only Shrishti's cabin were on..... he walked towards that taking long steps.....but halted at the door abruptly as the door was of glass he was able to see her totally frustrated unconsciously he was adoring her cute and messy look. Soon he realized what he was doing..... he scratched his head and to grab Shrishti's attention he knocked at the door, she abruptly looked up and seeing Kabir there her lips automatically curved in a beautiful smile.

"Kabir!... you.... Happ.... Come come sit"

"yes me.... By the way, why didn't you leave till now.... Why are you sitting alone here"

"Actually I have to finish my work... So that's why..... well what about you... why are you here at this time"

"I'm here to talk to you"

"talk to me.... About what" she asked confusingly

"Shrishti are you angry with me....."

"What the hell are you saying Kabir.... Why would I..."

"Then why are you not talking to me since we came back from paris...... why are you ignoring me..."

"no no..... nothing is like that Kabir..... please don't think anything like this"

"Then tell me why are you ignoring me"

"I'm not..... actually I was busy with some very important work that's why.... Maybe I didn't have time...."

"soo..... can I ask which important work you were busy with"

"Now how do I tell you yrr" she thought

"sorry.... It was personal " she said looking down trying to hide the truth from him.

"If you don't mind may I tell" she looked at him in utmost shock.

"Wh.... What will you tell"

"That work with which you were very busy I guess.... So should I tell you about that work"

"Oh god by any did he got to know about everything" she thought

"I know everything shrishti" she looked at him with wide eyes and finally uttered "means" she was still trying to pretend oblivious to everything he was trying to say. "Why are you this good yrr shrishti" "what are you saying kabir"

"Truth.... I have never seen a person like you in my lifetime.... Who can solve the biggest problem of someone's life and then react like she just doesn't know anything" she silently looked at him "I know since we came back from Paris you were busy for me only.... Right.... You made almost impossible things possible for me and here me idiot was thinking you are angry with me and don't wanna talk to me..... I seriously don't know how I should thank you....." he was not at all in mood to stop any time soon.... To stop his rant Shrishti picked a big piece of chocolate and put it in his mouth without any warning and consequently his speaking session halted.

15

He was looking at her innocently as his mouth was stuffed with chocolate. "Now only you'll keep speaking or give me honor of speaking too SIR!!" he nodded cutely while chewing the chocolate.

"First of all.... Whatever I did, I did it for my friend.... I did it for you.... Because I... I can't see you sad and disheartened, the day you expressed yourself in front of me at the lake side in Paris the same day I decided that the love you want from your parents, the care you want from them you'll get that as your birthday gift..... I try my level best to make it possible because you deserve it kabir and that's the reason I was ignoring you not purposely because after coming back I was left with very less time to make everything possible.... Now tell me, did I do anything wrong by ignoring you?" she huffed at the end and found him already on verge of emotional breakdown.

"I'm short of words shrishti..... I really don't know what I should say at this point, I just don't wanna cry right now.... You gave me what I had given up on years ago..... Thank you so much shrishti" he said, holding her hand. Suddenly he heard a loud growl at which he squinted his eyes and looked at her in a questioning manner. In response she looked here and there to hide her embarrassment.

"Are you hungry?" she hummed cutely, pouting a little.

"wind up your work.... Fast....."

"noo.... I have to finish my work"

"Who is the boss...?" he stood there, crossing his arms at his chest.

"You" "That's it.... Wind up your work right now"

"Ok sir right away" she said sarcastically which was not unnoticed by him. "Very good" a sly smile formed on his face. While packing her things something mischievous came in her mind.

"Kabir" "yes" "I want a party" she said crossing her arms.

"Party but why?" "Oh actually today's my birthday" she said looking straight at him. "Oh it's my birthday too today..... What a coincidence yrr.... Happ" she exclaimed. "OH genius.... I'm asking for a party for your birthday" she huffed and made a grumpy face.

"Oh that, so tell me madam..... Where do you wanna go...."

"Beach... the weather is also very beautiful, see." she said dreamily.

"But what I remember is you were hungry weren't you?"

"Ya ya, well we'll order pizza there na.... Now please let's go there"

Seeing her pleading like a baby he was not able to resist himself from agreeing, Soon both of them were on the beach as the beach was near their office. After taking their order both of them proceeded towards the beach and found that coincidentally there were very few people.

Finding a peaceful and a beautiful area they sat on the sand.... The view itself was magnificent...... The full moon was shining in the sky with its complete glory and its replica in the sea water was looking even more beautiful. The slow but cool breeze was enhancing the beauty of the environment. First few minutes both were sitting in complete silence and observing the environment, but another growl of shrishti's stomach grabbed their attention.

"Now have you ordered this for eating or before that are you going to do some rituals with these?" Kabir asked, chuckling at her embarrassment.

Shrishti, opened her pizza box happily and in excitement she picked one slice and was about to put it in her mouth but stopped midway, Kabir asked her the reason for raising his eyebrows.... In response she smiled sheepishly and held his hands after keeping the slice back in the box.

"I'm sorry kabir..... you know na I'm a little crack head..... the very main thing I forgot" she pouted. "what..... you forgot what?"

"HAPPY BIRTHDAY KABIR..... aur maybe I should say HAPPY BIRTHDAY KABIR THE ARTIST" for next few seconds he was continuously looking at her with moist eyes.

"THANK YOU SO MUCH......MISS. DON...... I'm really glad the underworld don wished me on my birthday..... What more do I need..." She was listening smilingly but when his words registered in her brain he earned a slap on his head.

"Hey hey.... What?"

"Don..... am I don.... Do I look like a don to you.... From where tell me"

"You tell me who beat an innocent like this han" he was trying to suppress his laughter but failing miserably.

"you know what? you are impossible..... huh.... You keep sitting like this... I'm hungry and I'm not talking to you, huh" She started eating her pizza and he was enjoying looking at her innocent face which was looking cuter in the moonlight. Eventually he started staring at the moon.... And here our shrii was done with her pizza.... To tease him she joked. "Oye... do you wanna eat or may I do the honors for you" not getting any reply from his she picked his box too, "I'm eating this and now don't blame me later that I didn't warn you.

She was really hungry because she ate Kabir's pizza too. Finally she burped and looked at him and found him staring at the moon without even blinking his eyes..... She also started staring, not at the moon but at Kabir's face. The calmness on his face was giving peace and calmness to her heart.... She was feeling good and relaxed seeing him relaxed..... somewhere her heart was praying for the moment to stop right there so that she can adore that calmness and peace on his face for eternity. Coming out of her own dreamworld she slapped her forehead and patted Kabir's shoulder.

"Kabir, what are you thinking?" she asked calmly.

"Kuch khwahishein hoti hain chand ki tarah..... Jise hum dil bhar ke nihar to sakte hain par paa nahi sakte..... Par fir is samudra ko dekh ke lagta hai..... Vo asman ka chand bhi akss ban ke jiski lehron pe utar ata hai..... Agar kismat main ho to chand ko bhi paya ja sakta hai......"

"You know in my case the moon is my parents and the sea is you.... The sea who brought the reflection of the moon on itself.... And I'm that innocent kid who wanted to witness this since forever sitting at the shore"

"kabir.... Please don't I repeat please don't let anyone snatch your smile, you don't know but you are one of them who holds the best smile..... and no one has the right to snatch it from you got it" she said looking at him at which he smiled warmly at her and nodded slowly.

"Ok sir" he saluted her comically which made her laugh at him, with him.

"Very good" And both burst into laughter..... but suddenly shrishti made a face.... And he raised his eyebrows to ask her the problem.

"Sorry kabir" "But for what" "I thought I won't get a chance to meet you today so..." she became silent "so what shrii" "so, I don't have anything to give you as a gift for your birthday" she said looking down.

"Are you even serious...... You gave me the biggest gift of my life and here you are saying you have nothing to give ...."

"but"

"no if no but......now lets go..... You'll get late to reach home right" she nodded "so get up, let's leave for now"

"Ok boss" she earned a glare from him but she pretended oblivious. Both were walking side by side on the beach because of that, waves were brushing their feets suddenly shrishti stopped and found something under her foot.

"what happened" "wait" she crouched down to look at the thing which came under her feet. She found that it was a very beautiful and shiny shell, a beautiful smile crept on her face seeing that.

"See.... today god also wants me to give you a beautiful gift.... See what I found" she showed him that beautiful shell. "it's beautiful"

"I know..... so this is your birthday gift from my side to you..... Here accept it please" She held his wrist and softly placed that shell in his hand.... He smiled at this and after that they moved towards their car. In the car both were silent but a serene smile was there on both of their faces....... Abruptly shrishti spoke up.

"Ohh.... I forgot to tell an important thing"

"What?"

"Today you were on your day off right.... HR department has appointed a new designer in my team"

"Ok, so what is his name"

"I don't know.... But he is going to join from tomorrow only"

"Ok, we'll see tomorrow," he said, focusing on the road.

"Hmmm......." she sighed. Soon they reached her home but Kabir left from outside only after dropping her because his parents were waiting for him at home.

Shrishti happily entered her house and directly entered her room as she was full after having 2 pizzas alone..... after changing her clothes she picked her dairy and sat on the couch placed in her balcony happily writing her whole day experience..... Meanwhile she was writing there was a bright smile on her face. All the time monika was noticing her when shrishti was about to close her diary she entered her room.

"Wait wait madam, show me also what you wrote that make you smile like this"

"Not happening"

"But why?" she gasped dramatically.

"My diary my choice"

"Ok ok fine, now leave all this and tell me did your plan succeed?"

"Yes di, it succeeded, I saw him smiling wholeheartedly and I can't tell you how content I felt" she said with a serene smile on her face.

"Great, if you are happy then what more do I need..... ok then go and sleep it's getting late...." listening to this shrishti showed her puppy face "what... no drama.... Sleep" she glared at her finally she raised her hands in surrender "ya ya going to sleep no need to glare a poor person like me" Switching off the lights monika left for her room..... shrishti layed on her bed hugging her teddy and was continuously thinking about kabir..... she didn't even realize when sleep took her over.

Here Kabir happily had his dinner because shrishti ate his pizza also…. He went to sleep with a very calm and peaceful heart and mind when he laid on his bed chiku also climbed on his bed following him and without making any noise she slept near him, he smiled at her behavior and thinking about shrishti he closed his eyes and soon he was in deep slumber.

Next morning

Kabir's dad and mom went back to their home taking all the luggage of Kabir with themselves and Kabir left for his office.

After reaching the office, Shrishti and Kabir were discussing something important about their upcoming project. All the while Kabir was looking happy wholeheartedly and seeing that shrishti couldn't resist herself from saying something. "Kabir" He hummed while he was finding something in his laptop.

"please always stay like this" this caught his attention and he finally looked at her and smiled more widely at her, Before he could say something khushi knocked the door. "Yes khushi"

"Sir that new employee is here should I send him" "Sure" "Ok then I should leave….. You meet him hmm" she was about to get up from her seat but kabir stopped him. "Why…. He is going to join your department only na." she nodded in response "then stay"

Listening to him she kept on sitting on her seat…… A few minutes later a boy in his mid 20's entered the cabin and he wished kabir and when he turned towards shrishti to wish her also. The moment both of them looked at each other a big and bright smile crept on both of their faces.

"You" both of them exclaimed. They shared a quick hug..... Finding them this happy kabir cleared his throat to gain a little attention and in response both looked at him.

16

"It seems you both know each other already," Kabir asked.

"Yes kabir.... This is Vicky.... And we both were in the same batch in college," Shrishti replied.

"Oh I see.... Take your seat Vicky," Kabir said.

"you both carry on. I'm leaving to finish my work" Kabir nodded and she walked out of the cabin.... Kabir noticed that Vicky was looking at shrishti in a strange way, he wanted to ask but brushing his thoughts away he asked a few questions from Vicky and then allowed him to join his job.

Days were passing well but somewhere changes were coming in kabir's behavior...... Vicky was getting more frank with shrishti day by day, But his strange glares on shrishti was not unnoticed by kabir and that was the main reason which was troubling him..... but he was unable to talk about the same with shrishti because she was totally oblivious about anything.

One fine day Kabir was working in his cabin around 2 in the afternoon. He thought about going to have his lunch.

"Damn this stomach of mine, can't we eat together for the whole day" he sighed dramatically "I think I should go and eat first..... Will ask shrii to join also, it's been long we ate together" Thinking all this he walked towards her cabin but found her already coming out.

"Hey don.... Where to,"
"It's lunch time, so to eat I guess" she shrugged.
"Great, great I was coming to ask you for the same.... Let's eat together come"
"Sorry no.... Kabir, Vicky is already waiting for me in the cafeteria" he made a plain face "but we all can have it together na.... You also join us"
"No, no you go, your friend must be waiting" saying this he moved back towards his cabin. "Hey..." But before she could stop him he left. She felt bad for him but she thought to let it be for the time being.

Here Kabir was sitting with a grumpy face in his cabin he was feeling betrayed.... But he calmed his mind down saying that she didn't only have him as a friend there can be others too..... but his empty stomach was not letting him calm his mind down.

Shrishti entered the cafeteria and found Vicky sitting there with two plates filled with food, she was lost in her thoughts, first she was about to sit but changed her mind. "Hey what happened shrishti sit"

"Sorry Vicky, we'll have lunch together some other day.... Right now I have to go, sorry" she said, going away. "But at least eat your food..."

"I will.... Just going to fill one more plate" he looked at her confusingly. Meanwhile she came back and after picking up her already filled plate on the other hand she left towards Kabir's cabin"

Here to distract his mind Kabir was chewing mouth freshener and was typing something on his laptop.... After a few seconds shrishti entered his cabin with 2 plates in her hand and directly went towards the couch which was placed in the corner of his cabin.

"Come kabir let's eat.... What are you waiting for huh"

"why are you here.... Don't you want to eat with your friend....." he said, stressing the last word. "Oh someone is jealous...... I see"

"I'm not...."

"Oh yes, you are...."

"I'm not shrishti"

"Is it, then why are you sitting with this grumpy face"

"My face My choice..... none of your business" saying that he hid his face behind his laptop. "Ok, ok.... Carry on this grumpy face session after lunch, firstly eat you must be hungry"

"No, I'm not" at the same time his stomach growled loudly, taking their attention. "But your stomach is saying otherwise" she said, raising her eyebrows "Now, no more drama.... Come here and eat..."

"OK, fine"

Closing his laptop he got up and moved towards the couch where shrishti was sitting with his and her food seeing his plate his grumpiness flew away out of the window.

"How do you know I like this?" "I'm interstitial...." she smiled comically at him squinting her eyes "Now eat" When both were done eating shrishti thought why not to tease him as he was already riled up.

"Well, well I didn't know Mr. mehra got jealous too," said innocently with a teasing smile.

"There's nothing like that," he said, stuffing a piece of cake in his mouth.

"Is it?"

"Yes, now no more discussions on this" She felt that it's enough teasing for a day so she left for her cabin.

"Are you stupid kabir... why are you behaving like kids.... What she'll be thinking about you" He slapped his forehead and continued his work.

Here Vicky who got to know that shrishti went to have lunch with kabir leaving him was filled with rage... but he calmed himself down somehow.

Few more days passed but strange stares of Vicky on shrishti were disturbing Kabir more..... here shrishti was totally unknown about anything because of that kabir was not able to talk to her as if he'll say anything suspicious she'll grow worried.

"I don't know but I don't feel that Vicky is a good person.... I seriously wanna talk to shrishti about this but if all this is my mere suspicion she'll get tensed unnecessarily.... Oh god what do I do" Talking to himself all this he left for his home.

****

One fine day Kabir announced that the anniversary of the company is next day and on that occasion the company was organizing a party, listening that there was a cunning smile on Vicky's face which was not unnoticed by Kabir at all. And now this was high time kabir finally decided to talk to shrishti.

"shrishti... please come to my cabin" she nodded and he left from there. When she reached kabir was already walking back and forth..... shrishti asked in a concerned voice.

"What happened kabir..... everything is alright....?"

"God I don't want to scare her..... What do I do?" he thought.

"say something yrrr.... Are you fine?"

"Ya ya I'm totally fine, see shrishti I just wanted to say..... please be attentive in the party ok" "what are you saying"

"Umm...... actually I wanted to say that......" before he could say anything Vicky knocked the door.

"Come in" he gave permission to come in the cabin with a straight face.

"Sorry to disturb you both.... But I need shrishti's help in one design"

"We are discussing something important.... She'll come in a while"

"Sorry kabir.... We have to complete that design today itself.....because we have to send that design tomorrow positively..... I'll come back to you..... hope you are ok with it" shrishti asked genuinely.

"Ooo....ok... but please come back fast ok....."

"Ya ya" Both Vicky and shrishti left from there leaving worried kabir behind. Whole day passed but she didn't come back and here Kabir was getting restless to talk to her but finally it was time to go back home.

At home

Kabir was sitting in his room in a totally confused state, he was contemplating whether he is overreacting or if there is an actual problem to arise for her.

"Arghh.... Oh god, isn't it so that maybe I am overreacting, it can be possible that there is nothing like what I'm thinking about vicky..... But... but that negative vibes I'm getting from his constant stares on her, what do I do about that" he thought for some time and then finalized one thing "Now I can do only one thing, I'll be with shrishti all the time during the party" He sighed deeply and fell into deep slumber thinking all this.

The other hand, Shrishti was busy selecting a perfect dress for the party and her mom and di were giggling seeing her frustrated state. "Mamma, di.... You both are laughing at what, don't you guys have a tiny bit of mercy for poor me" she whined literally like a 5 year old.

"Then what do we do" monika teased "means" shrishti fake glared at her.

"Means, you are selecting dress for past one hour and you haven't selected yet" her mom intervened

"Its because its a official party and worried If I got overdressed then, I'll feel embarrassed no" "ok look, if this seems good" monika said while showing a black plain simple yet elegant gown and finally shrishti exclaimed in approval and after lots of confusion, frustration, teasing, threatening and laughing her dress for the party was locked.

"Ok, now both of you girls go and sleep it's almost midnight"

"chill mamma..... Tomorrow is a holiday and I have to go directly to the party and that too in the evening so relax." Shrishti tried to convince her mom. "Then also, it's still very late so keep your mouth shut... go to sleep... fast" Both the sisters mumbled ok and left for their rooms.

Next day.

Whole day passed in the blink of an eye. Kabir was checking the preparations of the party while other guests and employees of the company also were coming..... When Vicky entered, Kabir automatically got attentive.... Whole time there was a cunning smile on his face and Kabir was completely focused on him only... till the time shrishti entered the hall with a heart warming smile on her face......

Seeing her in that black elegant gown Kabir was dumbfounded..... he was looking at her without even blinking his eyes.... Everything was looking blurred in front of her.... He came out of trance feeling a jerk on his hand.... And it was shrishti only who was shaking his hand.

"Kabirhhh.... Are you even hearing me"

"Shit man..... stupid kabir what was that.... How can you zone out like this..... what she'll think about you" he mentally scolded himself and unconsciously he again zoned out. "Oh god will you speak or should I call the doctor" she exclaimed. "Oh.... Yes yes..... actually I was thinking something deep" he said pretending to think something.

"OHH....."

"Well, why are you late madammm?" he dramatically spoke stressing on madam more.

"I was getting ready sirrrrrr......." she replied in the same manner and they shook their heads unbelievingly at their childishness.

"you girls"

"what we girls...." she crossed her arms in a challenging way.

"In what time girls get ready.... In the same time 4 guys get ready and come back after attending the event also"

"Whatever.... Oh wait you were saying something yesterday right, say what were you talking about?" "leave it no.... Sometime later, just be with me ok" he said looking in her eyes, there was something she saw in his eyes and agreed nodding her head.

While all the time Vicky was staring at shrishti from the other corner of the hall..... Soon the party started and kabir was busy meeting some important guests but his one eye was on shrishti all the time..... after sometime he saw that Vicky was nowhere to be seen......so he started searching for him.

Kabir was moving towards the corridor but his steps halted listening to the sounds of laughter coming from the washroom and that laughter seemed like vicky. He immediately moved towards the washroom and stood quietly outside the washroom door to listen to what Vicky was saying…. It seems like he was talking with someone on the phone.

17

"Today by hook or by crook I will surely take my revenge from this shrishti" These words escaped from Vicky's mouth making kabir froze at his spot, his mind suddenly started asking only one question "revenge from shrishti but WHY?"

"She rejected my proposal in the college no, she is has this proud of her beauty right, today i'll make teach her a lesson in a way that no one will propose her ever, she crushed my roses that day right now I'll crush her, badly very badly" he paused for some time maybe to hear the person other side, "ya ya, I'll execute my plan as soon as possible just looking for a good opportunity"

Here Kabir was standing stunned at the door of the restroom, he felt that Vicky was coming so he immediately hid behind a pillar, when Vicky left from there Kabir came out and was still in shock and was trying to register his words.

He suddenly realized he didn't have time to save shrishti..... he should be with her right now, in a moment he literally ran from there but his bad someone stopped him midway, out of courtesy he stopped but his heart was yelling to leave from there asap.

Here shrishti was enjoying a soft drink with khushi by her side and at the same time Vicky saw her and approached towards her.

"Hey shrishti.... Whats up"

"Hii.... All good... you tell" she replied as usual with her sweet smile.

"Actually I need your help" "What help...?"

"See, tomorrow is my sister's birthday and I want to give her a beautiful dress as her birthday present.... But I was not able to find that..... please can you come with me to choose one for her" he pleaded

"But, right now.... How can we go the party's still going on"

"I agree it's still going on but it's about to end soon.... See... please, please come with me no please" he said showing fake puppy eyes. Being an innocent and pure soul, shrishti agreed.,

"One minute, let me say goodbye to kabir at least then we'll leave"

"oh that, actually he's busy.... I saw him talking to someone" "ohh, ok then.... Khushi, if kabir will ask about me then please can you tell him about me``

"oh yes, you carry on shrishti mam, I'll tell him bye" khushi assured her and then Vicky and shrishti left from the party venue.

Kabir finally got rid of that person and he again ran towards the hall and found shrishti nowhere..... his heart stopped for a second.... He was searching for her like a maniac and at last he found khushi.

"khushi..... srishti..... Where is shrishti?"

"Sir she left just 5 minutes before you came with Vicky"

"Vickky....." he gritted his teeth in anger as he was very well aware of the intentions of vicky.

The other hand Vicky was driving a car at a fast speed..... to move away from the venue asap, shrishti noticed that he was driving towards the isolated area of the city so she asked, "Vicky..... where are we going..... I don't think there is any mall or clothes store on this side of the city" "you just sit quietly" he said in a stern voice, making her feel something wrong, some sort of insecurity was rising in her heart..... she again spoke, "Vicky, where are you taking me?" "just telling"

His dangerously slow voice made shrishti's heart beating fast. but she stayed strong.... She didn't want to show her weak self. He stopped the car with a sudden break, In the middle of the road where not a single person was visible.... Her heart was beating now at a faster rate. In a very fast speed he stepped out of the car and coming to her side he dragged her out also forcefully.

"What the hell is this behavior Vicky" she said raising her voice at him and the next moment she felt a hard slap on her right cheek, she took a few seconds to register the fact that he just slapped her. "Dare you raise your voice at me"

Kabir was trying her phone constantly but she was not picking because her phone was on silent mode. his heart was becoming restless by every passing second. He called one of his friends who was a police officer to track her location asap. Within 2-3 minutes he got a call from the police officer.

Kabir: yes.

Officer: xyz location it is....

Kabir: thank you.... I'm leaving from here. You also come fast with your team.

Kabir sat in his car and started driving at the speed of light and Here shrishti was trying hard to stay strong in front of Vicky.

"What is this Vicky...." there was rage filled in her voice

"What did you think, what did you do with me? I'll forgive you, no, never.... You are very proud of your beauty right, now I'll make your beauty your misery..... You just wait and watch" he fisted her hair tightly making her wince in pain. A tear escaped her eye..... but she didn't give up she was struggling hard to get out of his grip, But in response his grip on her hairs grew more tight.

"Vicky please leave me.... You don't know what you are doing..... you'll face consequences"

"I'm not scared of your whatsoever consequences, I just want to teach a lesson and that I will" Now shrishti was completely filled with anger as she had had enough of him..... So she slapped him hard on his face..... and this action of hers made him more mad. He left her hairs and slapped her harder than before because of the hard slap she fell on the road and blood started oozing out from her lips.

"Enough of your drama..... Now you see what I'll do with you" he said dangerously, taking out a sharp knife from his pocket.

Seeing that shrishti heart stopped for a moment. Tears started forming in her eyes, but she still was staying strong. He grabbed her hair and stood her up forcefully, she whimpered in pain but he was heartless. None of her tears or whimpers were making him have mercy on her. He was waving that knife in front of her eyes. "Please let me go...... please don't do this..... Please" she pleaded crying, But he paid no heed to her pleadings, he was about to make a big cut on her face but before that shrishti collected her whole courage and strength and kicked him hard because of that he fell down and groaned in pain.... Taking this as a chance to run she immediately started running seeing her running away.... He somehow got up and ran behind her..... but her speed was more than him.

She didn't see a big piece of stone as she was running looking behind.... She tripped on that and fell on the road. She groaned in pain and tried to get up.... But her wrist twisted, because of that she again fell, she looked behind and found that Vicky was just a little distance away from her.... She looked forward again and this time she found a person standing there.

She sighed in relief and without even looking at that person she started pleading to save her. Seeing her pathetic state... that person softly held her hands and helped her to stand up. Because of tears in her eyes she was still not able to see the face of that person still but she was continuously pleading to save her in her shivery voice.

"please.... Ppp....pp...lee..aase... save me..... please I request..... Please help me.... Please save me" by now tears were falling from her eyes like a waterfall. Seeing her so broken immediately that person cupped her face with both hands and wiped her tears with his thumbs..... and then she realized who was him.

"Ka.... kab....iir....rhhh.... Kabir you....." Realizing his presence she broke down badly, losing all the strings she was holding and hugged him tightly...... like her life depends on that only, automatically he also hugged her back to console her.

"Kaa.... bbirh...hh.... You know.... That..... He.... vic..ky... he's very bad" she sobbed hard and he rubbed her back to sooth her pain "he.... He slapped me... and also... he has a knife..... Please save me.... Please save me" her hold on him tightened more as she weeped harder.

"Shh..... You are safe.... You are safe shrii.... Don't cry.... He can't do anything, see I'm here no.... Look, he's even arrested.... Look". he said, moving her a little but she held him more tightly. "Nooo..... No I don't wanna see anything, you are lying…. He has a knife…. No". she shook her head vigorously "No shrii I'm not lying see he's really arrested they are taking him away"

Finally she looked at the side where Kabir was telling her to look and found that he was really arrested by the police… and they were taking him away in the police van.

Now only shrishti and kabir were left there, she was still crying holding him like a baby cries holding his mom, he was trying his level best to console her, but she was not ready to stop and her this state was piercing his heart, finally her cries turned into little sobs and he sighed in relief. He again cupped her face and saw blood coming out from her lips and finger prints on her right cheek. His blood boiled, he wanted to beat the shit out of Vicky but he couldn't do that.

"Shrishti look, your lips are bleeding…. Come let me do first aid" she was not moving from her place, Somehow he managed to take her towards his car and he took out a first aid kit. He dipped a cotton ball in antiseptic…. And placed it on the corner of her lips, because of antiseptic her skin burned and she flinched, seeing her in pain he immediately removed that cotton ball and blew at the same place.

"Now ok" she nodded with tears still in her eyes.

She was trying hard to hold back her tears, but some traitor tears fell from her eyes and he immediately wiped them off, he hugged her and caressed her hair to console her. "Shrii…… you can't be weak yrr…. And don't you worry at all I'm here with you right, you are your dad's tigress no, then tell me that tigress ever feel defeated this easily, Be strong and don't think about that psycho…. He can't do anything"

When he felt that she was a little calm he asked her to sit in the car. She did the same and after sitting beside her he started driving at an average speed. She was quiet for some time and he also didn't say anything giving her some time, but after a few minutes she abruptly said..

"Kabir..."

"Yes"

"What will I tell at home..... they'll be tensed for me...." she said, looking at him with hope filled eyes.

"Don't worry I'll talk to them" he said with a warm smile on which she nodded.

After that again silence occupied them..... after almost 40 minutes of driving they reached shrishti's home. Before he could climb down the car she held his hand..... he looked at her and understood her unspoken words, "Don't worry I'll handle everything" Both of them climbed down the car and pressed the doorbell. Shrishti's mom opened the door and seeing shrishti's bruised face she was stunned.

"Shriii..... My child what happened" Seeing her mom she was not able to control herself and she burst into tears hugging her tightly..... her mom got more worried.

"Kabir, at least you say why is my baby crying like this?" her mom asked kabir as shrishti was not replying to anything. "Aunty can we please take her in... then I'll tell you everything" Both of them took her in the living room and listening to her cry her dad and monika also came out hurriedly.

"Hey..... shrii.... My child.... What happened..... Why are you crying" her dad exclaimed looking at her miserable state. All of them were worried seeing her crying.... to handle the situation Kabir told them the whole incident.

"now he is in jail uncle..... and I'll make sure he'll get more than good treatment you don't worry"

"Thank you so much kabir, if not you then I don't know what would have happened today" her dad genuinely thanked kabir but he stopped him, "please uncle don't thank me like this, shrishti is my best friend and if not my friend then also I would have done everything because as a human being it's our duty to help the other human being..... For now please you all try to cheer her up a little so that she could come back to her normal self.

Kabir got up to leave as it was already past 11 at night, he looked at shrishti who was already looking at him with something unsaid in her eyes..... something broke in his heart seeing her teary swollen eyes. He didn't want to leave her but he couldn't stay there so he half heartedly left from there with a heavy heart.

18

Monika took shrishti in her room and asked her to sleep so that her mind can get some peace. "Shrii... you sleep ok you'll feel good hmm". She silently lay down on her bed and turned her face to the other side, monika thought she was asleep so she went out of her room.

Whereas shrishti was completely sleepless. Not because of what happened to her.... But because of the feeling rising in her which was somewhere suppressed under many layers in her heart......... she was thinking about KABIR..... how he handled her in her worst situation..... how he didn't let her feel insecure.... How he held her in his arms securely to make her feel safe..... She tried to sleep but his thoughts were not letting her sleep...... and suddenly her phone flashed and she noticed that it was a message from kabir only saying.....

"take a day off and rest..... and be strong like a tigress.... I'm with you...."

These words of his made her more sleepless. she drowned again in his thoughts only forgetting everything around her, she let out a huge sigh "what kind of feeling is this... which I'm experiencing today.... Why is everything making me think about him only"

"because you are fallen for him shrii....." her heart said

"What...? how can even this be possible..... it's not true"

"*if it's not true, then think about all the moments you spend with him.... What you feel*" her heart said again

Considering this she closed her eyes and started thinking about the time she spent with him since they met...... their first meeting... then jaipur trip...... meeting at his office... than chilling at the beach.... Winning world level competition with him...... how he took her proper care.... How he gave her surprise in Paris everything flashed in front of her eyes. She opened her eyes in jerk and hugged her teddy tightly.

"What is this, how can I remember each and every moment spent with him, why all those moments are so special for me and.... And those deep talks which I don't even do with my family and the comfort which I feel with him, what is all this..... God please help..... Is this what is called love just in case?"

"*yes..... you are in love... shrii*" her heart exclaimed

She closed her eyes and his face flashed in her eyes with a heart warming smile on his face. She opened her eyes shyly and unknowingly her cheeks turned into a light shade of pink, thinking about him all the time when sleep took her over she didn't even realize.

On the other hand Kabir was tossing on his bed continuously but sleep was miles away from him, his mind was struck on only one thing. Her swollen teary eyes, which was not meant to drop a single tear...... he was not able to forget her tears which she shed hugging him, He was not able to forget how relaxed he felt embracing her in his arms after searching her like maniacs. Finally he got up, started sighing and sat on his bed resting his chin on his palm.

"Oh god what do I do, why I'm feeling so restless, why I'm not able to forget her teary eyes, why it was so difficult to look at her crying face, why her tears were making me feel like something is breaking inside, why I was feeling like to kill that bastard vicky...... just WHY?"

"Because you love her kabir" He heard this and looked towards the source of the voice, it was his mom who was standing at his door....... He hesitantly looked at her then patted on his bed to ask her to sit with him. "What are you saying mamma"

"The truth"

"But I have never thought anything like this mamma, how can you say this?" he asked, confused at his mother's statement.

"You tell me, don't you feel good about the time you spent with her, don't you feel at peace with her, don't feel like be with her all the time or the maximum time, don't you adore her childish acts, and like you said by yourself you felt hurt seeing her crying the you tell me what is all this"

He closed his eyes and took a deep breath, he sighed deeply and opened his eyes again with calmness evident on his face. "I'll not lie, yes I feel all this, I really don't have any idea from when but I feel the utmost peace with her and only her, and today......" he sighed and looked at his mom "and today when I saw her crying like a little kid I was not able to control myself, I'm feeling helpless that I can't erase her tears stricken face from my mind"

"A true idiot you are my boy..... I'm saying the same thing no, that you love her and that you have something for her in your heart" He looked innocently at her mom..... she cupped his face. "Go and talk to her don't roam like a confused puppy"

"How she'll feel if I directly tell her..... Maybe she'll feel bad mamma" his mom looked dead in his eyes and then stood up to leave "You just keep on thinking ok, I'm going" she sarcastically mocked him and left.

He smiled and scratched his head and shook his head in disbelief. "I didn't know my mom was this frank and open," he wondered. "But the problem is still the same.... If I have feelings for her then how to tell her" he pouted. "We will see then, hope she'll be fine". Thinking about her, he drifted into deep slumber.

Next day passed normally.... Shrishti was ok but somewhere low as compared to daily basis and here Kabir was thinking about her only whole day if she is ok or not. The following day shrishti as usual went to the office and started working on her designs.... And Kabir was busy with his work... but oftenly he was looking at her as her cabin was just opposite his cabin. She was looking low but drowned in her work.

He decided to do something to cheer her up after the office hours..... luckily it was Saturday and half day for the staff too, so he ordered her favorite pizza at the time when employees started leaving.

Shrishti was so deeply engrossed in her work that she didn't even realize that it was a half day. She came out of her workaholic zone when she heard beautiful guitar music. She abruptly looked here and there in her cabin and then found Kabir sitting on floor pizza boxes on his one side with coke and he was the one who played guitar. She was looking at him confusingly for a few seconds then she asked.

"What are you doing kabir?" He didn't reply but started singing while playing the guitar. she was looking dreamily at him.... She didn't even realize when she sat beside him resting her chin on her palm. The lyrics of the song were somewhere true for both of them, Both were feeling that those words are meant for them only. she closed her eyes feeling the music and his soulful voice.

He ended beautifully and she slowly opened her eyes and looked at him.... There was silence for 2 minutes but that silence spoke more than 1000 words.

"I didn't have any idea you sing so well kabir". he just passed a soft smile at her, "well, what got you sing today all of a sudden hmm".

"About that, actually there's a don who happens to be my very close friend who was feeling low, so I thought why not do something to make him bring back to his usual mood" he innocently said looking at her.

"You know what, the talent of making someone feel so good and then spoiling their mood at the same time only you have" she huffed and turned her head to the other side. "What did I do?" he smirked, suppressing his smile.

"Can't you simply call me shrishti...... from where do I look like a don"

"See I can't call you Dada na your profile will look very low, so Chotu Don is best for me"

"Chotuuu...!!" she asked, squinting her eyes.

"Don't you like chotu? It's ok Miss. don is done then, nice name no?"

"whatever"

"Ok leave all this, and see what I have" he said placing pizza boxes between them "I'm not hungry"

"you are"

"I'm not"

"Oh yes, you are..... and I know this.... Now no drama.... You haven't had your lunch also..... eat it"

"How do you know that I haven't had lunch today? Why do you care so much for me kabir?" she thought, looking at him. He waved his hand in front of her eyes causing taking her out from her trance

"Earth to madam, where are you?"

"Here only, now you tell me why there are 3 pizza boxes, we are 2 right" "because you ate my pizza last time.... And I didn't get even a single slice of it.... So these 2 are yours and 1 is mine...... I'm already prepared... you see"

"So what, did I tell you to switch on your deep thinking mode hun, I was hungry so I ate all by myself"

"That's why I'm already prepared now," he said, raising his eyebrows to tease her, she shook her head in disbelief and both started eating. Meanwhile Kabir was cracking lame jokes to make her happier. After satisfying their hunger, both were looking out of the window as the sun was about to hide behind the clouds.

Kabir held her hand softly and asked in a concerned tone. "Shrii.... How are you feeling now" she silently looked at him for a few seconds and then spoke, taking a deep breath "I'm totally fine kabir..... Thank you so much for doing what you did for me.... Not only today... that day also..... I was really not in my state of mind.... I can't even imagine if you would not be on time then what he was about to do with me" A lone tear fell from her eye and he immediately wiped that off.

"Whatever I did, I did it for you and please forget all that hmm...... Just live in the present and yes one more thing, your eyes are so beautiful and it should shine like a star only, please don't ever let a tear escape your eyes." She smiled warmly at him and seeing her genuine smile he also mirrored her actions.

"Now let's go..... Your mom must be waiting for you at home, today is half day no". "Was there a half day today?" she surprisingly asked.

"Good morning Miss. Sharma". She slapped her forehead and they left for their homes.

After reaching home, Shrishti found that her mom was not home and monika was busy with work in her room so she directly moved towards her room and after freshening up she picked her dairy and sat on the balcony "Why everything which he did today was so special for me, Why I felt like that song should just kept going on and not stop..... Why everything was so beautifu......"

"you dumb head..... I told you yesterday also.... You love him, that's it...." Her heart said

"I know I was just confirming......"

"how many years you'll take to confirm...."

She got annoyed, closed her eyes and went to make tea for her and monika to distract her mind..... but in the kitchen she remembered her silly talks on tea with kabir. "Oh god, why everything coming over at him only"

"At whom?" Monika asked entering the kitchen, hearing her shrishti closed her eyes and started thinking of a way to save herself. "Nothing di.... Just like that"

After reaching home Kabir had tea and snacks with his mom and dad. when he went into his room all the things that happened in the office started revolving in his mind... a beautiful smile crept on his face.

"God!! I'm surely doomed, I am crazy but now I'm sure.... That I love her..... I love shrishti sharma". he said to himself scratching his head.

"But how on earth am I going to admit in front of her, and here goes a new problem, I'm in very serious need to talk to someone" he was thinking tapping the sides of his head.

"Now I'm left with one option only..... Aaditya... only he can help me now, but he'll directly murder me If i'll tell him about this all of a sudden" he pouted frustratingly scratching his head. Finally fighting with himself he called aaditya and after threatening him in different ways what will he do with him, Kabir cut the call smiling and sighing in relief And ran towards the kitchen to ask his mom to prepare special dinner for Aaditya and him. Within 30 minutes Aaditya reached his home and found Kabir already ready with the tray filled with snacks and 2 cups of tea..... when he saw Aaditya he stood up and hugged him.

"Finally you are here, this was my longest wait ever"

"Ok, ok now tell me what's the matter"

"Take a breath man, wait let's have tea and then we'll talk no" he said trying to ignore the topic for a while.

"okkk....."

Both of them sat together on the sofa and started having their snacks and tea while talking on some crazy topics, soon both were free and Aaditya again asked him the same question.

"Bro, tell me no, what's the blunder you created this time?"

"I'll tell you, can't you have some patience, sit quietly" Kabir shushed him as he was continuously contemplating in his mind how to start the conversation.

"you know what....." aaditya said in a bit annoyed voice.

"What.....?"

"you are impossible"

"I know" Kabir rolled his eyes, making Aaditya shake his head in disbelief. After passing some time talking about random stuff.... Kabir and Aaditya moved towards the dining area where his mom and dad were waiting for them to have dinner as time was already past 10 PM. All of them finished their food while enjoying each other's company after a long time, when they finished both Kabir and Aaditya went on the terrace.

19

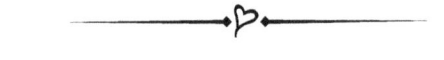

After walking almost 10 minutes on the terrace finally aaditya bursted.... He stood in front of Kabir, folding his hands on his chest with a serious face. "What? Why are standing like this"

"Are you really mad? On the call you were so desperate to tell me something and now you are not even ready to open this mouth of yours" he said, throwing his arms in the air.

"Hey, why are you yelling I'll tell you man, in fact I call you for that only right?"

"When? Now don't even try to beat around the bushes.... Just speak up." kabir looked at him with his lips sealed "will you"

"Um, actually.... The thing is.... I wanted to say.... That..... You know that right?"

"What on earth are you trying to say man, see.... Kabir.... Please have some mercy on this friend of yours and speak up" Finally Kabir closed his eyes, sighing and spoke everything in one breath only leaving aaditya completely confused.

"My lord..... What are you speaking.... No space, coma, question mark, exclamation mark, anything. How am I supposed to understand what you are blabbering about?"

"I wanted to say that I have fallen for shrishti and I want to confess but don't know how to do that so I wanted to ask will you help me" he said, as innocently as a child asking for an ice-cream. Aaditya was looking at him with his mouth touching the ground.

"Now will you say something?.... Hello sir, are you alive?" Kabir shook his shoulder a little just to check if he's alive a little dramatically.

"what you just say...... you..... kabir.... Kabir Mehra...... is in LOVE" he said making his eyes go wide as the same as a tennis ball.

"Do you by any chance think I spoke in french"

"Are you serious"

"No I'm joking"

"Then it's ok... you literally gave me a heart attack for a seco...."

"Are you mad aaditya.... Why will I bring this much serious topic if I'm not determined?" he said, getting annoyed by his dumbo friend's antics.

"Ok, ok cool cool...... got it got it" There was a silence for few minutes and again aaditya asked

"Means you.....The kabir mehra.....has fallen for shrishti whom I have never met" and here he earned a death glare from kabir.

"You know what, I should have not told you at the very first place... huh... I would have done something by myself" he was already annoyed and aaditya was not any help which was making him more mad in a dramatic way to be precise. "Ok fine, no need to go all furious on innocent me bro, you know it's difficult to digest information like this from someone like you"

"What do you mean by someone like me?"

"You leave this and tell me what's the main problem?"

"Told you already, I need to confess but I'm totally clueless how to?"

"Oooo... that you think on your own, how do I know?"

"You are just good for nothing.... Huh" he huffed looking at the other side, stuffing his hands in the pockets of his trousers.

"Now how can you say I'm good for nothing huh, when I don't have any experience in this field, you do one thing search it on google"

"One idiot was not enough that you are also behaving like idiots aaditya" Both of them got shocked and turned to find Kabir's mom standing there with a tray in her hand in which 2 bowls of ice cream was there. "I'm not idiot aunty, your son is making me one"

"Good, just very good now you both team up and prove me an idiot"

"There is not even a need to prove that it's already proven kabir" his mom said, riling him up more when he looked at her with his puppy eyes. "Now what?"

"I'm your own personal child and you'll do this with me?" he said while wiping his fake tears. "I'm not calling you an idiot because you are thinking to confess to shrishti about your love"

"Then"

"Go and propose to her directly, where will I find a daughter in law like her?" his mom said bluntly, making him choke on air.

"Correct" aaditya chided too, making kabir hold his head in shock. "You both are hell bent on making me get murdered by her, she's not less than some DON.

"But then also you love her right? If you have courage enough to love her then have this heart to ask her for the togetherness of your whole life" he was looking dumbfounded at his mom "Now will you say something"

"I seriously didn't know my mom is so open about all this" he said with his eyes widened in shock.

"Means you are going to propose to her right?"

"Now, when my mom is asking me to do something so confidently, the why to fear, let's do it guys" both aaditya and his mom well hell excited listening to this. "But if she denied because of all this rush up then you both get ready to face troubles because I'm not gonna let you both sit peacefully hehe" he threatened them with fake glare.

"Ya ya we will see" his mom said "so what, we are not afraid of you huh, let's go aunty we'll enjoy ice cream downstairs" aaditya teased kabir and urged his mom to go downstairs with him.

Both of them left after giving one bowl in Kabir's hand, here Kabir was left alone and confused about what he'll do exactly. After coming back to his room kabir was talking with chiku about what to do and that poor creature didn't understand a word he was talking about, he was half lying on his bed with chiku on his stomach.

"Chiikkkuuuuuu..... At least you give me some idea, see they are busy making my fun but not giving any idea" in response she was just staring at him cutely. "Means now you will also not tell me anything right?" she again looked at him with its puppy eyes. He was about to say something more but before that chiku got up and went out of the room silently. He looked at her unbelievingly.

"All are betrayers.... Huh.... see whom I used to think is only mine also left me here alone" And this time a cushion landed on his head.

"What the hell"

"Are you seriously gone nuts man, why are you behaving like drunkards, how can you expect from poor chiku to answer your stupid questions, you ask her for hifi she'll give, you ask for handshake she'll do that also now you'll ask stupid things then what she'll do..... Idiot" And then a pillow landed on Aditya's head too. "Now what is this for?"

"For your not very much asked lecture you just gave me, I asked one single idea and except that you said all the hell lot of useless stuff"

"Now, when I don't have any idea what, your shrishti's favorite is, where she wanna go likes the most what catches her attention the most then how should I give you suggestion tell me" Listening this Kabir's face lightened up like a bulb and he threw one more cushion at aditya. "Now you throw this damn pillow one more time and you are dead," "you stupid,idiot, nonsense man you gave such a good idea why didn't gave me the idea earlier hun"

"What idea, when did I give you an idea?"

"You just go and sleep and don't disturb me"

"Look at you, you ungrateful man huh..... No time for goodness is left nowadays.... You continue sitting like an idiot I'm going" he dramatically glared at Kabir and left for the guest room.

Kabir lay down on his bed looking straight at the ceiling. "I'm doing right no, if shrii felt bad then, what would she think about me"

"Nothing will happen..... Just be focused" his heart said

"Yes, it's just I hope whatever I have decided I implement rightly, shrii madam you'll be surprised tomorrow" With determination in his eyes and heart he fell into deep slumber with a sweet smile on his face.

Next morning

Shrishti was getting ready but today she was getting ready putting more effort into looking beautiful, unknowingly her heart was so happy and she was also humming some song. "What's the matter, someone is very happy today" monika said, coming into her room with breakfast of shrishti in her hand.

"Nothing di, it's just I'm feeling very content today.... Nothing much"

"Well, well..... you are looking beautiful shrii" she said pulling her cheeks. "Ok, bye I'm getting late"

"Where to, finish your breakfast first, I know you well you escape like everyday that's why mom told me to bring your food in your room only"

"You and mamma"

"What.....?"

"Nothing." She had her breakfast quickly and left for the office because she knew there was no room for argument.

On the other hand Kabir, also getting ready in his most presentable way, was ready to leave for the office when his mom came with his breakfast.

"You are looking handsome my son, come back after completing what you are going" He smiled at her shyly and after having breakfast he left for the office... Soon he reached the office and while moving towards his cabin his gaze fell on shrishti's cabin and he found her working already. He struck there only because she was looking more beautiful today.... Atleast to him. He came out of his trance listening to Khushi's voice.

"Excuse me sir..... your meeting is in 10 minutes"

"Sure, tell everyone to gather in the meeting hall" She nodded and left.

Whole day passed and after working a lot everyone was tired. Kabir had to implement his plan so he went towards Shrishti's cabin, Only to find her daydreaming she was smiling idiotically.

"Now what happened to her" he mumbled comically "shrishti" no answer. "Shrishtiii..... Shrishtiiii.... Is she going mad or something" Finally he shook her shoulder and she came out of her lala world.

"What happened?" she said, jumping on her seat.

"Nothing madam, you just zoned out"

"Ohh"

"I don't know why but listening "madam" from you is a different kind of happiness" she thought smiling at herself.

"Not again!!..... Shrishtiiii" he exclaimed. "What?" she exclaimed in the same way. "Ok leave it, see..... How beautiful weather is, let's go to the beach also sunset is also going to happen soon"

"Umm.... you are right, Ok then let's go let me just call at home so they'll not wait for me," "ok you wind up things here I'm waiting in the parking ok," "sure sure" After nodding he left.

Soon both reached the beach. The weather was really very awesome. Both of them sat on the big stones dipping their feet to the peaceful side. They were silently looking at the sun which was about to hide behind the sea. Still after sunset shrishti was staring at the sky and looking at her who was again zoned out a mischievous idea came in his mind. without thinking twice he splashed little water at shrishti and she suddenly came out of her trance. She gave him the most dangerous look.

"What was that?"

"Water," he said, splashing some more water.

"Youu.... Wait let me show you" She also splashed water on him and here begins the war. After 5 minutes they stopped, in fact Kabir made her stop. "Stop, stop, I surrender...... Just why, why I even thought to mess with the underworld don, you won and i lose now happy" he said joining his hands comically.

"Very happy" she raised her fake collars in pride. Both of them burst into laughter at their kiddish behavior. "God knows why we are acting like kids" she mumbled laughing hard. "One should never let the child die within us," Kabir said, looking forward. "yes you are right" suddenly she exclaimed as something caught her attention.

"Kabirhhh"

"Ya, say"

"See there, how beautiful.... Come let's see it from closer." she said pointing towards an isolated area where lights were decorated beautifully.

"It's for you only," he mumbled under his breath.

"Yes yes..... why not" Both of them started walking towards that area but in between they found a little boy selling beautiful flowers seeing his hard work. Kabir bought a big bunch of flowers from him and handed it over to shrishti, before taking she was looking at him dumbfounded. He waved fingers in front of her eyes.

"Don't you think you are zoning out too much today?" he asked, raising his eyebrow. "None of your concern" she squinted her eyes at him.

"Are you really a little crack or there is some other problem.... Well whatever..... see how beautiful flowers are...... hold it."

"Are these for me"

"No, actually these are for me, I was thinking to decorate my hair with these, how's the idea"

"Oh is it, c'mon give these to me, let me do the honors of decorating your beautiful hair my lord" she said, taking flowers from him.

"are you serious" she nodded cutely "its confirmed now"

"what?"

"That you forgot your brain somewhere" hearing his sarcastic comment she slapped his shoulder playfully. Talking about these silly things they reached the area which was decorated beautifully. "My god, it looks thousand times better from here than it looks from far away" she exclaimed dreamily adoring the beauty.

"Thank you so much god, she liked it.... Now I just hope she also likes what I'm going to say..... What more I want in my life" He was also lost in his dreams when he realized someone was shaking his shoulder.

"Someone was saying that I'M ZONING out today..... what do you wanna say now" she asked, squinting her eyes. He smiled sheepishly at her while scratching his head. "Ok then, I think we should leave, it's already around 9 what say" she asked looking at her watch. "Now what are you waiting for, say otherwise you never know you'll get the chance or not" his heart exclaimed. "Umm.... shrishti.... Actually I wanted to say something"

"Then say, what are you waiting for now, don't tell me you need my permission to say something" she casually said while fidgeting with her bag.

"Same but I don't understand how to say" he said with little confused and nervous expressions on his face. "Why are you stressing so much? Just say it, otherwise I'm not asking you for any atomic formula, say whatever you wanna say comfortably." He closed his eyes and took a deep breath and started.

"See..... the thing is that sometimes certain things happen to us, which we can't share but we are helpless to retain it with ourselves too, but the person whom we want to tell that thing we just lack courage and not tell them.... But you know that thing is so nice that we can't help to hide it..... Now the problem is that thing.... It happened to me, how I don't know, are you getting me what I am talking about?" she looked at him all confused and clueless "see, when that thing happens everything starts looking nice, what comes goes automatically.... Then if we are going or coming we get any idea..... World is moving around or not no idea" before he could blabber anything more she stopped him.

"Wait wait wait, what are you speaking kabir, what actually you are trying to and what on earth is that 'thing' which happened to you and you didn't told me till now and what are you blabbering say clearly"

"That only I'm thinking what the hell I'm uttering which is even not making sense to me" he thought scratching his neck in embarrassment.

"See again you zoned out.... Come here.... Sit" she dragged him and made him sit on one of the big stones there. She literally started checking his head from all the sides.

"What are you doing shrii? "Checking if you have hit your head somewhere" "Nothing happened like what you think"

"Then why are you blabbering stupid things..... Have you any idea what nonsense you just spoke making my head hurt" she said pouting cutely.

"Ok let me try again" she looked at him squinting her eyes "don't worry this time I'll speak clearly" earning her nod in approval he started.

"See shrishti...... I don't like to beat around the bush, I'm a very straightforward person so whatever I'm going to say please listen carefully" she nodded. "I really don't know how and when you became such an important person for me whom I want in life forever.... I don't know when I got addicted to those deep and serious talks of yours.... I don't know from when your tears started affecting me they started giving me pain.... I don't know when I started finding peace in the moments spent with you...... I don't know when you became this important for me that....." he gulped the lump which formed in his throat. "That.... Now I can't imagine myself without you.... I don't know how, when, where...... But I've already fallen for you shrishti.... Fallen very bad" all the while his eyes were holding her's not for a moment he moved his eyes from hers.

She was standing there numb with the tears of happiness in her eyes, still she didn't utter a single word.

20

She was standing there numb, not able to react to his words.... She didn't realize when he bent down on his knees and brought out a beautiful ring from the pocket of his coat.

"I LOVE YOU SHRISHTI...... really love you to my death...... and as my mom says if you have courage to love someone then you should have courage to accept it in front of that person..... And that is what I'm doing.... So...." he raised his hand showing the ring "WILL YOU MARRY ME SHRISHTI SHARMA"

Listening to these words shrishti was totally out of words. She had never thought that for whom she had fallen for the first time in her life has also fallen for her only and even proposed to her. From the very first moment till now all the time they spent together, all the memories ran in front of her eyes, emotions were flowing out from her in the form of tears, she was about to make him stand and hug him and hold him forever.

BUT— at the same moment she realized and more of remembered the biggest truth of her life...... she felt a ping in her heart and that's when she started stepping back with tears in her eyes but this time those tears were not of love but of pain.

Kabir was confused at the fact that a moment before there was a serene smile on her face but suddenly what happened. Before he could register anything she started running from there.

"Shriii wait.... What happened.... At least let me know.... Wait, listen"

He was also running behind her but she didn't pay heed to his words....... While running a dairy fell from her bag and Kabir noticed that he stopped and picked that dairy and before he could again run towards her he saw her taking a taxi on the main road and seeing her going away his heart became numb. He was standing there on the beach for 30 minutes holding her diary in one hand and the ring in his other hand. He was not able to understand what just happened.

"Why, why... why..... Just why every time with me only, why everytime the thing or person I love the most is snatched from me why god" he said looking up at the sky A teardrop fell from his eye. "I know it's not necessary if I love her then she should also love me in return, but at least she should have denied it to my face.... Did I hurt her to the extent that she doesn't even want to talk" He came out of his thoughts hearing his phone ringing on loop..... it was his mom.... He picked it hesitatingly.

"I'm coming home after sometime, please don't wait for me It's getting late you sleep" without even listening to his mom he hung up the call.

He finally made himself strong and moved towards his car..... Within 30 minutes he reached his home and found that her mom and dad were already asleep. He silently went into his room and after changing he sat on his balcony hugging his pillow.

On the other hand when shrishti reached home she found her family was waiting for her only for the dinner but making a lame excuse she went directly to her room.

The moment she stepped into her room she burst into tears. She locked the door and directly layed on the bed hugging her teddy and started crying her heart out muffling her cries so that no one could hear her.

Finally after 30 minutes of continuous crying she was tired, she got up and sat on the couch which was on the balcony still hugging her teddy. she was silently staring at the moon only lost in her thoughts but suddenly spoke to noone but to herself.

"I'm sorry..... I'm really very sorry kabir.... I should not have left you there all alone, today I'm feeling really happy after knowing the fact that the person whom I love also loves me back" by now again tears welled up in her eyes and her voice started choking. "I can't tell you how much I love you... I can't tell you what you mean to me.... It's me ill-fated kabir.... I love you immensely but.... But I CAN'T LOVE YOU"

And again she burst into tears, while shedding tears she didn't even realize when she fell into deep slumber sitting there on the couch only.

Kabir was also starring in the moon continuously...... somewhere now his consciousness started rising again.

"Godd, I get lost in my thoughts to the extent that I forgot to ask shrii if she reached home safely..... Why are you always an idiot kabir"

He immediately called her but as she was already fast asleep she didn't pick his call. He started worrying for her, he thought for a minute then called monika to confirm that she reached home or not.

On call

Kabir: Hello di.... Kabir here

Monika: hi kabir..... what's up

Kabir: all good.... Sorry for calling you this time.... But can you please tell me that shrishti reached home safely no.

Monika: No problem kabir..... and yes shrishti reached home almost 2 hours back, what happened why are you sounding tensed

Kabir: nothing like that di, it's just shrishti left before me today suddenly I thought to ask if she reached home safely even I called her but she didn't responded that's why I disturbed you

Monika: Oooo..... Actually today after coming from the office she went directly to her room and I guess she's asleep that's why she didn't respond to your call.

Kabir: thank you di..... and yes sorry for disturbing you.

Monika: no problem kabir.

Kabir: good night di

Monika: Good night.

After talking to monika he felt a little relieved that at least she was fine. He was also tired the whole day. He didn't subconsciously go towards his bed and dozed off.

Next day, Shrishti woke up with a heavy headache. Her eyes were red because of continuous crying last night..... The moment she saw her phone again her eyes welled up because there were almost 20 missed calls of Kabir and many messages saying "are you fine", "do you reach home properly"..... many more like this.

"Why are you like this kabir"

Her head was throbbing like hell. She hardly got up and went towards the kitchen, her mom was busy preparing breakfast, but seeing her condition she ran towards her.

"Shri... what happened child, why are your eyes red...hmm"

"Nothing much mamma just a little headache, can you please make a coffee for me"

"Why not, right away, you do one thing, go to your room and take medicine I'll bring your coffee there" She nodded and went back to her room.

Here Kabir as usual got up on time and after getting ready he was just about to leave but his mom stopped him. "Where to Mr.CEO who will eat this breakfast"

"I'm not in the mood mamma, please let me go" he said, looking the other side trying to hide his face from his mom.

"What 's the matter kabir, why are you looking upset... ok at least look at me no" she made him look at her "what happened"

"Noth....nothing mamma, let me go no"

"Definitely there is something, you come with me" She dragged him into his room with her. He was sitting on his bed and she was standing keeping her hands on her waist. "Now will you speak up, no drama in front of me ok, I know there is something... wait don't tell me you fought with shrishti"

He looked at the floor like there was the most interesting thing in the world to avoid his emotions. "Is she angry, speak up, what did she said"

"That's the problem" "means" Then he told her the whole story.

"I accept that it's not necessary that if I love her she should also love me in return, at least she should have said no on my face but no she just ran away from there like.... I don't know"

"Kabir.... You are very innocent my son... maybe you are misunderstanding her, it can maybe some other reason for not saying anything, you should not directly jump onto the conclusion, and before everything you both are friends right then there should be no hesitance you can directly ask her the reason"

"Hmm, maybe you are right"

"Ok now have your food and then go" he nodded and then went out with mom.

Here shrishti was not feeling well even after taking her medicine and her mom had already announced not to go to the office so she was sitting on her balcony with her dairy.

"Mamma is right, maybe I should not go to the office today... In fact I'll stop going to the office, because now after knowing everything it'll be difficult for me to ignore him, the closer I'll be to him the more will be the pain.... For both of us.... It'll be better if I stay back at home" She closed her eyes and tears fell from her eyes.

"kabhi kabhi hume unse bichadna padta hai..... Jinke bina hame humara guzara mumkin nahi lagta...... Dukh hota hai dono ko shayad umr bhar..... Par us samay bichadne se zada kuch sahi nahi lagta........"

She wrote these lines in her diary and fell into a deep slumber because of the effects of medicine.

In the office Kabir was waiting for her arrival impatiently but she never came..... he again started feeling guilty about his deed. 3 days passed like this but she didn't come.

Everyday he used to come to the office with the hope that she would come today but she didn't come....... He used to call her, massage her daily many times but she didn't reply even a single time..... 10 days passed with the same routine.

Day by day shrishti's health was deteriorating. She was not like earlier.... Happy, cheerful and full of life.... And monika was noticing this all the time..... due to something Important their parents had to go out of town for almost 10 days so they give responsibilities of taking care of shrishti to monika only as she is mature enough to take good care of shrishti.

Shrishti was in her room only when monika entered with their dinner in the room, she adjusted the food and then sat in front of her crossing her legs.

21

Shrishti and monika were sitting silently after finishing their food in silence all the time there was pain on shrishti's face and this was high time for monika she immediately went to keep the plates in the kitchen and after coming back she sat exactly in front of shrishti to confront her.

"Shrii"

"Hmmmm....."

"look at me....." she asked in a very calm voice "what's the matter"

"Nothing di, I'm fine"

"Fine? You are everything but fine shrii..... And you know very well, you can't lie to me.... Com on fast speak.... What happened"

"There is nothing to tell di, I'm fine why are you stressing this much"

"See I have already had enough.... I can't see you like this... just speak what has happened.... You never behaved like this ever.... You were never ever this silent..... you were the one who used to cheer everyone up and now you are sitting in the same room for 10 days and you are saying nothing happened"

"Done, I seriously don't know why everyone starts lecturing me like I am 5 years old" she did a very unsuccessful try to make the situation light but in return she earned a death glare from monika.

"I'm serious shrii.... Now it has become such a thing that you will not even tell me, no problem.... I'm going" she got up to go as she was genuinely feeling hurt but shrishti stopped her by holding her hand.

"Please don't say something like this"

Before she could say more her phone started ringing and it was of Kabir only..... she didn't pick and again and again her phone rang but she never picked.... And now monika was somewhere getting the point.

"Why are you not answering his call, wait is everything fine between you two" she gets nothing as answer but silence. "Have you both fought or something, shrishti please speak...... why are you ignoring him like this..... Poor guy called you 10 times and you didn't even answer a single time," "Because I don't want him to get hurt," "Hurt what do you mean?"

"Dii.... I really don't wanna talk about the thing which doesn't have any future... but if you are hell bent to know then listen. I really don't know how but I fell for him, he became that special one for me but...." by now she was holding herself back but it was difficult for her to control her emotions she hugged monika and cried her heart out.

"If this was it only then I would not have felt this bad but it hurts to know that he too has the same feelings for me, you know what from the day I am at home night before that day he confessed and even he proposed to me too..... But just look at my fate.... I can't take a step towards him even If I'm dying to do that" she paused for a while but her tears never stopped. "That day I left him there all alone.... Then also see how pure his heart is he calls me daily, I don't respond then he messages me..... Poor him he thinks he has hurt me, he doesn't know how much has my life already hurt me"

"And this is the reason why you are ignoring him and not even going to the office" monika asked, caressing her hair while still hugging her baby sister. "How di, how do I go..... When I know we both will get hurt and only hurt"

"Jab pata hai naseeb main kya hai to usse ladne ka kya fayda..... Dukh likhe hain zindagi main to fir mukarne se kya fayda....."

"But while trying to save him from getting hurt you are hurting yourself, mamma papa is already very tense for you, now you say what do we do for you.... Where is our fault in all this"

"Sorry di, I don't wanna make three of you upset but somehow the things unfold in such a way that you all end up getting hurt because of me"

"Ok now enough don't stress out more, otherwise your headache will start..... Hmm.... you sleep and don't think much"

She patted her head for sometime and she slept keeping her head in monika's lap, after comforting her on the bed monika left to complete some work.

On the other hand after dinner Kabir and Aaditya were sitting in Aaditya's room. "What's the matter man, why are you looking so disturbed is there any problem?"

"Yes bro there is a problem and that problem is me only"

"What nonsense are you speaking"

"Then what do I say.... You know I'm like this only I always end up hurting people around me, I can never keep my people happy"

"Hey no..... What are you saying... see I know you are hurt that's why you are saying all this, now tell me what's the problem," He told him everything happened till then.

"You know I'm not sad because she didn't accept or reply to my proposal, I'm sad because I lost a friend like her....

She's not even talking to me, not even responding to my messages.... I hurt her to the extent that she even stopped coming to the office. Listening his defeated voice aaditya scooted closer to kabir and kept his hand on his shoulder to give him some much needed support.

"First of all, calm down and listen to me.... It can also be possible that the situation is something completely different, do you know about her address?"

"Yes, I know"

"Then just go and meet her..... At least check if she is fine or not"

"But she's not ready to talk to me then how do I go"

"See, don't think much.... Just go and meet her and clear everything.... I can't see you like this"

Kabir started thinking deeply and contemplating if he should go or wait for some more time.

"Now don't think so much and go to meet her tomorrow after office" He nodded in approval and went to sleep as time was already past 12.

Next day kabir was just waiting for the day to pass soon and finally his work was over around 7 in the evening and he determinedly moved towards parking and took his car to go to shrishti's home. While he was driving suddenly his gaze fell on the dairy in the small section of the car where other things were also kept.... He stopped the car at the roadside and held the dairy in his hand.

"This is her diary" he was observing the cover of the dairy and a sudden urge rose in his heart to open the dairy. "Is it right to open someone's personal diary.... No problem she's my friend I can see" He opened the dairy and started turning the pages.... Almost the whole dairy was filled on each page where a thing or place name was written and below that one pic of shrishti doing that thing or at the place was there. Only the last 4 pages were left to be filled. He adored the dairy and closed it again.

"I think this diary is precious for her. I'll return this to her today" Thinking about her he again started driving towards her home.

At Shrishti's home there was a complete mess. Both the sisters were busy convincing each other.

"Di, you go without any doubt... I'm not a baby who can't take care of itself"

"But how can I leave you alone, shrii..... But what if something happens"

"Nothing will happen...... You go... your work is also important, I'm all right"

"Are you sure"

"Damn sure"

"Ok fine, I'm going and I'll be back within 2 hours max"

"Ok now go don't waste time here"

Caressing her head she moved out of the room.... when monika reached the main door she found kabir was coming out from his car.

"Hii di"

"Hello Kabir, you here at this time?"

"Um, actually di I wanted to meet shrishti, I think I have done something wrong because of which she is upset with me, I'm worried about her she didn't even came to the office since 10 days"

"I think I should give both of them their time.... Maybe if they'll talk it'll help them"

"Whatever you wanna ask you can ask her directly she's inside only, she is in her room currently and thank you we'll you came at a very good time"

"Why so"

"Actually I'm stuck with important work and I have to go for sometime.... I didn't wanted to go leaving her here alone but she initiated you know very well how she is but now I'm relieved that you came now I will be at peace"

"Oooo...."

"Please do me a favor, please don't leave her alone until I come back, please take care of her" He nodded and she hurriedly left.

"Take care of her? What has happened to her..... God is somehow she is sick" He stepped in the house and taking slow steps he moved towards her room as he already knew her room was on 1st floor so he climbed the stairs and directly went towards her room. He was about to knock the door but the door was open and his gaze directly fell on the beauty sleeping peacefully hugging a huge teddy in the exact center of the bed.

His heart was feeling relaxed, after many days he was able to breathe peacefully looking at her and finding her all ok, But when he moved near her bed his eyes widened in shock. Her face was looking pale like never before.... There were dark circles under her eyes..... she was looking so pathetic and her eyes were also swollen and there were fresh marks of dried tears. His heart stopped beating for a moment. He was not able to register the fact that a girl like shrishti could be in such a condition, his heart twinge looking at her swollen eyes.

He desperately wanted to wake her up and talk to her, and clear all the misunderstandings but he chose against it and sat on the couch to wait for her to wake up on her own. She was sleeping soundly but she felt someone's gaze on her so she woke up cutely rubbing her eyes. Her gaze directly fell on Kabir who was directly looking at her only..... she rubbed her eyes more to make sure that is he for real.

She thought she was hallucinating so she cutely pouted. "God, why are you doing this with me, what peace do you get hurting me like this.... Now what is this.... How can I see Kabir here..... Are the problems already less that you also added hallucination in the list"

She looked at him and now he was smiling at her, unbelievingly she shook her head and covered her eyes with both her palms

"Now I'll remove my hands and he won't be here" Kabir mischievously got up and went to the other side– she opened her eyes and found no one there.

"Huff.... See no one is here.... That's what I think about how Kabir can come here and.... And why won't he come" she sadly mumbled to herself. And the very next moment she felt someone patting on her shoulder, her eyes again widened in shock.

22

She gulped the lump formed in her throat and turned her head only to get shocked. There was Kabir sitting just beside her. she finally came out of shock.

"Kaa....kab...iirr... you here"

"What do you think..... where should I be" She was fighting with her thoughts in her mind about what to ask him, how to start the conversation.... But this problem he sorted himself.

"Shrishti what happened yrr...... why are you looking like this first of all...... and why are you not coming to the office..... Are you ok" She didn't answer him but looked on the other side to hide her tears filled eyes.... She can't let him know the reason behind her actions.

"Don't worry I got it..... You are not coming to the office because of me right? See if I have hurt you then you give me punishment but please start coming to the office." She still didn't say a single word.... And kept on looking out.

"Shrishti have I made such a big mistake that you can't even forgive me...... please don't do this shrii.... See if you want me to join my hands.... I can do that too for your forgiveness" he said joining his hands together "please forgive me" listening this she turned her head and immediately held his hands.

"What are you doing kabir?"

"Then what do I do.... I don't beat around the bush and you know this, so I'm directly coming to the point, I can't lose my best friend because of my love.... Please come back yrr..... I want my DON back"

"Sorry kabir but..... but now this can't be possible....... I can't come to the office" she said with her trembling lips and moist eyes.

"Means you are still angry with me, but shrii as long as I know you, you are not someone who can sit at home like this leaving her career at stake.... Now tell me what's the problem, why you don't wanna come to the office"

"There is no problem, it's just I don't want to"

"That's what I am asking no... why.... Shrii please speak up"

"Now what do I say that you are my problem that I can't handle staying in the same office as you" she thought, closing her eyes to avoid his questions.

"Please say something?"

Now this was high time for her, holding back is not there in her nature, so finally words slipped from her mouth leaving Kabir shocked.

"I can't come there because you are there and also I don't have time"

"Can't come because I'm there.... What do you mean" she again looked the other side "shrishti speak..... see only you and me are here..... I need answers" She again kept quiet

"Please say it shrishti.... What does it mean that I'm there" he turned her face towards him and made her look directly in his eyes.

"BECAUSE I LOVE YOU...... LOVE YOU TO MY DEATH..... BUT I CAN'T LOVE YOU..... AND CAN'T EVEN IGNORE YOU...... SO ITS BETTER WE STAY AWAY FROM EACH OTHER" she said each word with tears falling down from her eyes.

After listening to this, he was looking at her dumbfounded. He was not able to process the fact that she too loves him, so where is the need to stay away or ignore.

"You said....that.... that you too love me..... then why you'll ignore me..... why you can't love me"

"Because I can't," she said, closing her eyes.

"But why?" she kept quiet "shrishti I need an answer, if you love me and I love you then where is the problem, why you can't, shrishti speak"

"because I don't want to ruin your life... I want you to be happy in every single moment of your life, not pathetic"

"And why do you think that you'll ruin my life..... The person who cleared my messed up life in no time how can that person ruin it..... May I know how..... And even if my life would be ruined than I want it to... now say"

"Kabir, why are you not understanding..... I can't..... Can't you understand these 2 simple words" "But why...?" "Because I don't have time" finally she blurted out and hung her head low.

"What do you mean shrii" he cupped her face out of concern and made her look at him. He could feel the pain, the fear in her eyes. Her tears filled eyes were piercing his heart a million times at the same moment.

"Please say it......"

"I'm dying kabir...... every second, every minute, every hour, every day...... I'm just a step away from my death....." tears brimmed in his eyes hearing her unconsciously his hold on her tightened "I'm suffering from ASTROCYTOMA- last stage of brain cancer"

By now she was strongly holding back but now it was difficult for her to control...... she burst into tears and immediately he hugged her tightly in a secure hug. She let out everything in the forms of her tears but this time she was not alone who was crying. Kabir was also crying with her, their tears were saying thousands of words which their mouths were not saying. After not knowing how long Kabir parted away and cupped her face.

"How much time do you have"

"3 months"

"It's enough.... To complete the bucket list of "my don" it's enough, to write my love story it's enough, to enjoy teasing you it's enough, to get beaten up by you it's enough, to make you mine forever it's enough" Saying this he again hugged her tightly to never let her go. They were sitting like that only for a long time. He caressed her head and she sighed deeply, feeling relaxed and calm after many days.

"shrii"

"Hmmm......"

"Why didn't you tell me this before?" She parted away and directly looked into his eyes. "because I don't want anyone to look at me with a sympathetic look..... I can't tolerate that.....never..... I don't want people to think that I am weak..." she wanted to speak more but her throat was not helping.

"Who said you are weak..... you are the strongest underworld don I have ever met" and here he earned a death glare from her.

"What do you get, after annoying me huh?"

"Peace...." He said looking the other side he was trying his best but was not able to control his traitor tears, Shrishti noticed that and wiped them off immediately.

"What is this kabir, time is less with me and the person who is crying is you" he looked at her with tear filled eyes. "Well it's nice there won't be anyone in this world to eat your head right?"

"Because my world would be finished after you" he thought.

"Ok enough….. I don't know what is there in our future but yes….. For whatever time we are together, it will be the best time of your life, and I promise I will try my level best to complete each and everything left in your bucket list" She was looking in his eyes and when she registered what he said at last she came out of her trance.

"Wait, how do you know about my bucket list"

"I know and that's enough for you to know" he said with innocent smile on his face

"Kabir I'm damn serious, now tell me how do you know, no one knows about this only my dairy knows… wait my dairy…. It's missing" she was freaking out like her biggest secret was revealed.

"Calm down madam calm down….. Your secrets of the underworld are nowhere leaked…. Your dairy is safe with me, that day you dropped it on the beach, before I could return it to you you left"

"Huff…… thank god….. But" she squinted her eyes "how dare you open my diary"

"And here you go again with your don mode… you are my friend girl….. I have complete rights on your everything….. Whatever is yours is mine…. And whatever is mine is also mine ok, so thinking it as my right I just read it once…. And now I think I did correct, at least I got to know all about this….. Now don't worry I'll help you in completing them"

"Really" there was hope in both her eyes also in her voice and he knew she's again on one of her emotional trips, to lighten her mood he pulled her cheeks. "Of course"

"Pull my cheeks one more time and then I'll show you the consequences" she said with an angry yet cute pout. "Is it, then show me the consequences" he pulled her cheeks again and here our don came back she picked a pillow and threw it at him.... But he was quick to move, before he could register another pillow came..... and now he also stepped into the match...... both were pillow fighting and at a moment they were pulling a single pillow from the either sides and with a chrrrrrrrrr...... sound it tore into 2 pieces and whole room filled with feathers including their hair.

Before they could cover up they heard a loud gasp and turned their heads simultaneously.... And found Monika standing at the door of the room with her hands on her waist, with a frown on her face.

"Diiiiiiii........" both of them exclaimed as they were clearly caught red handed destroying the beauty of the room.

"Yes, diii..... Now tell me fast who started this" Both of them immediately pointed fingers towards each other while looking at monika.

"Tell me one thing, I left you both to clear your misunderstanding or to destroy this once pretty room" Both of them looked at her with an awkward smile and then looked at each other.

"Sorry di"

"It's ok.... Now come downstairs, for dinner" Both of them followed her like lost puppies as they were nowhere in condition to argue. On the dining table 3 of them were eating in silence. Kabir hesitatingly broke the silence.

"Di, I.... actually I wanted to share something with you"

"Whatever you wanna share I already know Kabir" she said with a teasing smile "what? I mean what do you know" the nervousness was rising in him from her comment. "That you both love each other..... Right?"she asked, raising her eyebrows. Shrishti acted like she was eating her food with full concentration whereas Kabir choked on his food.

"Umm.... actually yes, apparently you are right" And with this three of them burst into laughter but soon three of them were emotional to lighten their mood shrishti spoke.

"Ok guys now don't get emotional right now, you all still have to bear me 3 months you know"

"Shut up..... don't you dare say this" both kabir and monika exclaimed at the same time making her look innocently at both of them.

"Di, i need some help from you" he asked while taking a small bite from his food.

"Yes say"

"There is a bucket list of shrishti..... I hope you know about that" she nodded. "So yes This is my promise to her that I'll make her complete her bucket list, in all this you have to help me, will you please talk about this to uncle aunty"

"No no no kabir I can't both of them are very possessive about shrii and I really don't know how they are going to react"

"Ok don't worry I'll talk to them, when they'll come back?"

"Maybe in 3-4 days"

"Great, now I should leave and yes if you both need any kind of help I'm just a call away, Okay" he literally ordered them like a teacher.

"Okay" both the girls exclaimed like kids.

"And you don ji.... Don't stress this little head of yours ok.... Just chill...." First time after hearing "Don" from him she smiled or it can be said she actually smiled after many days because of him and only for him.

23

After kabir left shrishti went into her room and she immediately slept, very peacefully after many days. Seeing her it looked like she was actually at peace after sharing everything that was in her heart to him. Seeing shrishti happy monika was also happy for her but emotional for her sister too.

"I think I should tell mamma papa about shrishti and kabir, it'll be difficult for both of them to tell and if mamma papa already be knowing everything then It'll be easy for both of them"

Thinking about all this she called her dad and talked with both of them very calmly and told them the sensitivity of kabir and shrishti's relationship and unexpectedly both of them accepted instantly and they were also emotional for their daughter.

On the other side after reaching back home Kabir directly went into his room and ran into the bathroom. He turned on the shower and stood under it...... he was numb..... not able to understand what just happened in his life, he tried hard to stay strong but failed miserably.... Even after trying very hard those traitor tears started escaping from his eyes one after another eventually his hold on himself lost and he cried his heart out..... his legs were giving up to make him stand anymore, he sat down on the floor with the thud and closed his eyes. After 30 minutes he came out, changed his clothes and he sat on his balcony all numb,only one thing was running in his brain....... 3 months......

He was continuously staring at the moon like he was trying to find something in it, don't know after how long he mumbled no one in particular but more likely to god

"jo likh diya hai tune hanton ki lakeeron main, unhe main badal to nahi sakta..... par ye mera wada hai..... jo main badal nahi sakta....Use behtareen banadunga...."

"What you wanted to give me you have already given, now I don't even have any complaints from you, but now It's my promise to myself that these 3 months will be the best 3 months of her as well as mine life, now I'll not waste even a single day...... there are 4 wishes of her left no, no problem mission will start from tomorrow"

A lone tear fell from his eyes helplessly. He determinedly closed his eyes, soon he didn't even realize that he slept in the balcony only.

Next morning

On the dining table.... Kabir was eating his food in complete silence...... his mom and dad both were noticing the change in him but before they could say anything kabir himself started speaking

"Mamma, papa I want to discuss something big with both of you and it's very important" sensing the seriousness in his voice both of his parents understood that there is something big that's why he is behaving this way assuring him both of them nodded.

After finishing breakfast. Three of them were sitting in the living room. His mom and dad looked at him in a concerned way that what just happened suddenly which made him this serious.

"What's the matter son, why are you looking so troubled and disturbed, everything is alright right?" his dad asked in a very concerned way which made him more weak.

"Papa... mamma.... I'm going to say something in which maybe you both will not support me, but now I'm not going to back out and it's final for me at least"

"Why are you creating so much suspense? Kabir say it clearly whatsoever you want to say then only we could say something no" his mom said.

He closed his eyes first and after taking a deep breath he started.....

"I..... I love shrishti" Both of them looked at him with a serious expression and then smiled warmly.

"Then what is the need for this suspense Kabir, otherwise also I this already, your mom told me and if you are scared because of me that I'm against this then you are wrong, do I look like a mad man who will say no for such a nice girl" Kabir smiled sadly.

"This is not the matter papa, there is something big"

"Whatever it is tell me clearly"

"she don....n't have..." he was trying so bad but by now his eyes started pooling "she don't have time"

"What do you mean?" both of his parents asked in confusion.

"She is suffering from ASTROCYTOMA- the last stage of brain cancer" saying that a tear fell from his eyes which he didn't even bother to wipe off.

"What are you saying Kabir, how can this be possible" his mother asked in utmost shock.

"I'm telling the truth only mamma, I got to know about this yesterday only, that.... After sometime she won't be with me.... With us.... She won't be near us"

He was losing his control on himself and he again burst into tears.... Seeing their son crying miserably in front of them for the very first time. Both of his mom and dad were feeling their hearts clenched. His father stood up and hugged him tightly.... Kabir hugged him back like a small kid. To console him he was rubbing his back and finally he calmed down a little.

"Shh...... no, son don't cry like this, you can't lose hope like this, we'll try our level best"

"Now there is no option left papa, but yes there is something which I want to do for her"

"what?"

"There is this bucket list of her, and I want to help her completing her list, she had never shared about this to anyone but somehow I got to know, maybe god wanted me to help her and If I'm not even able to help her then what's the point in me claiming that I love her and finally.... I cried enough" he wiped his tears and took a deep breath "now It's time for me to smile for her to make her happy"

"I salute you kabir..... Nowadays no one has this kind of determination. If there would be someone else in place of you he must have run away leaving her..... But you didn't did anything like that and that's show how pure soul you are"

"I need you help dad"

"I'll do anything son...... just say it"

"Can you please handle the office for these few months"while asking, there was hope in his eyes as he was not at all ready to lose this time.

"Anything for you two, go and enjoy this precious time, make those memories which will stay with you forever" "thank you so much papa" he hugged him tightly. Apparently he was feeling weakest emotionally for the very first time in his life. After Kabir's dad left for office, he ran in his room and took out the diary of shrishti and pen down the 4 remaining things left from her bucket list.

He was reading those things seriously and thinking from where to start, after contemplating for quite a time, finally he decided on something. He determinedly closed the dairy and went to call someone.

On the other hand, Shrishti woke up late, and for a change she was looking a little better today, maybe she slept peacefully last night, she was stretching when monika entered the room with morning tea and breakfast for her.

"Here you go shrishti madam, finish your breakfast quickly"

"Diiii...." she pouted cutely

"Yesss...." monika imitated her, making her more annoyed than she was.

"I'm getting bored sitting here at home, should I go back to the office"

"Of course, now you have talked to kabir also then what's the problem in joining the office back" she said in a teasing way.

"There is nothing like that huh" she said looking the other side trying to hide her blush.

"I know everything and now there is of no use pretending all innocent in front of me, well even after all I'm not going to give you the permission to go out"

Shrishti again pouted but she knew there was no way to argue with her so she quietly had her breakfast. After that she took her medicine and tried to call Kabir but his phone was busy.

"Maybe he's very busy in the office" she sadly kept her phone aside and went into her room where she only used to paint.

Whole day passed but she didn't get any chance to talk to kabir. She was trying hard but some negative thoughts were coming in her mind..... like he left her..... why would he love a girl who is not there for more than 3 months.

"It's ok shrii.... What is in your heart no one can snatch it from you, have faith, he can't do anything which will hurt you" she closed her eyes and then opened frustratingly "then why he didn't talk to me since morning"

She became sad again after using all the ways to distract her mind. She went into her room and slept directly and Monika too went into her room.

Around 12 at night. A car stopped in front of shrishti's house and kabir stepped out from the car..... After locking the car carefully, he stretched a little and went under the balcony of shrishti's room.

"It's time to fulfill your first wish and here I am madam... but how the hell should I go up?" he pouted, scratching his chin and finding ways to jump in her gallery. But he was determined for what he came so he looked here and there to confirm if no one is noticing him.

"If anyone found you like this then boy be ready to get beaten up by the whole colony, but no worries, anything for my Don" he pep talked with himself and finally he started climbing the wall when he was in the middle it was getting difficult for him to climb fast as he was not professional after all.

"For god sake why on earth I'm climbing the wall like thieves, I could have pressed the doorbell and di must have made me enter the house without any problem, mom and aditya is correct I'm a serious idiot" he mumbled more like scolded himself moving a little upside. "But it's ok, it is also adventurous."

Finally with great difficulty he jumped on her balcony, trying to not make a loud sound. Luckily the door of the balcony was open so he easily entered her room and the moment he stepped in the sight in front of him was mesmerizing for him. The lights of the whole room were off and star shaped fairy lights were on which was elegantly decorated on all the walls. The dim light was enhancing the beauty of the room many times, when he noticed he adored the moon pasted on the ceiling with the many stars. It was giving the feel of an open sky. And finally when he looked at her he was in awe, she was sleeping peacefully hugging her teddy, he didn't have the heart to wake her up but to fulfill her wish he had to so he moved towards the bed and caressed her head softly.

"Shrii..... Wake up" she stirred a bit he thought she'd woke up but she turned to the other side "and here you go, madam is not even waking up, don't give up kabir try again" he mumbled under his breath. And again moved towards the other side of her bed. again caressed her head and she did the same thing again.

"Here I'm standing taking risk on my life and this madam is not even budging, now I'm left with only one option I have to snatch this teddy" he whispered to himself preparing himself mentally for waking up the don, ultimately he snatched her teddy which she was hugging with a jerk, she woke up in a shock, Because of darkness she was not able to see who was the person in her room. fearing her reaction kabir put his palm on her mouth but he regretted his decision, she bit his palm hard to make him take his hand back.

24

Kabir screamed in pain as shrishti bit very hard, to muffle the sound he put his free hand on his mouth.

"Shrriiii, yrr it's me.... Me Kabir.... Ahhh leave my hand girl"

"Kabirhhh...." she widened her eyes registering the fact that it was kabir only. Hurriedly she switched on the lights and took his hand in her's.

"I'm sorry kabir..... Is it hurting"

"No no I'm enjoying...... obviously it's hurting no, who bites like this yrr" He was rubbing his hand and shrishti placed a quick slap on his head.

"Now what"

"Now If you'll enter my room like thieves that to at this time then what do you expect me to do, otherwise also I'm angry with you and I don't wanna talk to you"

"Why angry, why angry?"

"I've been calling since morning and someone didn't even have time to answer my calls" she complained like a kid pouting at the end.

"May I know who is this someone" and here he earned a death glare from her "I know I know... its me"

"Would you like to explain"

"ya ya.... For how much marks..... 5,10 or 15"

"I'm serious kabir. And by the way what are you doing here on the top of it at this time" she asked, raising her eyebrows.

"About that, it is someone's wish to sneak out of the house after 12 at night..... so here I am helping someone" he said pretending innocent.

"and I know who this someone is" Kabir raised his eyebrows comically asking her "it mee"

"I know" he said smiling widely and here he earned a slap from her on his head "now this is what for"

"what I know...... are you mad..... First of all you decided to appear at this time on the top of it using the balcony, mr. if you get caught no you don't have any idea what people will do with you entering room of a girl like this"

"Very good, bravo..... I came here taking this big risk and now making a fool of myself by listening to the lecture" he pouted in disappointment, fake disappointment to be precise which worked on her. "Ok ok now no need to make this face"

"See it's already about 1 if you wanna come then come, otherwise I'm going"

"this time.... How..... if di woke up then"

"you wanna come or not..... I know it's your wish" she looked at him cutely "don't hold yourself back.... Come with me..... It'll be fun you'll surely enjoy" She was hesitant, But thinking about the least chances of doing this craziness again.... On the top of it with him she got up from her bed.

"Let's do it, this was one of my biggest fantasies" she said dreamily looking at the sky through her window.

"Let's go then"

Both of them looked down from the balcony to confirm if anyone was there, shrishti said she'll go first and surprisingly she climbed down within a minute, whereas our hero took good 6 minutes to climb down, when he finally came down he looked at her in amusement.

"Oye, How do you climb down this fastly, seems like someone is very experienced... by any chance do you this way for enter and exiting house on daily bases, oh wait how can I just forget it You are underworld don, you must have experienced this a lot"

"Hello Mr. stop your babbling...... it's just that I got rock climbing training in my school days"

"Ooooooo....."

"lets goooo..."

"Here is the car sit"

"Means what, you made me escape at this hour from the house to sit in the car?"

"Oh god!!..... are you seriously dumb shrishti..... we are going somewhere that's why I'm saying so.....now sit"

Getting excited she jumped inside the car and so did he. He started driving at a normal speed enjoying the calmness of the night. Both were silent to avoid getting bored. Shrishti turned on the radio. Some poetry was going on enjoying the poetry she leaned on the window closing her eyes.

"Yun to mujhe zaroorat hai nahi kisi ki, Tumhare sath hone se sukoon ki kya baat ho..... Rahon pe chal to leta hun main khud bhi magar, Rahein manzilon main badal jaye agar tum saath ho....."

Shrishti didn't notice but these lines were piercing Kabir's heart..... he was feeling each and every word. He averted his gaze at the road and a lone tear fell from his eye, he immediately wiped that off to get it unnoticed by shrishti. Soon the car halted on the famous Juhu beach.

"Don ji..... we are here so, wake up"

"I'm already up" she said with an annoyed expression

But noticing the surroundings she forgot that she was annoyed. Her face lit up with happiness which brought a smile on Kabir's face too. Whole beach was decorated beautifully with lights and there were many food stalls. It was a full moon night...... shrishti was amused seeing all this and she was looking everywhere dreamily. She felt a pat on her shoulder and she looked towards the kabir.

"hmm"

"Wanna sit"she nodded cutely "come" Both of them were moving towards the big stones to sit on, But stopped in their tracks seeing pav bhaji stall in between.

"Shrii, pav bhaji here is the best, come lets eat"

"This time..... I haven't even brushed my teeth"

"Damn you girls, eat just like that nothing will happen"

"As you say my lord" she bowed down dramatically in front of him. Getting excited, Kabir ordered pav bhaji for them coincidently the stall vendor served them in a single plate only. They also didn't say anything and started eating together. After their beautiful and peaceful eating pav bhaji session under the open sky they got up and moved towards the sea. They silently sat there for a few minutes adoring the beauty of the beach late at night.

"shrii"

"hmm...."

"How do you like it?" She looked at him with utmost calmness on her face.

"Do I really need to tell you...... how much I liked it.... You have no idea how peaceful I'm feeling right now. Just live in this moment and feel this cold breeze."

She rested her head on his shoulder authoritatively and hugged his arm and closed her eyes feeling the cold breeze. Seeing her happy he was feeling relieved and peaceful too. He was staring at the moon and didn't realize when he rested his head against her head. No one of them moved and eventually they fell asleep in that position only..... whole night passed like that only and around 5 in the morning Kabir opened his eyes and got confused first but then he realized that they slept there only. He realized she was still hugging his arm seeing that a small smile crept on his face and a lone tear fell from his eye.

"How can someone make everyone happy by suppressing the pain inside his heart, how you like so selflessly shrii, I really don't wanna think but how do I imagine myself without you.... I can't" he was thinking, closing his eyes, feeling the silence of the morning.

"Jo bas main hota mere Is waqt ko yahin rok leta main, Na khud uthke kahin jata, Nahi tumko kahin jane deta main....."

He mumbled looking at her still sleeping figure. He noticed the sun was about to rise so he slowly patted shrishti's shoulder to wake her up. she stirred a bit and then cutely opened her eyes unknown to the surroundings.Before she could say something kabir pointed towards the sky and looking at the sunrise her eyes lightened up with happiness..... After a few minutes of silence she spoke.

"Oh, I didn't even realized how I fell asleep and you didn't even woke me up" she pouted cutely yawning

"If I had woken you up then I would have missed this beautiful view also one more thing with that"

"Oh, well what would you have missed?"

"Leave it, it's not of your use anyway"

"You are telling me or not"

"Ok ok listen, i would have missed the chance to see the sleeping rabbit" he suppressed his smile while saying which was unnoticed by the innocent shrishti.

"Rabbit! Where is it" she said while looking here and there and then she realized to whom he was saying that "do you wish for getting a beating session right in the morning from me"

"Oh no no no" he said, raising his hands in surrender.

"oh my goddd" looking at her horrified expression suddenly he became serious. "What happened?"

"I was not at home the whole night, if di didn't find me in my room she'll create havoc in the whole damn society" the way she was panicing made him worried so he tried calming her down as he was well aware about the whole situation.

"Hey, hey calm down nothing will happen" she shot a question glare at him. "Actually I had informed di about this beforehand, even I took permission from her so that I can take you out at night"

"Now I understand, you too joined their team huh" she asked, squinting her eyes at him.

"I just took permission so that we both don't get all the scoldings together and here you are getting mad at me"

"I know kabir..... you are very sincere that's why you asked her in advance..... Now get up.... Let's go or you are planning to stay here only"

"sure"

Both were going back home but something came in shrishti's mind so she asked a little hesitatingly.

"Can I ask one thing"

"You can ask two, you know"

"I never got chance to visit, there is a very beautiful temple of lord radhakrishn and it's also time for morning prayer can we go there for a while please"

"Your wish is my command madam" he said with a sweet smile on his lips "thank you soooooooo......much.... I guarantee you'll also enjoy there" she said getting excited like a baby

Within 10 minutes they reached the temple as it was really near, the whole premises of temple was radiating calmness and peace, when they stepped in they found the morning prayer was just about to start and luckily both of them got opportunity to stand exactly in front of the idol of the radhakrishn. The curtains were still on and within no time with the sound of a conch shell the curtains opened and seeing the beauty of lord radhakrishn everyone was mesmerized.

Shri krishn was wearing a dress of plain fabric of yellow color and a simple turban decorated with fresh flowers and a beautiful peacock feather and radharani was wearing a simple lehenga choli of blue color and along with both were wearing the same type of white pearl jewelry.

Both kabir and shrishti were looking at them with tears in their eyes.... Soon prayer started and they joined their hands and closed their eyes, they started praying and in between kabir opened his eyes and looked at shrishti and a tear fell from his eye, he controlled himself and closed his eyes again to not let her find him being emotional that way. The moment he was back to the same praying position, Shrishti opened her eyes and looked at Kabir with tears filled eyes,

"I know you are in pain kabir and I'm feeling guilty for giving you the pain which you don't deserve even a bit" she thought controlling her tears but some stubborn ones fell from her eyes too, prayer was about to finish she quickly wiped her tears and resumed smiling like before.

25

When prayer was over, kabir and shrishti were about to leave but the priest stopped them. "Don't go without prasadam, this is a special one"he said, forwarding 2 bowls towards them. They smilingly too took those bowls and after joining their hands in front of radhakrishn they came out of the temple and sat on a bench in the premises of the temple only, they noticed in shrishti's bowl there was maakhan (butter) and in kabir's bowl there was kheer (sweet rice pudding)

"*I want maakhan*" he thought "*I want kheer*" she thought.

"Shrii" he tried to sound extra innocent so that she could not deny what he was going to ask. "Hmm" "can you exchange maakhan with me?" She smiled brightly at him, showing her perfect teeths. "Why this much happy huh"

"Actually I wanted to ask the same"

"Then do it" Before he could take the bowl from shrishti's hand she took some maakhan and ate that kabir looked at her with twisted eyebrows. "If you didn't want to give then why did you agree?" he said with puppy eyes.

"Ohh little kiddo, why are you crying like baby? It's maakhan only chill, otherwise also I was just tasting if this is sweet or not" before he could register her words she took some portion again in her hands and fed him. He was looking at her in amusement because this was unexpected for him, she smiled genuinely at him and before she could take a bowl of kheer from kabir's hand he did the same thing she did earlier. "hmmm...... its yummy" while eating he winked at her and eventually both burst into laughter. "Ok if you are satisfied then please give me now I too want to taste it na" Finally they exchanged their bowls and enjoyed their favorite Prasadm After finishing they left for shrishti's house.

When they reached home they found monika was already done with preparing breakfast and morning tea for them.

"finally you both remembered the way towards home"

"sorry di..... We....actually" kabir was about to explain the scenario but monika cut him in between.

"ok ok now I'm not asking for the details...... just sit and have your breakfast and tea"

While having food, Shrishti told her about their visit to the temple and all and they further talked about some random things.

"Ok di, now I'm leaving, and you shrishti madam take care of yourself ok" she nodded and smiled at his concern "and di as you both are alone earlier I didn't knew but now if there is any problem I'm just a call away......ok" Both the sisters looked at him with a warm smile.

"Don't worry kabir...... we are good and surely will tell you if there is any problem" he got up from his seat "wait, I forgot to tell you both something important" Both kabir and shrishti looked at her in excitement.

"When you were not here, papa called me, they are coming tomorrow.... so"

"Soooo...." shrishti exaggerated.

"So you both are going to talk to them about yourself"

"What? How, how we'll talk to them just like that" she panics slightly.

"I'll do" he said with utmost calmness on his face

"How"

"don't worry..... just relax" he said with complete determination In his eyes. He said calmly and left for his home.

After he went, Shrishti and monika both did little preparations for the comeback of their parents and then they decided to watch a movie

On the other hand after coming home kabir was thinking in different ways about how he will talk to shrishti's parents, for the first few hours he was totally confused and finally giving up he ran towards his mom who was working in the kitchen.

"Mammaaa......" hearing him whining like kids his mom came out of the kitchen. "What happened"

"Tomorrow shrishti's parents are coming back, and now I'm confused that how am I going to talk to them"

"Why are you getting confused, go and talk directly and otherwise also whatever you wanna do is for shrishti, their daughter why would they don't accept you and your suggestions"

"Hmm, well actually you are right, I'll try my best to make them understand" After talking to his mom he felt relieved and went to sleep with little calmness.

Next day around 11 in the morning Shrishti's parents reached home, four of them sat together to have tea and snacks. They were talking about some random stuff. Meanwhile shrishti was totally engrossed in the thoughts of kabir... how he'll manage the situation, what he will say and many more things.

Finally she came out her trails of thoughts listening to the voice of Kabir, she noticed him touching the feets of her mom and dad.

"Come son sit, monika go bring tea for kabir too"

Looking at Shrishti's nervous and confused face Kabir's confidence also started to fly away, but he composed himself and diverted his gaze towards her mom and dad. Soon monika was back with the tea and snacks for Kabir also. All of them started talking again but finally collecting all the confidence in him Kabir started to speak for what he was there.

"Uncle, aunty.... I wanted to talk to both of you about something very important." He tried to maintain his calmness to the extent it was possible for him and not to show his nervousness.

"Of course kabir, say what's the matter" her dad asked in complete obliviousness but as a matter of fact he already knew about what kabir was going to talk about. Kabir looked at shrishti with love and concern filled eyes and then again looked at her parents. He was struggling hard to begin the conversation about what he was there for. Seeing him struggling more, her dad finally spoke up.

"Kabir," he said calmly, making Kabir look at him "I know" listening to this kabir shot questioning glare at him "I know that you both love each other" Listening to both Kabir and shrishti was shocking like anything, Before they could say anything her dad continued.

"This is not important how do I know this, I really don't know how I should react..... I know that you know about shrishti's condition, if after knowing everything you both love each other, specially you kabir then I don't know what can be more pure than this, in today's world people leave each other on minor problems and here after knowing everything you are standing by her......" he was trying hard but as a father of a daughter his heart was already clenching for his daughter and the new found information was more overwhelming for him "I really don't have any idea how do I thank you kabir...." Before he could say more, Kabir rose up from his seat and hugged him.

"Thank you so much uncle, for understanding us.... I can't talk about others but yes, what is between both of us is not going to fade away in any situation, I can say this with complete surety that I don't care about anything and I'm with shrishti in everything..... Doesn't matter for how long" he tried to speak everything boldly but at the end his voice broke which was not unnoticed by any of them present there.

"I'm speechless.... I don't have words for you two" her dad said with tears in her eyes. All of them were listening to Kabir's and shrishti dad's conversation very calmly and patiently.

"Uncle I need your permission for something"

"Yes, say for what?"

"There is a bucket list of shrishti, which she never shared with anyone and I want her to complete that, only three wishes are left, please will you allow her to fulfill that"

"Is it shrii, why didn't you tell me about this" she hung her head low but her dad knew his daughter enough that he could guess her answer "no problem"

"Please uncle don't say no"

"I trust you kabir..... and you know this, how and why would I say no, and on the top of it when this is for the happiness of my princess then how can I ever say no"

"That means you are giving your permission right," Kabir asked with hope in his eyes. He didn't say anything for a complete one minute and all were looking at him with their whole concentration. Finally he nodded with a warm smile. Seeing that shrishti exclaimed like a little kid.

"yeahhhhhhhhhhh........ Thank you.... Thank you.... Thank you......sooooooo much papa" Seeing her this kiddo mode on all were looking at her in amusement with tears filled eyes, finally when she calmed down, she looked at all of them and she shook her head in disbelief.

"What happened to you all, why are you guys making this face hun.... I'm not going to leave you all so easily you know"

"Shut up shrii" everyone exclaimed together. She threw her arms in the air and ran in her room leaving all of them numb.

"I'm thanking you again uncle thank you so much, I'll start working from today only that how all the things will be set up I want her to live her wishes as soon as possible"

"Don't say thank you again and again son.... Come" he hugged him warmly "I know kabir it's tough for you... very tough..... but we have to do it together for her" he caressed his head to make him feel better.

"Ok then uncle I should leave, I need to prepare a lot"

Finally Kabir left from there and directly went to meet Aaditya, on the way he called him.

On call

Kabir: hellooooooo.....

Aaditya: yesssssssss......

Kabir: can't you speak slow

Aaditya: who started?

Kabir: Ok fine, now tell me can we meet now?

Aaditya: yes but where?

Kabir: In the cafe near your house, I'm on the way. You also come fast.

Aaditya: ok coming.

Kabir: ok ok...

Call cut

Soon both of them were sitting in the café

"So yes, say what do you wanna talk Mr." aaditya asked kabir while playing with his phone.

"As you already know about me and shrishti... and about shrishti's condition also"

"Of course, then"

"There is a bucket list of her... and I want to complete it with her, before she...lea..." his words choked in his throat. Aaditya keeps his palm on his shoulder to comfort him.

"I can understand kabir, now say what you want"

"See I'm alone so I need your help in some arrangements..... Will you do..?"

"Do you really need to ask me now for any help"

"I know you'll do...."

"Ok now enough of your drama, now tell me what I have to do"

"I need you to find an academy who can teach ballroom dance in least time"

"That's all, get the job done, I'll let you know max bye evening ok"

"Thanks bro"

26

After meeting aaditya kabir went home and started searching further about his plan..... whole day passed like this only finally around 9 in the night kabir got a call from aaditya.

On call:
Kabir: yes bro,
Aaditya: done.
Kabir: thank god.
Aaditya: thank me.... leave it.... I'm sending you the address and proper details etc. from tomorrow there will be classes. ok
Kabir: ok ok... thanks thanks
Aaditya: ok go and sleep now it's getting late.
Call cut

After talking to aaditya he called shrishti to tell her about their visit.

On call:
Shrishti: hellooo.....
Kabir: hii.... Someone is very happy.... Any specific reason....
Shrishti: Well there is nothing particular.... But I don't know why I'm very happy today.
Kabir: ok ok.... If you still don't have any reason.... Then don't worry I'm here to give you.

Shrishti: What do you mean?

Kabir: I'm taking you somewhere tomorrow.... Be ready by 11 in the morning.

Shrishti: where? Tell me

Kabir: nope....

Shrishti: please.....

Kabir: no no no.....

Shrishti: you know what, you are very bad huh

She cut the call, getting annoyed.

Here Kabir chuckled listening to her annoyed tone.

"She is unbelievable, wait wait, if she'll come tomorrow or not, let me text her also"

shrishti was making her bed when she received a message from Kabir saying "you are coming tomorrow right, please don't do this, I have worked very hard, well I know you will come, so be ready on time, bye good night" She shook her head in disbelief

"This boy is unbelievable, if a person is angry and you wanna make him more mad then do take notes form Mr. Kabir mehra, but anyhow, I liked it" She smiled at herself and went to sleep.

Next morning after many days, shrishti after getting completely ready, came out of her room. her face was glowing and she was looking happy wholeheartedly, seeing her all ready to go, her mom asked.

"Where to madam"

"That I also don't know mamma, at night kabir texted that he want to take me somewhere, where I really don't know, that's the reason I'm ready"

"It's good though, at least you'll go out of the house, now come and have your food otherwise I know all your dramas"

Shrishti happily sat for breakfast. around 10:15 shrishti listened to the sound of a horn.

"Shrii, kabir is here, now go"

Shrishti happily got up and picked her bag. She left the house, she was feeling very happy as was leaving home after a very long time. She happily climbed in the car and adjusted herself.

"so ready"

She nodded, getting excited and he started driving. First few minutes, Shrishti was sitting quietly holding her curiosity. but finally she bursted

"kabirhhhhh......"

"What on earth happened girl" he said holding his heart "I nearly got a heart attack"

"Now tell me no, where are we going?" she whined but failed to convince him.

"You'll get to know, patience is the key you know" he said holding back his smile.

"If you'll tell me then your height will reduce or something?"

"If not then will your weight be reduced or something?" he asked the same way as her making her all worked up, She twisted her nose left right and started looking out.

"You are very bad"

"You are very good"

"You know what....? You are impossible..... huh..."

"Thank you..... but now leave this grumpy face of yours and see we are already at our destination"

She annoyingly looked out and was awestruck seeing the place where they were.

"Kabir this is—"

"I know come" he smiled. Both of them were looking at her building with a wide smile, shrishti looked at him and he also looked at her smiling warmly.

"As it is your wish then how It'll not be fulfilled, now look.... There will be a personal tutor for us and he/she will teach us only and you know what" she raised her eyebrows cutely "they'll teach us ballroom dance in just 10 days with choreography on a song choose bye us"

"you know what......?"

"what......?"

"You are the best."

"I know..."

"Really"

"Oh yes, because you are bestest and bestest like best only right?" he said, raising his collars.

"What logic.... Kabir, impressive"

"Now let's go in or we are going to stand here only" She nodded and both of them happily entered the building. shrishti was very happy with the anticipation of learning ballroom dance. They entered a hall which was looking like a rehearsal hall. Both were observing the surroundings and finally a girl and a boy around the same age of kabir and shrishti entered the hall.

"Hello..... welcome to our academy. I hope you both will enjoy the learning process here.... Myself rajat" he introduced himself smilingly.

"hi I'm roshni.... We both will teach you guys the ballroom dance" Both kabir and shrishti introduced themselves also and four of them shook hands to start the practice.

They began teaching kabir and shrishti with the very basic steps. Both of them were really enjoying learning the new dance form, 4 of them were working hard, 2 were teaching and 2 were learning. They were taking proper rest intervals because of shrishti's health.... So that she doesn't get exhausted.... Like this their first day finished and Kabir and shrishti were heading back towards shrishti's house.

"Seriously, we enjoyed a lot today right, I never thought this would be so much fun," shrishti said while enjoying the cold breeze coming from the opened window.

"Sometimes reality is more beautiful than imagination, that's why we should not keep lots of expectations"

"Yes, expecting from life that life will correct everything is the biggest misunderstanding of humans" she said unconsciously zoning out. Hearing this from her..... Kabir froze for a moment.

"It's you saying this shrii, the one who taught me to have faith in life" he thought and suddenly stopped the car at a roadside and held her hand softly, feeling his hand on hers as she looked at him.

"What happened? Why did you stop the car"

"Why did you say that?"

"what?"

"You know what I'm asking......"

"Then what do I say.... I'm tired, tired from keeping myself positive, I'm tired being strong all the time kabir, now It's difficult for me to do the same, I don't know what do I do how should I make myself understand" By now tears were threatening to slip out of her eyes "when I know.... Know that.... I.. I'm about to.... Di...." Before she could say anything further Kabir covered her mouth with his palm.

"Please..... Please.....don't say this" his lips were trembling as he was controlling his emotions very hard "you are my strong girl shrii.... You can't lose yourself like this...... Don't forget I'm here for you..... Say anything to me, anything you want.... But just please don't be weak like this." he said cupping her face.

She couldn't hold it back as she was breaking every moment. She hugged him tightly but didn't say anything. He was controlling himself with great difficulty as he can't become weak in front of her as his first priority was to handle her and to console her.

Finally after almost 5 minutes she parted away and wiped her tears..... And said something which left Kabir speechless and proud at the same moment..

"Now enough, I cried enough, no more, whatever life is giving I'll accept that with whole heart, now no more crying you also no crying hmm" she said cupping his face. He smiled with glistening eyes.... And nodded, wiping her tears too.

"yes..... Now no more crying..... Now we'll live our time to its fullest.... Hmm."

"Hmmm." He started driving again but she interrupted him.

"Wait wait"

"What happened, Anything serious."

"Let's eat that"

"what"

"That, see there na"

"Gol gappe" she nodded, smiling widely with her glittery eyes.

"NO"

"what no....?"

"I'm not gonna allow you to eat this....."

"But why.....?" she asked like that disheartened kid from whom his favorite candy is suddenly snatched.

"Because it's clearly mentioned in your diet plan that you are not allowed to eat street food"

"Who told you....?"

"Monika di.... Who else"

"But I wanna eat it.... Please na.... Just 1 plate.... Please" she whined like a baby and tried literally hard to convince him.

"No shrishti.... I'm not gonna allow this...." she made puppy eyes ``now this will also not work.... Try to understand yrrr..... I can't take risks with you."

"You also joined that.... Let's annoy the shrishti gang right?" she said with a grumpy pout.

"Now say what you want.... But I'm not allowing this"

"please na." she said on the verge of crying.

"No.... Means no." He started driving determined on his decision. But shrishti was totally pissed by now.

"You are very bad, no not only you but everyone, everyone is just lecturing me.... Who am I a kid..... I'm not gonna talk to you" she pouted angrily and started looking out of the window.

"shrishti yrrr..... try to understand"

"Nope"

Kabir didn't say anything for the time being as he knew she'll not understand, finally they reached shrishti's home, before she could climb down the car he held her wrist.

"Now what?"

"Are you angry with me?"

"No"

"You are"

"I said no"

"Then why are you not talking to me"

"Because I don't want to, now please let me go"

He left her wrist and gave her a heartwarming smile. But in response she made an angry pout and left the car.

"Oh god, my don is angry now what do I do? " Thinking about something he left for his own house.

After entering home shrishti was roaming here and there with a grumpy face then monika came to ask her.

"What happened shrii, why this long face"

"Congratulations"

"For what...?"

"That, Mr. Kabir, he also joined your and mom's team"

"What are you saying, say it clearly"

"I wanted to eat gol gappe and he didn't let me"

"So this act of his shows how much he loves you"

"I don't wanna talk to anyone" She ran into her room and slept immediately hugging her teddy.

Next morning around 9 shrishti felt some chaotic sounds coming from the living room but she didn't bother to get up and see, she again closed her eyes and hid her face under her teddy. After another 5 minutes she felt someone was in her room and even playing guitar. She lazily got up to see and was shocked to find Kabir sitting on the couch with her guitar, he was playing some random soothing tune.

"you"

"Good morning" he smiled in amusement looking at the shock evident on her face.

"Good morning, but what are you doing here.... At this time."

"You forgot we have practice to go for"

"Yes but that is at 11 no"

"I know...."

"then"

"Then just go and brush your teeth..... I have something for you"

"what?"

"can't you do a single thing without bombarding 1000 questions" She lazily got up from her bed and dragged herself towards the bathroom. she was out after 10 minutes, all freshen up. The moment she came out her eyes widened with shock.

"Now what is this?"

"You forgot this early, yesterday only you were whining for this like small kids"

"But someone was saying no for it" she folded her arms in front of her chest in an interrogative manner.

"Because that was not hygienic...."

"And this is....."

"Definitely, it's homemade I requested mamma to make this and rest is in front of you"

"You are impossible..... First you never agreed and then troubled aunty too, great"

"Oh hello madam, I have also helped her equally don't say like this"

"Really"

"Of course, ok now c'mon eat it or you are still angry with me"

"I'm not angry..... I know that you are concerned for my health, that's why you did not allow me"

"Means I'm forgiven."

"You are idiot"

She dragged him towards the couch and both of them enjoyed gol gappe together. Soon after the eating session they left for their practice.

27

Their days of practice passed with the blink of an eye, both of them enjoyed a lot and surprisingly they learned the dance form very efficiently.

"You both are very good dancers.... Do you guys even know this?" Rajat praised them, making both kabir and shrishti smile widely.

"He is right.... No one can learn this form precisely within just 10 days..... we as a trainer feel very proud after teaching you both" roshni joined too.

"Thank you so much, well it means a lot that professionals like you both are praising us" kabir spoke feeling happy with all the praise. "Really thank you so much," shrishti said.

After completing final formalities both of them came out of the building..... Soon kabir dropped shrishti at her home and he went to make some arrangements with aaditya.

"Bro, can we arrange a vacant hall for some time" Kabir asked while starting the engine of the car.

"What you have to do in a hall man"

Kabir told him his whole plan and aaditya looked amused after listening to him.

"See I can arrange a hall but..."

"but what"

"Are you sure..."

"I'm damn sure bro…. I know she will love it"

"As you wish my lord," he said dramatically and both of them burst into laughter.

After making all the arrangements kabir came back to his home, nowadays kabir was looking happy in front of all but something was breaking inside him bit by bit, he was trying hard to not show any emotion in front of anyone but as it is said you can hide anything from anyone in the world but not from your mother. His mom was noticing his every action. She tried to ask him many times but he ignored the conversation making lame excuses.

After dinner he went into his room and laid straight on his bed. Finding him sad, Chiku jumped on him and he hugged her instantly.

"Chiku, everything will be alright no" She looked at him with cute puppy eyes. She didn't understand what he was saying but she knew he was sad so she started licking his face and rolling all over him.

"Ok ok fine, I know you don't like me being sad" She barked cutely at him and then ran towards her cute little bed as she was sleepy. Kabir thought of talking to shrishti as he had to tell her about the next plan, he picked his phone and directly called her.

On call

Shrishti: hello….

Kabir: hi….. all good…

Shrishti: yes yes….

Kabir: I wanted to ask….. umm…. No no tell you something….

Shrishti: and what is it……

Kabir: I want to take you somewhere tomorrow…. Will you come?

Shrishti: Obviously I'll come…. Happy.

Kabir: very happy.

Shrishti: ok then goodnight go to sleep it gets late.

Kabir: shrii.... You are ok no, any problem or anything.

Shrishti: nothing.... I'm all ok..... why are you asking

Kabir:Actually you agreed for the first time without any interrogation so that's why I asked.

"Means wow, don't let me have peace anyhow, if I ask a question then you have a problem if not then also, and when I already know you are not going to tell me then why do I waste my energy."

Kabir: smart......!!

Shrishti: very smart

Kabir: ok then, if you are doing this much then do one more thing.

Shrishti: what?

Kabir: I'll send you a dress please wear that "she didn't answer for a minute) it's ok if you don't want to.

Shrishti: no no.... I'll love to wear.... Now I'm curious what you are cooking.

Kabir: you'll get to know, tomorrow now sleep... good night.

She happily went to sleep wondering what Kabir was planning. Kabir also slept thinking about his plan.

Next day Kabir didn't call her even for once but she didn't mind. she was waiting impatiently for the dress sent by him.... Whole day passed and around 5 in the evening a parcel came for shrishti.....with a note saying

"get ready and car will be there in a hour"

She happily went to get ready and when she finally looked herself all ready in the mirror she was mesmerized by herself while she was fixing her final look monika entered in her room.

"Someone is looking very beautiful."

"Really"

"Really, kabir will go mad after seeing you" She playfully slapped her shoulder. Both of them burst into laughter, within 5 minutes they heard the sound of a horn.

"Now leave..... and enjoy" She smiled widely and left towards the main door after hugging her mom.

There was a car at her main door. Shrishti was wondering where is kabir. while she was thinking she got a call from kabir itself.

On call

Kabir: car is there....?

Shrishti: yes.

Kabir: Then hop In what are you waiting for..... I'm waiting.

Shrishti: ok ok... well someone is very impatient.

Kabir: I truly am.

At this shrishti chuckled and cut the call.

Soon, shrishti reached a familiar place. But she was curious to meet Kabir but he was nowhere to be seen. She pouted cutely looking here and there and again her phone rang.

On call:

Shrishti: Kabir man, how much drama do you want now where are you?

Kabir: calm down Miss. Don, have a little patience.

Shrishti: I don't have patience or anything (he chuckled) I'm serious kabir....

Kabir: ok ok..... follow the directions you'll find me soon.

Shrishti: I know your soon very well which never comes....

Kabir: trust me this will come.... Just breathe in, breathe out.

She huffed and cut the call and started following the directions made for her.... Soon she was standing in front of a door. On which push was written. Without wasting a second she pushed the door and entered and again there was some mystery. Whole room was dark.... Nothing was visible.... She was about to burst but she became awestruck when a spot light fell in the exact center of the room or hall we can say.

And finally there was Kabir standing with his million dollar smile on his face..... he was looking as handsome as she was looking beautiful. Both of them were looking at each other without blinking and even without uttering a single word. Alas breaking the trance, Kabir started walking towards her, when he was finally standing in front of her without uttering a word. His eyes were saying a thousand things, he extended his hand out and looked directly in her eyes. she understood in a second what he wanted. Smiling widely she placed her palm in his.

He led her back where he was standing earlier, both of them stood there at the beginning position of their dance. Both were looking into each other's eyes when the beautiful mashup of her favorite songs started playing in the background.

She looked at him wide eyed as all the songs used in the mashup were her most favorite ones, she had not a single percent idea how he managed to get to know all of them. They started dancing to the music, she was swaying to the rhythm of the music effortlessly with his lead, she tried to focus on her surroundings but the impact of the songs and him dancing with her that way was so much that she couldn't decide if it was reality or a magical dream. After not knowing how long the music came to the end and for the finishing touch he twirled her multiple times and they took final position, he kept his hand around her waist in a very secure way and she also held him in a warm hug and placed her head on his shoulder.

They stood there in the same position for a long time until Kabir felt her little sobs..... he cupped her face out of concern.... And she looked at him with tears filled eyes.

"Hey shrii.... What happened" she shook her head "then are your eyes leaking? Just tell me what happened"

"How can you love someone like me this much?" she asked in a cracking voice.

"What do you mean by someone like you?" he asked, showing fake anger "Don't you dare say something like this again, how can you say this about my don....huh....."

She didn't say anything more and hugged him tightly, hiding her face in the crook of his neck. He hugged her back and they stood there like that for somewhat like eternity saving the moment for forever.

Still holding her he asked in a soft voice. "Miss. Don are you planning to leave me anytime soon" he asked mischievously and earned a slap from her on his shoulder. "You know you should start giving classes about how to waste someone's good mood, leave it I don't wanna talk to you,huh"

"You seriously won't talk to me" he asked to rile her up a little more.

"no..."

"Really?"

"No means no"

"But you are talking no

"Youuu" by now she was completely pissed to provoke her more, he ran from there and she started chasing him lifting her dress a little..... he ran out of the hall but she never gave up.... Finally their tom and jerry chase came to an end when kabir stopped at a very beautiful place.

"Now where will you escape huh?"

Before she could say more her gaze fell on the place which was decorated very elegantly And then she again looked at Kabir who was standing there folding his hands with a mischievous grin on his face.

"Can't you do anything straight?"

"Who am I, kabir..... How can I do anything straight" he said, raising both of his eyebrows playfully.

"So tell me SIR! What do you want"

"Now what I want is to sit here peacefully and have dinner with you," he said, making her sit on one of the chairs.

After her he too took his seat and both of them were adoring. Shrishti was adoring the place which was decorated so beautifully and here Kabir was adoring his don. After sometime their food came and shrishti was amazed seeing that each and everything was of her choice.

"So much hard work.... impressive"

"Anything for you.... Now eat"

Both of them started eating happily and after their beautiful somewhat like date they left for shrishti's home. Meanwhile in the car, Shrishti was completely silent. She was overwhelmed by the love Kabir was showering on her. She was feeling like the most loved person in the entire world. Thinking all these tears automatically dwelled in her eyes.

"shrishit"

"Hmm..."she simply hummed, controlling her sobs.

"Was there glue in your food?" She gave him a very confused look.

"What are you saying?"

"Then why are you so silent"

"Just like that, nothing specific" she paused making him look at her "to be very honest kabir...... I have never felt this much loved before.... I was truly overwhelmed today..... Seriously, I can't even describe what I'm feeling right now..... And Today I don't want to spoil your efforts by saying thank you, because thank you is very small in front of whatever you are doing, I'm just" she was going on and on to stop her emotional express he exclaimed comically.

"Ok enough, enough... this much praise, I can't digest bro" she glared at him annoyingly "Ok listen.... There is no need to thank me yrr..... I did what I did for my shri, my don, my rabb..." shrishti exclaimed before he could say further.

"Don't you dare, I repeat don't you dare..."

"What.....?" he asked smirking "do you want me to not call you rabbit" he asked innocently "ok if you don't want me to call you rabbit then I won't call you a rabbit but what's the problem in calling a rabbit a rabbit" he stopped looking at her deadly glare.

"You already said rabbit 5 times... huh.... You are very mean, I'll not talk to you" she looked out angrily.

"you will, I know"

"In your dreams"

"Mam you house is here, please have some mercy and get down" he playfully said.

"Bye..." she said, annoyed yet softly which made him chuckle. After she went inside her house, his bright smile faded away like it was never there on his face, Pain took place in his eyes, controlling himself he drove off for his home.

Around 10 he reached home and found the lights of the house were off..... so he thought his parents must have slept already, taking slow steps as he walked towards his room. He changed into comfy clothes and laid down on his bed on his back, staring straight at the ceiling, a lone tear fell from his eyes he didn't even bother to wipe that off. He was staring at the ceiling only when he heard the opening of his room's door, he looked and found his mom was coming towards him only. She silently sat beside him as he was laying in the center of the bed. For a few minutes there was silence but his mom abruptly started speaking.

"kabir"

"Hmm"

"You're fine right?" she asked very softly, caressing his head.

"Hmmm...."

"Really"

"Hmm.... I'm fine mamma" he said in a very low voice.

"No... you are not" listening to this he looked at her while still laying. "A child is not needed to tell his mom if he's fine or not, now tell me, anything you want.... Take it out kabir whatever is in your heart" she again caressed his head.

This was the last nail in the coffin he lost his control on himself, he placed his head in her lap and cried his heart out hugging her like a small kid, she was continuously rubbing his back to make him feel a little calm but he was not in his self control, he cried and cried only forgetting everything. seeing her son like that she was also getting emotional but she controlled herself for her son.

"Mamma.... She is going, going away from me, everyday, every hour, every minute.... I don't want to cry but I'm helpless, I don't know how to control myself, I don't know how to fix everything."

"I know son, it is way harder to do than saying, but now when you have taken this huge step then you have to handle yourself and yes don't think like she's going away, she is not going anywhere, she'll live here in your heart forever....

hmm"

She wiped his tears and caressed his head to make him feel relaxed. He was tired so he didn't even realize when he fell into a deep slumber keeping his head in his mom's lap.

28

Next morning he woke up and was strong as before. He got ready and after having breakfast around 11 AM he left for shrishti's home to talk to her about next things.

On the other hand, shrishti was alone at home. She was feeling bored so she decided to go and paint to keep herself busy and also she felt relaxed while doing so. She went into the room where she used to paint. While she was busy painting with music, suddenly she heard the main door bell ringing, her both hands were filled with colors and she didn't want to go, hence she whined annoyed by the sudden appearance of someone at her doorstep.

"God, can't I have my me time... now don't know who is here to disturb me" She grumpily went out and walked towards the main door and what she found there was enough for making her all grumpiness fly away. Kabir was standing there with the brightest smile ever..... even today someone also came with him...... it was chiku.... Looking at shrishti she started wiggling to free herself so she could jump on her. Seeing Kabir there she immediately hid her hands behind her.

"You here, at this time"

"Yes mee.... Well what makes you take so long to open the door..... and what are you hiding behind"

"Nothing nothing" she said nervously while shaking her head vigorously.

"It means there Is definitely something…. Show me no…. otherwise you know I have my own ways" he said smirking.

"Ok fine" She took out her hands from behind and showed him like kids show their hands. He looked at her all amused.

"what were you even doing…?"

"Umm….. actually I was painting"

"You paint?" he asked, totally shocked with the new found information.

"Why are you getting this shock? First come inside" he came inside and kept chiku down so she could play.

"Then miss. Painter….. Can you show what you were painting?"

"A big noooo"

"But why…..?" he asked with fake hurt expressions.

"Because I'm not pro like you…. You'll make fun of me."

"I'll not…. Now please don't test my patience and show me, I want to see"

"You are way more than stubborn, come with me I'll show you. but dare you laugh at me" he nodded genuinely and excitedly at the same time.

She took him towards the room…. The moment he stepped in the room he was shocked to the core. The whole room was decorated with the different artworks made by her. He was speechless for almost a minute and here shrishti was confused why he was silent.

"Hey, are these that bad that you became speechless"

"Sometimes I really feel you are mad. How can you even say such masterpieces are bad….. it's just beautiful"

"Are you serious"

"I'm damn serious….. but hurt also"

"Why so?"

"You know na how crazy I am for painting and you didn't even tell me that you too paint on the top of it with this perfection."

"I thought It's just normal. Nothing special to tell you." while she was telling him, he was checking all the paintings. Suddenly his gaze fell on a portrait which was totally covered.

"What's in that cover"

"No, That's a secret, Please if you'll not see one then what will happen"

"Ok madam, chill"

Listening to their talks, Chiku too came into that room. and started jumping on her place so that one of them could pick her up, finally shrishti picked her and caressed her softly.

"Is there anything specific for which you are here"

"Actually yes"

"Come then, let's sit in the living room..... I'm going to make tea also" hearing about tea his face lights up, Like a kid is going to have its favorite chocolate. Soon both of them were sitting in the living room with tea and snacks.

"So yes what were you saying"

"That I'll tell you, but tell me why are you all alone"

"Dad and Di are at work and mamma has to visit some relative so that's why"

"Oh.... ok listen, let's talk clearly.... There are 4 things in your bucket list, 2 are already done and 2 left, so now we have to plan for them..... because you know those are big ones"

"Hmm...." she hummed zoning out but he didn't let her dive in her thoughts very deep.

"Earth to madam"

"You know what, I have went to vrindavan before also, but why this in my bucket list"

"why?"

"Because I find peace there, I feel the actual love and affection there, because I feel being alive there in true sense"

"True…. I completely agree."

"And the last wish…. Which is going to kedarnath…. That is because I love nature and the way bholenath has protected nature's true beauty there is immense." looking at the dreamy expressions on her face he smiled feeling content.

"Get ready madam…… we are going there very very soon"

"Mamma papa"

"They don't have any problem. they had already accepted us….. and even gave permission for fulfilling all your wishes"

"hmm"

"Then why are you thinking so much…… just chill yrr… and even if you want I'll talk to them again about it….. now happy"

"Very happy" She smiled showing her teeth like kids and he shook his head at her childish behavior.

Whole day both of them played like kids….. both of them were very happy with each other. They were busy playing ludo when Shrishti's mom and monika entered and both of them burst into laughter looking at them and the reason was that they were fighting about who cheated in the game.

"Ok enough guys" monika exclaimed while still laughing at the poor kiddos. And then they realized someone else was also there.

"When you came back?" shrishti asked.

"When you were busy fighting like kids" She looked here and there to hide her embarrassed face.

"Why are you feeling embarrassed? It happens" he said comically and here he earned a slap from her on his shoulder.

"Dare you speak, first of all you cheated and then blaming me"

"OH hello madam.... You are the one who cheated" he shrugged his shoulders carelessly. And here goes World war 3

"Ok enough guys," giving up, the kiddos looked at them and finally four of them burst into laughter..... while their laughing session was going on shrishti's dad also came back from his work.

"What's going on, did I miss something?" Shrishti's mom told him also and he also laughed at their kiddish behavior..... Finally, after calming down they sat for tea and snacks as it was already past 5 in the evening.

"Uncle aunty, as you both know we are completing the bucket list of shrii, so from 4 things only 2 are left and for that we need permission"

"Well, what are those things?" her mom asked curiously.

"vrindavan aur kedarnath visit"

"But how both the places are far away from Mumbai, how will you both manage, what if something happ-" her dad cut in the middle and spoke.

"They are going, and very soon" everyone looked at him shocked "I trust kabir and only kabir with my shrii and if he's with her then there won't be any problem" he stated with the finality in his voice making kabir and shrishti both the happiest. Shrishti hugged his dad as she was sitting beside him only.

"Thank you so much papa"

"Anything for my doll"

Soon after spending a very good time with all of them, Kabir left for his home as he had to do lots of preparations for their trip. shrishti was really very happy and keeping all the sorrows aside she was dancing like a kid in her room with shinchan theme song on. Her family was also very happy seeing her happy and all good.

After coming home kabir also happily ate his dinner with his mom dad and then left for his room to do proper research about the places they were about to go. He was doing this almost the whole night, around 4 in the morning he was done with the research and he had decided many things also, in excitement he was about to call shrishti but realizing the time he slapped his head. "Idiot kabir, if you are a night owl that doesn't mean everyone is" He kept his phone aside he lay down straight on his bed..... but he was not at all feeling sleepy..... again to pass the time he picked his phone and opened insta and started scrolling. Suddenly he noticed Shrishti's story which was just 3 minutes ago.

"3 minutes ago..... that means she is also awake.... Should I text" He sent her a message and started waiting impatiently. she replied instantly and there started their chating session which continued till 5 in the morning in which they discussed every possible thing regarding their trip and finally feeling sleepy they halted their discussion and both the night owls went to sleep.

29

Next morning around 11 shrishti woke up and found her mom and monika busy in the kitchen, yawning and stretching until she reached there.

"Woah di, at home today how"

"Yo bro..... today is my day off."

"That's great..."

"and may I know how it's great"

"Last night kabir told me that we should leave tomorrow because of kedarnath schedule of closing"

"Ohh....." he mom nodded seriously and suddenly the same seriousness was on monika's face too.

"What happened, why so serious suddenly"

"Miss. shrishti, either you are crazy or you are thinking us to be one"

"Please have some mercy and don't confuse me"

"You dumbo, we are saying if you have to leave tomorrow then when are you planning to pack the day after tomorrow or something" her mom exclaimed making her realize the cruciality of the situation. And here she freaks out like anything.

"OH NO OH NO OH NO NO NO NO....... I didn't think about it, how can I be this idiot, but huff at least I have one day, I'll manage don't worry." she said proudly raising her fake collars.

Whole day she was busy deciding what to keep with her and what not, but not a single thing was kept in her bag by the end of the day.

Time was around 10 PM and she was hell confused..... here her mom and monika were busy making some quick food items for her to take with her while traveling. Alas she thought to put whatever comes in her mind first. While she was busy packing, someone jumped on her balcony without making any sound. It was not that difficult to recognize that it was Kabir. Before he could enter her room a very melodious voice fell in his ears....

And the voice was none other than shrishti..... She was happily singing her favorite song, not realizing that there was an invader in her room who was silently enjoying her singing. He was awestruck listening to her singing.... And she was totally unaware that someone was watching her..... here Kabir was engrossed in listening to her song that he didn't realize but accidently he pushed a little flower pot and it fell down. Hearing the sound of breaking something shrishti was just about to turn but at the same time lights went off.

"Who's there?" she asked a little sternly but no reply.

He was afraid that if he'd say anything she'd beat him. She was moving towards him in the dark while she grabbed a big pillow to hit him. When she reached near him unaware about her next move he placed his palm on her mouth so she couldn't shout, but regretted it the very next second, she bit his hand so hard, a painful whimper left his mouth and without giving any chance she started beating him with the pillow she was holding.

"How dare you enter my house, today I'll teach you such a lesson you'll think 10 times before entering your own house.... You bloody thief" During her beating session she awarded him with two punches and two kicks also. While she was busy showing her power, suddenly light came back and looked at the person on whom she was showing her power. Her mouth hung open in perfect O.

"Shit...... kabir!"

Without saying anything he sat on the place he was standing crossing his legs and resting his chin on his palm.

"I'm sorryyyy........ I thought it's thief" he was completely silent not even blinking "now say something, are you going to speak or not"

"Why should I speak, what will even happen if I speak, when You let me speak even"

"Sorry, I got scared, I thought It's someone else."

"You could have at least checked whom you are beating mercilessly, poor me.... I have never even got beaten by my mom this much" he complained like a kid pouting sadly at the end.

"Does it hurt?"

"Obviously" he said on the verge of crying and here he earned a slap from her on his head "now what?.... Are you still not satisfied with this beating session"

"Enough of your drama ok, I know you very well"

"Look at you, you are saying I'm doing drama huh, well tell me one thing why are you always into this violence and all huh" even before she could react he continued "oh how can I forget you are Don no"

"OH hello mr. first of all it was all your mistake, who told you to jump into my balcony like hero, and if you'll come like this then you have to be prepared for the consequences"

"Is it, I came here to surprise you and here I am sitting all blue and black" Both of them became silent for a minute and then burst into laughter.

"You are a complete idiot, wait let me bring ointment for you" She came back and applied that pain relief spray where she punched him. While applying the ointment, Shrishti asked him.

"Well why did you jump on my balcony, when the door facility is also available in my house" seeing the sarcasm in her voice he squinted his eyes comically at her.

"Hello madam, I don't have any experience in jumping on people's balconies. I just came to check if Miss. don only knows how to fight of she knows packing as well"

"I think there is still a need for some punches and kicks"

"Cool cool, why are they becoming so violent nowadays"

"My choice...." He stared at her in amusement, before getting up from his sitting position. "Okay now I'm going tomorrow around 11 or maybe 12 we'll leave ok" She nodded her head in excitement he smiled at her and went back using the way he came. Shrishti shook her head at her stupidity and after finishing her leftover packing she also went to sleep all excited.

Next morning Kabir woke up happily and after getting ready he went to have breakfast with his parents before leaving.

"I hope all the preparations are done and if there is any kind of problem directly contact me ok" his dad being a typical indian dad told him.

"No, no papa..... Everything is done now I just hope the trip goes smoothly"

"It'll be best, be positive" his mom encouraged him while filling a glass of juice for him. He smiled at her mom and the three of them had their breakfast while talking on some random topics.

Finally it was time to leave, "ok then I should leave hmm, take care both of you ok" they nodded at his protectiveness as he was not saying but ordering them to take good care of his parents. "Will meet soon," he said, hugging both of them.

"You also take care of yourself and shrishti hmm" his dad also said in the same tone like him making him smile shaking his head. "Of course papa"

On the other hand, Shrishti was hell excited; she was all set to go. All of them were sitting in the garden. Her family members were making fun of her that she was sitting all ready but still Kabir didn't reach. She pouted cutely and was about to go inside at the same time she heard the sound of horn and she was again as excited as earlier. Kabir came and after greeting everyone he kept her luggage in the trunk of the car.

"Take care both of you" shrishti's mom said, Both of them nodded together and smiled widely.

"Kabir there is no need to listen to her any odd demands, ok you can do whatever you think is good for madam hmm" monika told him like a good elder sister at which shrishti huffed in annoyance.

"Ya ya, he'll do exactly what you are saying di, after all he's your teammate right?"

"Hey, monika, don't annoy my princess, nothing will happen like that shrii don't worry" She smiled and hugged him. "You are best papa"

All of them laughed at the father daughter duo.... Finally after taking all the instructions both of them climbed in the car and taking god's name they started their journey.

"Finallyyyyyyyyyy......." she squealed like a baby making him chuckle at her behavior.

"Someone is already excited"

"I'll lie if I deny this..... I am excited and happy too.... Are you happy"

"Of course I am"

The car was moving at a great speed and soon they were on the highway, a cool breeze entering from the window was brushing on their faces.... The weather was also appropriate for traveling and if there are Indians who are traveling food can't be neglected. As kabir was busy driving, shrishti took out a big box from their food bag and there were sandwiches in the box... the aroma of sandwiches filled the car.

"You are already hungry?"

"What's new in this.... While traveling everyone used to feel hungry no,"

"Yes of course if you are an Indian" Both of them chuckled at the fact.

Journey was going really very well. Both of them talked a lot about almost everything, for both of them this was their golden time together. They stopped at many places and took little breaks and now it was almost the time of sunset..... by now shrishti was all energetic but he didn't realize when she slept he also didn't disturbed her. Soon when they were almost 20 minutes away from their resort Kabir thought to wake her up.... He called her name but she didn't budge.

"shrishti...... wake up" he said while focusing on the road.

No response!!

"shriiii..... Wakey wakey..... We are about to reach the resort"

Again No response!!

"Shrishti...." this time he shook her shoulder a little.

But No response!!

And this time he got a little doubtful, he stopped the car and opened his seat belt and Turned towards her and shook her again.

"Shrishti..... are you ok?"

She was not responding and slowly fear was rising in his heart, he called her many times but she was not responding at all. By now he was controlling himself but unknowingly tears started forming in the back of his eyes. He opened her seat belt and started rubbing her palms with moist eyes. Again he called her name this time more loudly than before and in response she opened her eyes with a jerk. The view she saw after opening her eyes was piercing her heart.... She found Kabir in a completely devastated state.

The moment he saw her opening her eyes tears fell from his eyes uncontrollably, before she could ask anything he engulfed her in a tight hug. She was completely unaware about what was happening but she also hugged him back giving him the comfort which was much needed by him at that time.

30

She could feel him sobbing holding her tightly in his embrace but she was still clueless as to what made him suddenly cry like that. She tried to part away but he never let her go. Taking a deep breath she rubbed his back a little to calm him down and asked in a soft voice.

"what happened.... Why are you crying Kabir...... are you fine"

"You just almost took my life a few minutes back" She gave him a confused look.

"At least tell me what happened?"

"You were not waking up. I was trying to wake you up but you know you are very stubborn.....you finally opened your eyes making me cry..... for a moment my heartbeat stopped you know" he said all while complaining like a kid and at the end she started laughing.

"Now what is so funny about this....."

"I was just sleeping.... Actually because of the medicines I sleep like a log.... Sorry for troubling you"

"You idiot.... You should have told me earlier about it"

"sorry no..... Ok tell me when we'll reach the resort."

"We are just about to reach.... Now don't change the topic.... I know your tactics.... Dare you scare hell out of me like this" She smiled at him sheepishly and at the same moment she got a call from her mom.

Soon they reached the resort and after freshening up they slept immediately as they had to travel early in the morning again.

Next morning, they woke up all energetic and after getting ready for the day they had their breakfast and left for their destination. Half a day passed and now shrishti was feeling totally bored she exclaimed, shocking kabir.

"kabirhhhhh!"

"what?"

"Let me drive na.... I'm bored. and even you also must be tired no"

"It's not like that... I'm ok"

"But I am not...... let me drive na please"

"Ok ok fine."

He stopped the car at a roadside and they exchanged their seats, now shrishti was the one in charge. She happily turned on the engine and started driving. Kabir also felt a little relaxed. He stretched his arms and noticed that she was driving at the speed of 30 only..... he thought she'd increase the speed in a minute or so but no she was driving like that only at the same speed. Merely 20 minutes had passed and Kabir was already feeling frustrated.

"Shrishti"

"Hmmm....." she said while focusing on the road like a pro driver

"We have to reach vrindavan today only"

"I know that....." she said in a duh tone.

"Oh..... but at the speed you are driving I don't think we are going to reach even in 3 days"

"What do you mean...." she asked innocently not getting what he was trying to say.

"yr we are on the highway.... Atleast drive at the speed of 50 to 60 km/hr"

"Oh is it..." Without any warning she increased the speed and now she was driving at 80 km/h. Kabir was totally confused.

"When she can drive well at high speed then why she was wasting time, god this girl is impossible" he thought. Within 3 hours they were on the outskirts of vrindavan.

"And finally we are here," she said proudly.

"Well, the transformation was good from tortoise to rabbit." he said comically.

"what do you mean....?"

"Hehe- nothing, nothing" he raised his hands in surrender. Soon with the help of google maps they found their hotel in which kabir had already booked 2 rooms for them. After keeping their luggage in the rooms first, both of them freshen up and then went to have evening tea. They were sitting in the eating area of the hotel.

"shrii"

"yesh...."

"look at your happiness....."

"Indeed I AM happy..... and all because of you.... from here onwards I just want to feel all the happiness which we both are going to witness."

"Ok listen.... As it's already evening.... So I think we should start visiting temples tomorrow morning"

"But... What we are going to do now..... sitting back in the room"

"Who said that.... We are going to roam In the local market..... remember you were the one who dragged me in the market in jaipur"

"Oh that's great.... Let's go then.... What are you waiting for"

After finishing their tea they left for roaming in the local market..... they enjoyed themselves there a lot. Kabir bought a pair of bangles for her, Which she wore immediately. Actually, he made her wear them by himself. Shrishti bought a flute for him as she knew he plays flute very well in a very simple language. He was all happy seeing her happy in front of him.

Finally after enjoying themselves a lot they decided to go back to the hotel...... They did their dinner and left to sleep.... As they had to wake up early in the morning to visit nidhivan.

Next morning they woke up around 4 AM and got ready as fast as they could. They decided to walk till nidhivan as their hotel was just a 10 minutes walk away from there.

The cool morning breeze was soothing their nerves and the divinity was all around their..... very few people were out on the streets..... They reached Nidhivan and found that they were the one who reached there first, obviously after the priests. The locks of rangmahal was still not opened. the head and the oldest priest noticed kabir and shrishti and signed them to stand near the gate of the rang mahal...... they did as told..... soon other devotees also started coming and finally the head priest opened the main lock of the rang mahal.

There were 7 locks which he opened one by one..... finally when the last lock opened all the devotees standing out including kabir and shrishti were stunned. As per the sayings the Prasadam which was kept for bihari ji and radha rani was partially eaten. The clothes which were kept there looked like someone had worn them and there were many things that were like that.

All the devotees exclaimed together.

"BANKE BIHARI LAL KI JAI......" "RADHE RADHE"

The priest started distributing the Prasad to the devotees but the head priest picked the saree of radharani and gave it to shrishti and the pan which was half eaten to kabir...... saying....... "MERE THAKUR THAKURAIN KI TARAH TUMHARI JODI BHI BANI RAHE"

Listening to this both of them were numb they smiled at the priest a little and after saying "RADHE RADHE" they left from there. The happiness was and somewhere sadness was clearly visible on both of their faces but they chose to be happy as they don't want to feel any sorrow at the moment...... they wanted to live the moment to its fullest.

"kabir"

"yes"

"I have an idea"

"about what"

"See how lucky I am that I got this beautiful radharani's saree of radharani...... I wanna wear this.... Can I"

"That's great, ok let's go to the hotel and after changing we'll start our day hmm"

"But there is a problem.... I need to buy blouse for this so we'll go to the shop first ok"

"As you wish madam"

They went to find a shop and luckily they found a shop open, very easily shrishti found a matching blouse for her.... Suddenly her gaze fell on a very beautiful kurta. Without telling kabir she bought that for him with a matching dhoti. When they reached hotel kabir was about to enter his room but shrishti stopped him.

"Kabir wait"

"Ya say, do you want anything?"

"Yesh" he raised his eyebrows seeing her excited face "here take this and wear it, go" she said, forwarding a carry bag towards him.

"What is this"

"Whatever it is just wear it please"

"You know right I can't say no to you..... ok I'm going you also go and don't take a lot of time ok, I'm hella excited to roam here"

"Ok ok..."

Both of them entered their rooms to get ready. When kabir opened the bag a smile broke on his lips seeing a yellow kurta and a matching dhoti with it, he happily wore that and after setting his hairs soon he was ready.

The other hand, Shrishti also wore that saree happily as it was a direct blessing of radharani for her. She applied a very little pink gloss on her lips and just a stroke of eyeliner. While she was wearing her footwear she heard a knock on her door.

"Cominggg......"

She grabbed her side bag and rushed towards the door..... When she opened the door Kabir was standing there in all his glory.... He was looking very handsome and cute at the same time in the traditional look and hence she was awestruck for a few seconds. The condition of Kabir was also the same as shrishti, she was looking like a diva in the saree. Both of them came out of the trance listening to the ring of Kabir's phone. It was his mom. He took the call and here shrishti locked the door and rushed towards him, after keeping the call he turned towards her.

"I didn't know saree suits on you to this extent Miss. Sharma"

"Same goes for you Mr. Mehra" she said sheepishly, Both of them laughed and left to visit the temple.

Firstly they went to banke bihari temple and after that they visited many temples. The whole day they enjoyed it a lot and after eating dinner early they went to sleep as the next day they had to go to barsana and nandgaon.

Next morning. They get ready and leave for barsana today. Kabir was more excited than shrishti.

"Someone is very happy today," shrishti teased him.

"NO doubt I am..."

"Then share your happiness with me too."

"We met your kanha ji yesterday and now we are going to my radharani, I have to be more happy no"

"Well it seems like you love radharani more"

"Obviously, you just go to radharani and kanha ji will automatically comes to you that's why prem se bolo radhe radhe"

"Well that's true, but when my kanha ji plays flute your radharani comes running all the way you know"

"I know, but you know the flute of which you are talking about also chants the name of shrimati radharani"

"Ok ok, peace..... Now are we going to fight on this, at last the eternal truth is we can never define them separately, they are one and that's what means the most right?"

He smiled widely at her in agreement.

They reached barsana within 2 hours and seeked blessings. Both of them were extremely happy and after clicking loads of pics they left for nandgaon. When they reached there, some function was going on. Everyone was dancing there and were chanting HARE RAMA HARE KRISHNA. They dragged Kabir and shrishti too in the group and both of them really enjoyed dancing there.

Around 2 in the afternoon they were free so they thought to return vrindavan as their luggage was in the hotel only. After coming back they went to the hotel and took some rest.

Next day they had to leave for the kedarnath trip so they packed their bags again properly around 7 in the evening. Shrishti knocked on his room's door. He lazily opened the door and found her standing ready to go somewhere. He asked in a half sleepy state.

"Hey, are you going somewhere? " he asked, taking out a small yawn.

"Not me, it's we are going somewhere"

"But where?" he asked tiredly as he didn't want to go and he was super sleepy also.

"You know it is said if you didn't had lassi (buttermilk) of vrindavan then you did nothing in life, so let's go to have it"

"We'll have it tomorrow no" she tried to reason but who he was trying to reason with, she stubbornly exclaimed.

"no no nooo..... I want to have it right now, now don't be this lazy kabir let's go." she forcefully dragged him with her.

"This girlllll!!" "you no what.... You are very stubborn" he said, pouting.

"Tell me something which I don't know" she said grinning like a baby showing her teeth. He shook his head in disbelief and finally after locking the door they went on the streets, there were many patli gali's (narrow lanes) where delicious authentic lassi was available. Soon they were sitting in the small shop holding glasses made of mud in which lassi was served, they cheered and started drinking it in a go as they challenged each other.

Kabir was the winner, while he was smiling proudly at himself. Shrishti also finished her glass.

"It's heavenly yummy,"she said dreamily, closing her eyes. And Kabir started laughing at her madly.

"What just got into you kabir"

"Well well white mustache is suiting you..... you are looking cute"

"hehehe..... not so funny, you should not speak without looking at yourself" "What do you mean.....?"

She opened the front camera of her phone and showed him he was also having the same white mustache and now it was turn of shrishti to laugh at him eventually he also started laughing. they clicked selfies for memory with their mustaches on. After that..... they thought to roam there casually as the weather was very beautiful. They reached the bank of Yamuna river and found it was empty. There were stairs made which gave a very beautiful look and the cherry on the cake was the full moon. Kabir held her hand softly and walked towards the stairs.

"Let's sit here" "why not?"They sat there and started feeling the cool breeze, unknowingly she rested her head against his shoulder and closed her eyes.

"Shrii" "Hmm...."

"You are happy, no...." She slowly opened her eyes and looked at the moon.

"Whatever you did for me since we met made me happy kabir..... you don't even know what all these things meant for me you are the one who understands me who understands that these wishes of mine are what for me and you are the one who is making it real for me. I have never thought that I'll be sitting here like this with...... all these things are surreal for me"

Listening to all this he rested his head against her head and closed his eyes, thinking about something for a few seconds as she spoke.

"Bade betuke se khwaab the mere, Tumne unhe apna bana ke anmol kardiya"

He smiled a little and replied in the same poetic way.

"muskurati teri ankhe dekh, Dil fir jee uthata hai mera, Ye sirf tere khwaab nahi, Khushion ka zariya hai mera"

They both sat there for almost till 10 at night then they left for their hotel as they had to catch the train for haridwar the next morning at 10 for kedarnath trip.

After coming into their respective rooms they laid on their beds but no one of them was feeling sleepy, mixed emotions were running in their heads. Both were facing emotional turmoil. They were happiest at the peak but somewhere there was hidden grief also..... but none of them was ready to let that grief destroy their true happy time.

Shrishti tried a lot but sleep was miles away from her so she thought of writing something in her diary. She grabbed her diary from her bag and started writing.

~ZINDAGI~

Badi ajeeb si hai ye zindagi.... Kabhi itna hansa deti hai ki insan rona bhul jata hai, Kabhi itna rula deti hai ki insan hansna bhul jata hai, Fir bhi bahut haseen hai ye zindagi.....

Tajurbe hazaar deti hai chahein hume kyun na tod de, Fir muskan lauta deti hai ek naya tazurba jod ke, In tazurbon ki daud mein insan piss jata hai, Fir bhi bohot haseen hai ye zindagi......

Kabhi khushiyan sari dekar gum bhula deti hai, Kabhi gum sehte sehte hum khushiyan bhul jate hain, Dil bahut udaas hota hai, Fir bhi bohot haseen hai ye zindagi....

Yunhi kisi se takra deti hai hume bin kahe Door karne se pehle batati bhi nahi, Dil tadap uthata hai, Fir bhi bahut haseen hai ye zindagi......

Badi ajeeb si hai ye zindagi Fir bhi bahut haseen hai ye zindagi.....

31

Next morning shrishti woke up on time and she was ready to go but here in kabir's room another level of struggle was going on. He was setting his hair for the past 20 minutes but not getting satisfied. Shrishti barged in his room and found all his bags ready but the one who should be ready was not looking like so.

"kabir..... how much time do you need?"

"just 2 minutes"

"ok"

She sat on the bed and started waiting for him to get over with his hair. After 15 minutes, shrishti was fuming like hell. She was feeling like pulling her own hair.

"kabirhhhhhhhhh......."

"Yes, yes"

"How much more time?" she asked in a dangerously soft voice.

"Hey, these stubborn hair are not getting set what should I do"

"Come let me help you" she stood up and went near him.

He innocently lowered his head a little so she could set his hair. She gave him an innocent smile and ruffled his hair in the very next second.

"Now fine?" she asked, squinting her eyes.

"youuuuuu......."

Without giving him any chance she sprinted and started running in the room. whenever he was about to catch her she escaped from him.

"I'm not gonna leave you today...... you destroyed my hair" he said while trying to catch her.

"Do you really think..... you are in any condition to fight on this topic...... who takes this long to set mere hair" Their Tom and Jerry chase was going on but it disturbed when Kabir's phone started ringing. It was his mother's video call..... he picked and smiled widely at her.

"hellllooooo mamma..... How are you"

"I'm good, but what happened to your hair?"

"I didn't do it she did" at this shrishti too entered in the frame to say hello.

"Then what else would I have done, he's wasting time in setting hair since half an hour aunty, we are already late he is not helping either"

"Very good, he deserves this, i'm also done with this habit of him"

Kabir pouted sadly at her.

"Very bad both of you, I'm not gonna talk to anyone of you"

"Cut it Mr. drama, now have a great journey and enjoy, bye"

Kabir made a sad face and looked at the other side.

"Are you seriously not going to talk" he didn't reply and continued being sad "say something yrr" She made him look at her and to her shock there were tears in his eyes.

"hey hey.... Yrrr why are you crying.... Please don't be sad. I'm sorry if I hurt you" He was on the verge of crying and seeing him that way shrishti started crying.

"I'm sorry na.... Please don't say something..... I won't do anything like this again" She literally started crying and seeing her kabir burst into laughter, she was confused seeing him laughing at her and then she realized that he pranked her.

"Youuu..... I won't leave you"

She grabbed a big pillow and started beating him. Finally he surrendered but he was still giggling like a baby.

"Ok sorry sorry, are you going to kill me with this pillow"

"You are very bad, I hate you... huh"

"I hate you too" She finally stopped and crossed her arms.

"Enough of drama. We are getting late lets go" He raised his hands in surrender and alas both of them left for the railway station.

Around 10 they were at the station and soon their train came and they were seated on their seats. This time both of them were in deep thoughts, both of them were observing the trees moving back while the train was running forward at full speed.

Abruptly both of them exclaimed "HEY LISTEN"

"You say first"

"No, you say"

"No, you say"

"You remember we met in the train only for the very first time" again they spoke at the same time. They shook their heads in disbelief.

"How unexpected was all that"

"Exactly..... Your saying "see you soon" at every meeting, when we even didn't knew that we are going to meet again or not"

"That's my trust"

"you are mad"

"yes I am...... actually everyone is mad"

***"ye duniya pagal khana hai, yahan pagal ate jate hai ,
Koi iska koi uska, par pagal sabhi ban jate hai"***

She smiled at him and the journey went on.

–Finally they reached haridwar around midnight, they had already booked a room for them so they went to sleep not before threatening each other to wake up by 4 AM.

Around 5 AM both of them were ready to go and their taxi was also ready so they started their journey, both of them were extremely happy as they were going to witness heaven on earth together. Shrishti was happy because her last wish was just a step away and Kabir was happy because his don was happy. Around 11 they reached the base camp from where the trekking of kedarnath starts, there was no bound to the happiness of shrishti.

"Finally we are here"

"Yes finally"

"So tell me how we are going to start the trekking" she asked, jumping on her place like a kid.

"Who said we are going to track"

"What do you mean?"

"My meaning is simple, we are not going to do trekking"

"But why....?? Everyone used to track only here"

"But we are not gonna do that..... we'll go up via chopper"

"But kabir...."

"no if no but"

"But why?" she asked in a defeated voice.

"Because I can't take a risk with you yrr..... we'll go via helicopter that's it"

"Ok..." she said in low voice "but I wanted to do trekking" she muttered under her breathe

"Ok ok now no need to be sad..... we'll go trekking" her eyes light up listening to this "but while coming down" "ok ok ok... no problem" she squealed like a kid getting all excited again.

"kiddo you are.... Now let's go..... we have to check first about our reservation."

"means you had already planned this right......(he nodded) then why didn't you tell me..."

"So that you could turn on your kiddo mode on then and start being fussy" She looked here and there rolling her eyes.

Soon they were standing in line for their turn to ride in a chopper, but someone was nervous, and without giving much stress to the brain it could be said who it was.

"goddd...... I'm gonna sit on this horrible chopper, please have mercy and save your child" Kabir prayed, closing his eyes comically. Shrishti sensed his fear and kept her hand on his shoulder. "Don't worry I'm with you" she said genuinely trying to assure him. She gave him an assuring smile and he nodded in response. Soon they were sitting in the chopper and Kabir was trying really hard to show that he is not frightened. But he was hell nervous, seeing him shrishti softly hold his hand.

"Nothing will happen...... just breathe in breathe out.... I'm here with you" He nervously smiled at her. The moment the chopper started rising in the air. He closed his eyes and here shrishti was super excited as she loves nature and even height too, soon they were flying high and the beauty of nature was unexplainable. She was happiest to the core.

"Kabir..... yr open your eyes man..... see the beauty" she said in a completely joy filled voice.

"please no...... you know I can't"

"Please for me" she said softly. He instantly opened his eyes and the first thing he saw was her beautiful pleading eyes.

"Thaaattzzz Raayyttt....... Now look at their" She made him look out of the window and the moment he saw the art of nature he was awestruck. He turned to look at her and found her smiling widely.

"How did you like it, now do you feel scared?" he nodded negatively "then, you were feeling scared for no reason, Now enjoy" She hugged his arm and rested her head against his shoulder and soon they landed at the nearest helipad which was 1 to 2 km away from the temple. The moment they stepped down. some other level of divinity in the environment they felt. Shrishti's excitement has no bounds. A very beautiful smile was there on her lips all the while.

Both of them started to walk towards the temple, the moment they were just 10 steps away from the temple shrishti stopped walking abruptly..... The feeling was surreal for her..... there were tears of happiness in her eyes which were falling uncontrollably.

"Hey hey what just happened..... why are you crying" he suddenly felt worried for her.

"Nothing... " she said wiping her tears "I'm just happy"

"Are you even serious.... Who cries out of happiness"

"I do.... Everyone does"

"I don't do"

"Now are we going to fight here on silly things kabir"

He raised his hands in surrender. And they again continued walking. There were 2 lines one for males and other for females, so according to that both of them separated but still they were almost together while standing in their lines also, because for some reason shrishti's line moved fast but kabir was standing at his place only.

After sometime shrishti came out after happily chanting "OM NAMAH SHIVAY" while kabir was inside the temple.

After coming out kabir was looking for shrishti but she was nowhere. He thought she'd be somewhere near but not. He was looking for her for the past 10 minutes but she was nowhere to be seen, panic started rising in him, he was feeling his heartbeats increasing out of fear. He was pacing madly there and suddenly something struck in his mind and he ran towards the backside of the temple and there he found his rabbit.

She was sitting there in 'sukhasan' , closing her eyes and meditating very calmly and silently. Firstly Kabir was furious for a minute but looking at her cute and innocent face his anger flew away but he sat there silently beside her with a poker face.

Around 15 minutes later shrishti opened her eyes and found Kabir beside her.

"When you came?"

No response!

"Say something, why are you silent"

No response!

"what just happened… why are you sitting here making this poker face" she asked, crossing her arms.

"I'm mad…"

"What….?"

"yes…"

"what are you saying….. say it clearly"

"Are you mad…... you were sitting here alone without even telling me that you are going to sit here and meditate. I was searching you like fools and here you were sitting so calmly" he said all in one single breath.

"OH so someone was tensed for me"

"I'm not in the mood shrishti"

"Ok sorry no, I agree I must have told you…. Sorry"

"you should be…."

"So AM I forgiven" she asked making puppy eyes

Finally a smile broke on his lips and she dragged him for the photoshoot. They enjoyed a lot and clicked loads of pictures of each other and together also, finally they were feeling tired so they decided to walk in their room, the room they booked for them was in the nearest resort from the temple.

"shrishti see it's already getting dark so we should go to sleep..... Otherwise" she cut before he could start giving her lecture about her health.

"otherwise bla bla bla..... I don't want to hear your lecture, no no mamma's lecture from your mouth again and again..... Let's go"

He shook his head in disbelief and they walked towards their room...... There were 2 single beds in the room so they changed and got freshened up turn by turn and then without wasting any single minute they landed on their beds and closed their eyes making themselves fall in the lap of sleep, suddenly shrishti remembered something she got up and grabbed her phone.

"What happened?" he asked, opening his one eye only.

"Alarm..." she said with a wide smile.

After setting her alarm she laid back again and immediately she was in deep slumber. Around 4:30 in the morning shrishti's alarm started ringing, as she was conscious about it she immediately got up and stopped it, while kabir was sleeping unaffected.

"kabir...... kabirhh.... Wakey wakey.... fast"

"Hmmm......" he merely hmmed without even moving an inch.

"God this boy...... hey get up" she said, shaking his shoulder.

"Hmm...." he turned to his side but never bothered to wake up.

"Are you gone nuts, hey wake up man..... Kabir last warning, are you getting up or should I do something"

"Hmmm..." still sleeping.

"Now don't blame me..... For the consequences"

She picked a water bottle and luckily that bottle had a very small opening. she started sprinkling water on his face drop by drop. Holding back her laughter.

"Damnnn its cold" he screamed his lungs out and got up in jerk. Shrishti was laughing at him like a maniac, where he was still confused about what just happened with his innocent soul.

"you are so cute"

"he he he.... What was that..... How can you do this cruelty with an innocent sleeping person" Listening to this she again burst into laughter, he got up adjusting his sweat shirt and then he wiped his face.

"So would I have done.... You were sleeping like a log..... to wake you up I took help from my favorite bottle."

"Now If you have already been successful then please have some mercy on me..... and tell me why you wake me up this early"

"I have to take you somewhere, wear your cap and jacket properly, it's very cold out there"

"Now where do you wanna go this early madam"

"Just do what I'm saying"

"Do I have any other option?" she shook her head and he raised his hands in surrender comically. Finally both of them were ready and they came out of the resort after locking their room.

"close your eyes," she said.

"Then how will I walk"

"I'm here to help and now no more questions, close your eyes and no cheating" He closed his eyes and she held his hand securely and started leading the way.... After walking almost 15 minutes Kabir was already annoyed.

"How long it'll take shrii"

"We are just here..... but don't open your eyes until I tell you. Have a little patience." He huffed and stood there obediently beside her..... Few minutes later, Shrishti patted his shoulder to signal him to open his eyes.

He opened his eyes slowly and the view in front of him was enough to dumbfound anyone..... The sun was still behind the clouds but the golden rays which were coming out were making the environment more divine. He turned to look at her and found she was also busy adorning the beauty of nature which can be said as heaven on earth.

"I don't have words to explain how calm and peaceful I'M Feeling right now"

"the feelings are mutual" she said smilingly wide at him.

"You could have told me na about this...."

"Then how could I have got this beautiful and serene smile on your face" she said winking at him. He too smiled widely and they started walking there peacefully for sometime and then it was time for morning prayer and also more devotees started coming there..... They took part in morning prayer and after that they came back to their room.

"So madam..... let's start trekking down"

"yesssssss....."

"ok then let's leave..... otherwise we'll get late" After getting ready they went to have food and stuffing some eatables in their bags they finally started trekking down. Whole trek was filled with only and only nature's wonderful art. They were feeling very peaceful and relaxed while walking. They took many pics and recorded many videos, played many verbal games to pass the time. All the while shrishti was happy and her eyes were radiating the satisfaction her soul got after all the moments she lived there with him, with HERSELF.

Kabir was also enjoying it and was happy too but somewhere he was a little worried for her..... as the track was not so easy..... to make her take rest he was purposely taking breaks saying he was feeling tired. Finally fighting on silly topics, talking about the whole world, making fun of each other, doing all this they came down. After tracking down they called the same taxi driver who brought them from Haridwar, while their taxi was coming they had some maggie with tea to keep their growling stomachs quiet.

Their taxi came and they climbed in tiredly as both of them were tired they immediately fell asleep when the car started moving. Around 11:30 at night they reached their hotel in Haridwar, and the next morning they had a train to catch for vrindavan because their car was there only. Without wasting any time they went to sleep so that they could energetically start their journey back to vrindavan.

Next morning both of them got up all fresh and less tired as compared to the last day...... After breakfast they left for the railway station.

32

Around 12 at night they reached vrindavan station. And after 30 minutes both of them were sitting in their hotel.

"huffff...... finally on earth"

"hahaha.... Now tell me what's the plan"

"See I know you and I both are tired so I think we should take a rest for one complete day and then leave for mumbai coz you have to drive...... so if you'll not feel good it'll affect your health.

"Ok ok..... Well, are you sleepy?"

"not at all"

"Then let's go"

"where.....?"

"Yamuna tat" (bank of yamuna)

"Now.... It's already 1:30 at night"

"So what.....? Are you afraid of ghosts"

"Hell no...." he raised his eyebrows in a questioning manner "ok ok lets go.... Happy"

"Veryyyyy......" After locking the rooms they came out of the hotel, seeing the beautiful weather they decided to walk down till the bank of Yamuna. Reaching there they silently sat on the stairs like before..... She rested her head against his shoulder and he rested his head against her head.

"May I say something"

"Of course"

"I never thought that someday my bucket list will be completed..... and even before I....." she stopped and took a deep breath to compose herself.

"please......." he said in a low voice which was audible for her only, and with the volume of his voice she understood that he didn't want to talk about what she was indicating, She didn't say anything and closed her eyes.... He did the same and the whole night went with the beautiful sound of flowing water and peaceful music of nightingale. The environment was so serene and divine that they never realized when they fell asleep sitting there only resting their head on eachother.

Next morning shrishti woke up first and tried to wake him up but how can he disappoint her being a sleeping log.

"Kabir wake up, it's already morning....." she patted his face a bit but he didn't even move an inch.

—The environment was filled with soothing flute music and the priest was chanting holy verses..... meanwhile all this I was looking for my bride..... my shrishti.... And my wait came to halt when I found her walking towards me holding a very beautiful garland in her hands.....she was looking no less than any goddess..... I was looking at her dumbfounded that I didn't even realize when she came and stood in front of me. I came out of trance seeing a hand waving in front of my eyes.

"Are you ok...?" she asked in a teasing manner.

"You are looking so beautiful"

"So you are"

Seeing the priest's indications she put a garland around my neck and the feeling was something else..... I looked directly in her eyes and put the garland around her neck also, the whole environment erupted with the sound of houtings and clappings.

The priest was doing all the things which were necessary and finally he ordered me to fill her hairline with vermilion, that moment was beyond any explanation..... she directly looked into my eyes and I filled her hairline..... tears of happiness fell from both of our eyes..... but still there was a big smile on both of our faces.

I was about to say something to her but splash..............!!!!.

"Flood flood......floooooddd...... save me save me"

"OH dumbo.... It's me.... Shrishti.... And yes there is no flood" He opened his eyes with a jerk and found her making an annoyed face.

"Why did you do this?" he asked in an irritated manner.

"Because you were not being less than any piece of log"

"I was happily getting married and you spoiled it.... huh"

"Married?" Suddenly she became almost silent.

"Yes, and what beautiful bride of mine was standing with me and you woke me up" he said more dreamily to irritate her.

"Sorry...." she said silently and looked at the other side..... she was trying hard but tears started dwelling in the back of her eyes.

Kabir understood that she felt bad because of his words but he thought to irritate her more, so he continued playing along.

"Are you mad?"

"No, why would I be, there is not reason to be one"

"So you are not?"

"Not at all"

"Ok, the do you wanna know about the girl whom I was getting married"

"I don't need to know.... huh"

"Means you are angry"

"I'm NOT, and if you say this one more time the see what I do"

"Wanna see her pic..." he asked, raising his eyebrows and earning a deadly glare. She was trying hard to show anger but thought of him getting married was breaking her. She was about to say something but before that tears fell from her eyes.

"Hey hey.... Why are you crying....?"

"I want to, so I'm crying, do you have any problem?" she asked, looking the other side. Finally he burst into laughter leaving her in complete confusion and shock. She was looking at him in disbelief but her anger got the best out of her at that time.

"Kabir, I'm seriously saying I'll start beating you If you don't zip this mouth of yours at this instant" He was laughing unaffectedly, by now she was emotional but seeing him laughing she really started crying and weeping like kids finally kabir stopped and side hugged her playfully.

"Why are you crying yrr....."

"I'm not crying..... otherwise also why are you asking.... Go and dream about your wedding" she again started weeping.

"Godddd.... Why do I always put myself in trouble on my own..... Now what do I do" he thought, slapping his forehead.

"Ok, first you see her picture and tell me she's beautiful," he said, forwarding his phone towards her.

"I'm not interested" she turned to the other side.

"See it na" He forcefully made her look at his phone and firstly she refused but when she looked at the mobile screen she became numb she was not in the state of saying anything, She looked at him with tears filled eyes.

"Isn't my bride the most beautiful?" he asked with the widest smile possible on his face. She didn't say anything but hugged him, hiding her face in the crook of his neck and again burst into tears. He hugged her back and caressed her head softly.

"Now please stop crying...... I was teasing you.... I didn't have any intentions to hurt you"

"I'm not crying"

"So if I'm blind or your dictionary is bad"

"Kabirhhhh...." she whined like a baby she was.

"Ok ok, I was just dreaming about our marriage. Now is it clear"

"hmm..."

"what hmmmm...... now"

"what now...?"

"You were jealous I see"

"Huh.... Jealous and me? Of course I was jealous...." she bit her tongue on realizing what she just said. Listening to this he again burst into laughter.

"You are just impossible" Saying that she got up following her he also got up.

"Look now nothing can happen, I'm a married man now" he said in complete seriousness "so you should not feel jealous."

"Are you even listening to what you are saying kabir"

"Obviously yes"

"You seriously gone nuts, not let's go, we have to reach the hotel" He was innocently following her while she was busy adoring the beautiful morning.

"I finally got married to you shrii, so what it was a dream, now you are mine only mine" he thought and in the meantime they reached back their hotel. Whole day they enjoyed roaming in the market and finally the next day they left for Mumbai by road.

After driving turn by turn they reached Mumbai, after dropping shrishti at her home and satisfying her parents about her well being he finally left for his home.

His mom was waiting for him so eagerly, the moment he stepped in the house she bombarded 1000 questions at a time, but he happily answered each one of them as he was missing her questioning a lot. After eating lunch he went to sleep in his room, before he could enter the room chiku jumped on him all excited.

"Hey my chiku...... I MISSED you too my baby....." She started jumping more but he handled her and sat on the bed taking her in his lap.

"damn..... I missed you too my dear bed"

Settling chiku on her little bed he went to take a shower to relax himself after that he came back and directly laid on his bed. Within minutes he was in deep sleep as genuinely he was tired.

On the other hand, shrishti was very happy and excited to tell her family about her trip but they forcefully sent her to sleep as her face was showing how tired she was. Somehow she agreed and went to sleep.

In the evening around 6 kabir was still sleeping, but his sleep was disturbed by continuous calls of Aaditya.

"God, who is this person not letting me sleep peacefully" he was totally annoyed by now, Without even looking at caller ID he picked up the call.

"Who is this, han... What's your problem man? Why don't you want me to live peacefully, means what can't I sleep, why are you messing with me when I wanna sleep so badly.... Now why are you not uttering for what you are torturing my phone since forever"

"If you are done with your blabbering then should I speak...." Now he opened his eyes to check the caller ID....

"Oh it's you aadi, I thought someone is messing around"

"See you have already wasted 5 minutes blabbering.... So can I come to the point"

"yes yes sure...."

"See there is going to be an all india level painting competition cum exhibition...... this is a golden chance for you.... So would you like to participate in this"

"Really...? why not.... Indeed this is a very big opportunity"

"But there is a problem"

"What....?"

"You can only participate in pairs.... So you have to find a partner first.... And asap because the last date of registration is today itself you have 3 hours only"

"Shit man, now who do I find at this short notice" suddenly something struck him "Aaditya..... You go do my registration. I'm sending you all the details of me and my partner"

"Great.... do it fast.... I'm online already"

"Sure"Kabir sent the details to Aaditya and again laid back on his bed and immediately he was in deep sleep.

33

Around 11 at night Kabir was wandering here and there in his home and the same was going on at shrishti's home. She was also not at all sleepy because she slept the whole day.

"Getting bore is another level of torture, what do I do now" she mumbled to herself. She went back to her room and picked her phone.

"Maybe kabir will be up so I can talk to him" she smiled mischievously at herself.

Here Kabir was stealing Ice cream from his kitchen without making any sound because his mom and dad were already asleep. Abruptly his phone started ringing and out of shock a bowl of ice cream was about to fall but he somehow managed it to himself for his mother's scoldings, he literally ran in his room holding the bowl and phone in respective hands.

After landing in his room he placed the bowl and immediately picked the call but he was out of breath so he didn't say anything for a few seconds.

On call:
Shrishti: helloooo.....
Kabir: he..ee...lll....ooo....(he sighed heavily)
Shrishti: What happened? you ok na.
Kabir: ya ya.... All ok.... It's just that I was running.
Shrishti: what?.... You were running at this hour.

Kabir: Actually I was stealing Ice cream and the phone started ringing so I had to run no.... before mom could catch me red handed.

Shrishti: Why on earth did you steal ice cream? That too in your own house man.

Kabir: About that, actually after coming back I caught a little cold and mamma was not allowing for ice cream and I was dying to eat that.... So what could I do more than stealing.

Shrishti: you are impossible kabir.....

Kabir: hehehe..... I know..... well well... is there anything you called this time..

Shrishti: yeshhhh....... (she said like a kid)

Kabir: what.....??

Shrishti: I'm bored.... Totally.

Kabir: why so..... Were you also sleeping the whole day....

Shrishti: You also?

Kabir: hmm..... (Both of them burst into laughter)

Kabir: Well, I have something important to ask you.

Shrishti: yes yes say it...... otherwise also we both are not at all sleepy.

Kabir: ok so I have already done something without actually taking your permission so.... (he said getting little hesitant)

Shrishti: what you did that you are feeling hesitant, say it

Kabir: Now you can't even back out.... It's already fixed....

Shrishti: at least tell me.....

he said everything in a single breath at which shrishti slapped her head in annoyance.

shrishti: I'm not a robot kabir..... say it clearly....

Kabir: : actually there is an all india painting competition I decided to participate in that but there was condition there should be 2 people so I also enrolled your name with me...... (he said innocently this time)

Shrishti: hmmmmm...... (she was quite for some time)

Kabir: Is this silence before the storm?

Shrishti: Do you really think I'll be angry with you for this..... not at all.... If you can do anything for me.... Then mind it Mr. Mehra I also can do anything for you.

Kabir: Damnnn........ You don't even know how happy I am...... so should I tell you the details.

Shrishti: sure...

Kabir: See, we have only 15 days to complete 5 paintings...... the theme we can choose on our own.... on the 16th day there will be a competition cum exhibition... and as you know 2 people are required.... That's it.

Shrishti: that all is fine but where we will do this work.... Do you have any particular place, because we need quite an area right?

Kabir: yes.... As you know when dad agreed for my painting career I started arranging an office to make my art gallery..... so yep I have one office.... Where we both can continue our work.

Shrishti: great great.... It means we are going to start the work from tomorrow morning itself no..... otherwise we only will be left with less time.

Kabir: oh damn..... I didn't think about it

Shrishti: very good..... now finish your ice cream and go to sleep.... I'm also going..... let's do it.... I want you to win this.

Kabir: I'll surely win if you are with me.

Shrishti: Very much confident I see.

Kabir: It's my belief.

Shrishti: Good night, sleep now.

Kabir: Good night.

Finishing the call both of them excitedly went to sleep.

Next morning shrishti woke up before her time and seeing her up early in the morning her parents were shocked.

"What a miracle shrii is up, that too this early" her dad asked dramatically.

"yes papa.... Actually I need to tell you all something important"

"Yes say"

And told everything to them and they also agreed as they thought she'll also feel good and happy with Kabir and doing her favorite work. Around 10 she was already ready with her painting stuff in case anything was needed. Kabir came and they left for his office.

Meanwhile in the car they started discussing their ideas excitedly. "Kabir..... have you thought about any theme" she asked

"Not yet" he replied while focusing on the road.

"why are you so lazy yrr......"

"coz I just found out about this last evening and I was tired so I didn't bother to think about that"

"Ummm.... well I have one theme in my mind"

"Tell me then"

"I'll tell you directly in the office"

"As you wish madam"

They reached the office within 10 minutes, the office was very beautiful and elegant, all set and maintained, the theme of the office was all wooden and aesthetic giving cozy homely vibes, Shrishti was already adorning the place and was dreaming about working there with kabir.

"Kabir, This place is so beautiful.... Really loved it"

"Well I too love this place..... coz it's MY SPACE"

"From where you copied this." he raised his eyebrows

"MY SPACE...."

"From your room's wallpaper.... Now do you have any problem with this... huh" she chuckled at his answer.

"No, and now no more stupid talks and seriously let's start our work"

"Why are you behaving like a teacher suddenly"

"Because I don't like work to be delayed.... Now let's go in the room where we have to paint"

"Sure madam"

Both of them entered a hall kind of room where all the painting stuff and many canvases was kept there. Both of them rolled their sleeves and sat on the floor to discuss their theme. Finally after a lot of thinking and all they decided with a theme and started with their paintings they decided to make. Shrishti played music along with them so that they wouldn't feel bored. Without wasting a single minute both of them were drowned in their work.

like these days started passing and one fine day..... around 2 in the afternoon both of them were tired so they thought to order pizza for them and from somewhere Kabir took out his guitar.

"Someone is in a whole mood"

"yo.... Let's sing together"

Meanwhile their pizza was coming and they started jamming on the songs which they liked the most. Around half an hour later they heard a bell ringing. Kabir went to receive their order and after that both of them enjoyed eating together, luckily she didn't snatch his pizza this time.

After eating, Shrishti was sitting resting her head against the wall and Kabir was busy with his painting as his little work was left. here shrishti didn't realize when she fell into deep slumber.

Finally when Kabir was done with his work he turned and found her sleeping cutely. He didn't realize it but he was staring at her from the past 10 minutes and automatically tears welled up in his eyes.... This time he didn't control himself.... He let his tears freely fall from his eyes. After a few minutes an idea struck him and he took a blank canvas and started doing something on it.

The way his hands were moving so fast his heart was beating at the same speed and side by side tears were falling from his eyes like a fountain.... He didn't realize but his tears were directly falling on the canvas and that was creating another level of magic in the portrait. Within an hour the portrait was complete and finally his tears also stopped flowing leaving the stains on his face, he felt she was stirring in sleep so before she could wake up he ran out of the room.

The moment he stepped out of the room she was finally awake and her gaze directly fell on the portrait in front of her. She got up and walked towards it. without her knowledge tears were forming in the back of her eyes. The portrait was of HER only. The way he had made the painting of her sleeping figure which was enhancing her beauty a thousand times was exceptional.

"kabirhhh....."

No response!!

"Kabir, where are you...?" (she yelled but no response)

She was completely in a very emotional state and out of her rational state of mind... she ran towards the balcony of the office as he used to go and sat there for some freshness.

She reached where he was standing near the railing and his back was facing her, she hurriedly stepped towards him and after turning him face to face she hugged him tightly, she was crying silently so he could not notice, he also hugged her back and asked her softly.

"Why are you crying...?"

"how do you know...?"

"I have supernatural powers you see..... Now tell me why are you crying?"

"Because you are suffering a lot and the sole reason Is me only me..... please kabir stop torturing yourself like this.... I can't see your tears, not even in my dream.... Please leave me"

"Here you are standing hugging me like your life depends on it and asking me to leave you, not fair madam" he said trying to sound comical but all went in vain.

"You are not going to get any better.... Are you?" He nodded negatively and earned a slap from her on his arm. After consoling her both of them left her house, dropping her at her home he left for his house too.

34

Days passed and only 2 days were left for the competition. Both of them were working hard to complete their work and almost finalizing was left of the paintings. Around 7 in the evening Kabir got a notification and he was numb for a few minutes. Shrishti was doing some work and she noticed him standing still so, leaving her work she walked towards him.

"Hey kabir what happened?" she asked in a concerned way, keeping her hand on his shoulder.

"Its finished"

"What....?"

"The competition"

"What are you saying kabir..... tell me clearly"

"We are disqualified"

"What....! Why....? We are already done with our paintings.... So why are we disqualified?"

"There was a very big miscommunication of the message"

"Kabir please yrr..... Don't beat around the bushes and say it clearly"

"We have prepared 5 paintings.... But it should be 6"

"oh shit..... this is a big blunder"

"It's finished, now nothing can happen" He sadly kept his phone on the table and sat down defeatedly, he felt like he came a very long way to meet his dream but it ran away from him again. She was also feeling bad as both of them had done a lot of hard work without even participating. Getting disqualified is more painful than losing. She was thinking deeply when she remembered something and a bright smile formed on her face.

"Kabirhhhhhh....." she exclaimed happily.

"Hmmm......"

"Problem is solved man, leave this cry baby face of yours"

"What have you got that you are suddenly so happy?"

"Why are you sad because you don't have a painting right?" he nodded "what if I give you my painting....."

"means"

"Very simple.... Do you remember there was a painting in my house totally covered and you were very curious to see that but I didn't allow you..... that is based on the same theme..... we can add that painting and huff we are again qualified"

"seriously....! That day you were not even allowing me to see and now you are giving it to me on your own..... woah great change"

"Excuse me... not a great change.... I just can't see you sad and can do anything for you..... that's why I'm giving you" she said pouting at the end. He was not able to resist and he ended up pulling her cheeks cutely.

"Ehhh...... I told you to not do this, didn't I"

"When?" he ask pulling them again

"You are so gone Mr. kabir mehra"

And with this started the Olympics race..... actually chase.... He was running to save his life and she was behind him like a tigress. Finally getting out of breath they stopped. She was again about to attack him but he raised his hands in surrender.

"Sorry madam sorry, please spare poor me"

"Good for you"

"Ok then let's leave, tomorrow we have lots of work as it's the last day and we have to finalize everything" she agreed and they left for her home. Meanwhile in the car, Shrishti was in a very pleasant mood all the time. She was humming songs but some weird feeling was running in kabir. He was feeling some pain rising inside him, he was getting confused by every passing moment as he was feeling restless but when he looked at her face filled with happiness he felt a little relieved.

After dropping her he left for his home and slept directly because he was tired mentally more than physically.

Next whole day both of them were busy finishing their work. Finally they were done with everything around 12 at night, both of them were completely satisfied with the work they had done. after placing all their paintings in a row both of them were adoring the paintings, Kabir abruptly spoke

"Shrishti...."

"yes"

"Umm...." he wanted to say something but stopped himself.

"what....?"

"Nothing, just like that"

"Say it no"

"Maybe later, well may I say something else"

"Yes, of course"

"Let's go to the beach"

"At this time"

"yes..... please no.... I don't know but my heart is dying to go there, Please" he said making puppy face "kiddo you are..... Let's go, no need to make this face like we are not going to get a chance to go there again"

"Means we are going right?"

"Obviously"

"Then let's go" he held her hand and dragged her out of the office happily.

"Easy easy..... I'm not running away!" They laughed and jumped in the car.

When they reached almost the whole beach was empty but the same pav bhaji vendor was there with his stall from whom they had eaten earlier.

"Let's eat first then we'll sit around the shore.... See it's getting late, I'm feeling hungry" she asked.

"Why not come.... But can you do me a favor" she raised her eyebrows in a questioning manner "we'll feed each other"

She shyly nodded and within 15 minutes their plates were in front of them, they fed each other with utmost love and after finishing they went towards their special spot, the big stones where they sat every time they visited the beach.

Somewhere in kabir's heart the weird feeling was rising again no matter how much he was trying hard to not distract his mind but nothing was helping him. keeping all the thoughts aside he moved towards the big stones and sat there along with her.

The sea shore was brushing their bare feets and soothing their nerves exceptionally. The full moon was adoring the dark sky along with the thousands of diamonds like stars. The environment was way more beautiful than anything. She rested her head against his shoulder and hugged his bicep. In response he also rested his head against her head and no one of them spoke even a single word. yet the silence was speaking a lot. Abruptly she started speaking, parting away from him and looking at him face to face.

"Kabir"

"Hmmm..." he asked, raising his eyebrows.

"How much will you miss me?" she asked in a low voice as she knew some or the other day it's going to happen. He wanted to reply to her instantly but he was taken aback by her question and was not able to understand how he's going to handle the most dreadful thing which is their reality..... "THE DAMN BIG REALITY."

"Why are you asking this....." he asked, controlling his breaking voice.

"Tell me no.... how much you'll miss me.... Or you'll even miss me?" she asked, pouting cutely.

"Yes I'll forget you..... now happy" he was trying to look angry but his voice was not helping in any way, unconsciously he turned his face to the other side.

"Then why are you looking there huh?"

"Why are you poking me shrii?"

"Will you marry someone else"

"Sorry, but I'm already married to a don. So no chance for anyone, Otherwise she'll not spare anyone you know"

"Hawww..... when this happened man?" she asked dramatically but he replied with utmost genuineness.

"The day you did something that no one can ever do for me, the day you cried in my arms, the day we shared our pain, the day we visited vrindavan together the land of love itself, the day radharani blessed you, the day I married you in my dream......." His words had already made her emotional and the tears were nowhere lacking in the race..... a teardrop was about to fall from her eye but he didn't let that happen.

"Kabir I'm telling you please..... please please don't torture yourself, just for me..... I'm nothing" before she could say more he cut her in between.

"You are everything shrii..... Now dare you say something bad about yourself" She smiled sadly.

"Well well you know I'm a little crack head...... Why are we getting emotional idiotically...... let's think about tomorrow....... it's a very big day for you"

"Ane wale kal ko koi rok nahi sakta vo aake hi rahega, Beete huye kal ko koi laa nahi sakta vo fir nahi milega, Jo ab hai use samet lo, kyunki ye lamha ab hai fir nahi rahega....."

"Tell me one thing, If you won the competition tomorrow what are you going to do?"

"Me, what will I do....." he started things actually very deeply but she started telling him.

"May I tell you?" he nodded, smiling at her, "you'll smile.... Smile wholeheartedly, you'll smile like no one is watching you but only me, because I know how adorable you look while smiling wholeheartedly and how beautiful is your genuine smile not that poker face you carry always" he squinted his eyes at her last comment but smiled eventually.

she asked, extending her hand in his direction "promise"

"promise"

"Pinky promise"

"Pinky promise madam, now happy"

She looked at the waves for some moments and again looked at him back. "Kabir"

"Hmm"

"Can you give me one more promise"

"Yes, promise... pinky promise"

"Listen to me first, what's the hurry"

"Ok say"

"You are not going to cry ever, got that" his eyes met with hers and he was able to see that unsaid pain, those unsaid words she never said. He was getting what she was trying to say but to keep her heart, he said in a broken voice. "I'll try my best shrii... I promise" she was looking constantly in his deep green hazel eyes but was contemplating if she should say what's going on in her heart and soul. Just by looking at her face he knew she wanted to say something so he himself asked her.

"Is something bothering you shrii, do you wanna share something"

**"Hoth hain khamosh, ankhe phir bhi keh rahi hai kuch....
Ho sake, to jhank lo inme, ho sake to padh lo kuch....."**

she sighed heavily and rested her head against his shoulder again.

"You know kabir, we can do anything, literally anything in this world if we want it to but the only thing which we can't do is..... Is to run from the reality, even after ignoring it like it doesn't exist but deep down we always know it's still there" she was trying to talk to him openly about her and the fact that she was not going to be there with him for a very long time, but he was not in the state to listen to her and her all those heartbreaking facts, he looked into her eyes and asked feeling like most helpless person in the world.

"Why are you saying all this? Please don't do this to me shrishti"

"because you are strong...."

"I'm not strong..... I'm weak..... without you...." losing his control over himself he broke down but she immediately wiped his tears reminding the pinky promise he just gave her a few minutes back. Suddenly a shooting star occurred and shrishti squealed in excitement.

"See, kabir it's a shooting star, make a wish fast" She also closed her eyes and like every single time this time also he didn't make any wish and stared at her with pain and love filled in his eyes for her only for her. She opened her eyes after a few seconds and found him again in the same state like always.

"You are very bad you know, you never listen to me, huh"

"I don't want to do, as simple as that" he was trying to sound stubborn but his voice was not helping him a lot.

She knew he's not going to change when it comes to this topic so she let it go, all the while unknowingly thousands of emotions were going on in heart, she wanted to tell him everything but she didn't have those words which can describe what she was going through and what she was actually feeling but along with all the chaos going in her there was some different sort of calmness in her and she knew deep down what that calmness, what that stillness says.

"Why are you so silent shrishti?" she came out of her train of thoughts feeling a pat on her shoulder.

"Kabir, what if this is our last visit here..... What if we are sitting here together for the last time, what if we never get this chance to rest our heads with each other and look at this sea endlessly........" he tried to stop her but she didn't let him "what if we are not going to meet again, what if this my last moment with you, what if you'll not be able to see me ever again" he was suddenly out of his mind after hearing her, he immediately kept his palm on her mouth to stop her.

"Why are you saying all these sad things today shrishti, I can't handle all this, please stop"

"Tell me kabir, what if"

"I really don't know, I really don't know..... I request please don't speak like this" he lost control over the last string he was holding and pulled her in a very warm and homely hug, he hid his face in her hair as he was well aware that by now those traitor tears would have made their way out of his eyes. She was silent for a few moments as she knew what pain she was causing him but she was helpless to stop herself either, in spite of trying to keep herself as strong as stone and hold herself back to not break in the moment she failed, her heart was about burst and the pain and helplessness starting making its way out of her eyes, for few minutes no one said anything, collecting all her courage she pulled back and cupped his face in her small hands.

"Jo puri na ho saki humari kahani to kya, Jo hai aankhon mein ye gum ka paani to kya, Tum udas mat hona Kabhi bhi ye vada karo, Laut kar phir tumhare pass aaungi main, tumhari thi tumhari hun tumhari reh jaungi main.....

Yad rakhna sada sath tumhare hun main, Aankhon se bhale nazar na aaun to kya, Jo puri na ho saki humari kahani to kya.... Jo aankhon main hai gum ka pani to kya....."

He was just looking in her eyes, without uttering a word. He knew that the words she said were holding the deepest meaning in them but the mere thought of losing her was breaking his innocent little heart which was familiar with her warmth only.

"There is no need to be disheartened kabir, don't be this week, let's face it with a bright smile on our faces, let's show it to the life that if it offers lemmon we are not going to sit holding them but will make yummy lemonade" he listened to her, but never said a word.

"This is not THE END kabir, this universe is very vast, very diverse, I believe if not this time WE'll MEET some other time, somewhere else, we just have to wait for that time and also this is just a materialistic world and no one is bound to be here forever, If not in the materialistic form maybe in some other form I'll be always by your side"

She paused for few seconds and that was it for him without wasting a second he pulled her hugged her like his life was depending on that mere hug, she closed her eyes suddenly she was feeling like all the silence, all the stillness, all the calmness was emerging in her, her breath was turning shallow and eyes was drooping, she tired to speak something but nothing came out of her mouth. With great difficulty she made him look in her eyes and the words which left her mouth were enough for him to realize that his world shattered right in his arms.

"SEE YOU SOON KABIR......I LOVE YOU......!"

Finally she closed her eyes and started her journey to the world from where she was expecting the PEACE she was speaking in this world.

He was numb— the full moon was shining in its whole glory, the waves hitting the shore were giving musical touch and the cold breeze was brushing his face. A teardrop fell from his eye and directly fell on her closed ones. He leaned down and kissed her forehead in a promising way like he was telling her that he'll wait for her even if the wait is going to be till eternity. He kissed her eyes and hugged her tightly, hiding her face in his chest.

"Ye jo aaj tum mujhse dur jaa rahi ho, duniya kahegi hum bichad rahe hain, Toote tare ki tarah har dua poori kardi meri, Koi kya jane...... hum toot kar bhi..... Tumse kis kadar mil rahe hain......."

A star shined as brightest as it could and it broke and fell from the sky. ....*a shooting star.......*

****

I can never understand still how she came into my life like a blessing and how she disappeared to never appear again in front of me, every single time I open this album it feels like I lived the whole journey again. All I wanted was a little more time with her but it never happened as they say LIFE don't wait for anyone , whether you are ready or not it'll take the decision the way it wants and without any other option you just have to accept it. The way SHOOTING STARS accept their fate to break down in the sky just to fulfill the wishes of the people who live far away from them.

Epilouge

8 years later–

It feels surreal when I find myself promoting my art on an international platform, this was my dream which I had given up once in my life but then she came into my life and everything changed. Now I know what the value of a small smile is, now I know what it takes to make people around you happy, alas I know how it feels when you so desperately want to see your home person but you can't just feel the presence around you....... And yet again I'm back to my memory lane, I can't just help whenever I sit idol and do nothing my mind automatically drags back to HER.

I was waiting for my flight to land soon in my motherland so I can run back to my home sweet home.--- finally I'm back in mumbai and walking out of the airport where my driver is waiting with my car but suddenly this thing called phone started ringing and again it was from my mom and I had to take it.

"Hello, mamma"

"When are you going to reach home kabir?"

"Soon mamma"

"I know your soon very well ok, now tell me clearly"

"I think in 2 hours as I want to visit 'MY SPACE' once as I was out for almost for a month"

"Do what you want, just come fast as this poor old lady doesn't have very much power to wait for you for long" she says dramatically.

"Dramatic much mamma"

"Hehe"

"Ok I'll try to come as fast as possible"

"Hmm, bye"

EPILOUGE

While talking to mom I reached near my car and directed the driver to start for the orphanage I started a few years back. Within few minutes I reached and like always all the kids were waiting for me with those grinning face and the sparkling eyes, I took out all the chocolates I bought for them and the happiness on their face were telling me how desperate all of them were for those chocolates, without wasting any second I started distributing and they all started munching on them forgetting anything around.

"So how's everything going on here Mr. Shukla?" I asked the manager who handles everything there.

"Everything is good sir, there is an update" I signed him to continue and he did so "there is a new little girl here which came when you left for london but-" he suddenly stopped.

"But?"

"But I think she's not ok, I means she's very much into herself and don't talk to anyone but ya she loves painting and kept on doing that only and If I'm not wrong she must be doing same right now too, I'm little worried for her actually"

"Tell me where she is I want to meet her" following his directions I went on the first floor of the orphanage where there are activity rooms and one of them is painting room where she'll be probably as per him, I don't know why but I'm having this weird feeling inside me about this little girls, we'll lets meet her first.

I am standing at the doorstep of the painting room where she was indeed sitting in front of a canvas and painting, her back was facing me but by looking at her I could tell she is around 8 years old not more than that, silently I went near her was shocked to the looking at the painting she was making– it was the same painting which

EPILOUGE

shrishti made years ago. How can a little girl make such a piece of art at this age. Composing myself I crouched down beside her and then she realized that there is an invader in her territory.

She was looking at me wide eyed but didn't ask anything. Finding her all silent I decided to start the conversation, I took out two chocolates from my pocket and forwarded towards her, she looked at them and then at my face, I blinked, smiling warmly at her and finally she took those from me. She was struggling to open them so I helped her. When she was busy munching her chocolates I analyzed the painting she was making in detail. It looked like it was made by some professional or well trained person, not at all by a small child. I don't know why but I wanted to talk to her she was not even looking at me, to gain her attention something mischievous came in mind— I picked the paint brush and showed like I'm going apply a completely out of the palate color on the painting and there I heard her soft melodious voice.

"Please, don't ruin my painting" I turned to look at her and there was this big fat tear in her eyes, immediately kept that brush back to the place and picked her up.

"Hey, little angel don't cry" I wiped her tears and started walking with her in my arms towards the balcony. "I wasn't ruining your painting baby,"

"Really?" she asked in a way which melted his heart to that instant.

"Really" I passed my biggest smile at which she smiled too and then I realized how a pure smile of a child can soothe your heart effortlessly.

"Why were you sitting here alone, don't you like to talk to others and make friends?" she shook her head.

"Why?"

EPILOUGE

"I like PEACE" her words suddenly shook me up as I knew who used to say these words to me. "Ohh.... so you can make me your friend you know" she looked at me with her twisted eyebrows and confusion dancing in her eyes. "Because I also like peace" hearing my words a beautiful smile broke on her lips.

"Really?"

"Yes"

"Can I ask you one thing?" she nodded a little "how did you paint that?"

"I had seen it once on TV, I liked it so I made it" I nodded my head in understanding.

While I was busy thinking about this little munchkin and shrishti's similarities she squealed in my arms suddenly bringing me back to reality. "See, there" she pointed at the sky. "SHOOTING STAR..... Make a wish fast, god always fulfills it " she immediately closed her eyes and started murmuring something, if this is what is called deja vu I was totally doomed. Helplessly I was staring at her when she opened her little eyes and slapped her forehead shaking her head.

"What happened?" I asked out of concern.

"You wasted your opportunity, why didn't you make a wish? " she asked in exactly the same way as shrishti used to ask and again I had that same answer. "I don't want to, " she looked disappointed by my answer and it broke my heart looking at the sadness on her face.

"Hey don't be sad na, I'll make it the next time, promise" and here comes her smile back, but what I just said, why I agreed to this, she waved her hand in front of my eyes and forwarded her pinky finger.

"Pinky promise" I don't know for how long but I was looking at her finger without blinking, and again

EPILOUGE

unconsciously I joined my pinky finger with her. "Pinky promise."

"So, you didn't tell me can we be friends? " she smiled wide and then nodded her head vigorously. "But there is a problem"

"What?"

"I don't know your name no"

"Why?" she asked, god this kiddo, how cute can she be? "Because you didn't tell me" this time I pouted.

"Shrii"

"What?"

"My, name is SHRII"

"We'll meet again kabir, maybe in some other way, maybe some other time" her words started ringing in my head and my mind stopped working. I made little shrii stand on her feet and patted her head. I left immediately without sparing a single more minute.

****

"Mamma..... Is everything ready?" I asked my mom nth time and her reply was also same for the nth time "For god sake kabir, just go and get her here and stop asking same question"

So, today I'm going to bring my little munchkin SHRII home as my daughter, it's a long story to tell some other time how I made my mind to adopt her as my daughter but I can say this is the second best decision of my life. Finally getting scolded by my mom I started for "my space" where my girl was standing all ready in her pink beautiful frock looking cute like anything. The smile on my face was telling how desperate she was to jump into my arms and she did the exact same thing the moment I stepped out of my car.

—soon after doing all the formalities at the orphanage we two started for home. All the way back home she was

EPILOUGE

chirping like a bird and It was like music to my ears. Soon we reached home where I found my parents and shrishti's parents along with monika di waiting for us with the excitement dancing on their faces. The moment we stepped out of the car all of them engulfed her in hugs and showered her with kisses. They welcomed her very grandly and looking at the happiness on her face I was feeling like the most content person in the world.

Playing the whole day with everyone she was tired so she went to bed early, and currently I'm sitting in my room's balcony. Suddenly I remembered something and went back to my room. I took out the diary, 'her diary' from the cupboard and walked back into the balcony.

Settling myself on the swing I opened the diary and I knew I'm going to meet her again, turning the pages of the diary I stuck on the last page which was saying 'we will meet again...... till then see you soon'

"I don't know when we are going to meet again don ji, but I met someone, someone as innocent, as cute, as bossy like you" a soft chuckle left my mouth and shook my head at myself.

"You know what..... you went that day.... Somewhere where I guess who has surely found your PEACE, I know you are always with me..... I can't see you but can feel you. This diary of yours talks daily to me, which is filled with nothing but letters for me only, as you had taken a promise to always smile.... I smile the way you always like.... Just remembering you"

"You were the one who was breaking bit by bit from inside but you taught lessons of life to everyone around you..... now I understand why you were the way you were"

"The brightest stars are those who shine for the benefits of others"

EPILOUGE

"I know our time together was just like a shooting star.... It may have been short but while it happened it was breathtakingly beautiful...."

"You came into my life like a blessing..... you are a blessing for me..... the way you taught me to fight with my problems..... makes me feel like the problems are no more problems either. The way you understood me and loved my soul.... Selflessly...... you broke yourself to shine in the sky of my soul which makes you my star. I can say it without any doubt that you are **'MY SHOOTING STAR'**

I THINK A PART OF ME WILL ALWAYS WAIT FOR YOU. TILL WE MEET SOMEWHERE BEYOND THIS MATERIAL WORLD TILL THEN........ SEE YOU SOON MISS.DON.

And yet again a shooting star occurred and this time I joined my hands and closed my eyes and wished, not for me but for you.

~THE END~

www.ingramcontent.com/pod-product-compliance
Ingram Content Group UK Ltd.
Pitfield, Milton Keynes, MK11 3LW, UK
UKHW041945230426
12048UKWH00008B/154